Roger Roffman's beautifully crafte
transporting story of the ways in w
generations to inspire and wound.

> --Kimberly Marlowe Hartnett, author of *Carolina Israelite:*
> *How Harry Golden Made Us Care about Jews, the South, and*
> *Civil Rights*

Roger Roffman's must-read story comes at a time when the COVID
pandemic has confronted us ALL with an existential challenge: do we
dwell on the things that hold us back, becoming prisoners of our own
minds? Or do we reach out, beyond ourselves, to find a new way of
being?

> --Dr. Marilyn Dexheimer Lawrence, author of *Trail Rides with*
> *Tequila: A Journey of Faith* and *Love, Dad*

This wise and beautiful book deals with issues we rarely pause to
explore: responsibility, moral obligation, the core of our humanity, and
the quest for meaning. *Looking Always* is about striving to be the best
version of ourselves, extending generosity and kindness, love and
forgiveness.

> --Dr. Pauline Erera, author of *Family Diversity: Continuity and*
> *Change in the Contemporary Family*

In a masterful treatment of the aftershocks of trauma, Roger Roffman's new
novel, *Looking Always,* explores how the violence of the Holocaust
reverberates down the generations.

> --Dr. Carol A. Mossman, author of *Writing with a Vengeance: The*
> *Countess de Chabrillan's Rise from Prostitution; Politics and*
> *Narratives of Birth Gynocolonization from Rousseau to Zola; The*
> *Narrative Matrix: Stendhal's Le Rouge et Le Noir*

Looking Always

Roger Roffman

Looking Always

ISBN: 9781737767145

Library of Congress Control Number: 2021948285

Cover Design by All Things that Matter Press

Cover image: *Facing West* by Cheryl A. Richey

Published in 2021 by All Things that Matter Press

On page 54, lines from a poem titled "given/over" by Max Regan, first published in TAKE by Hollowdeck Press in 2005, are used with permission. The title of this book, *Looking Always*, comes from the "given/over" poem and is used with permission.

On page 147-148, lines from a poem titled "Unnanounced" by Barbara Ann Carle, first published in CAVE DRAWINGS by Church Avenue Press in 2017, are used with permission.

Acknowledgements

I owe a deep debt of gratitude to Max Regan for his superb skill as a teacher of the writing craft, a dozen years (and counting) of his mentorship, and his unfailing confidence in my journey as an author. Thanks as well for their support to my fellow writers who attend the annual 10-day writers' retreat Max leads each June.

Being in writing communities with Dorothy Van Soest and Mary Kabrich in Seattle, and on line with Ann Loar Brooks, Sindee Ernst, and Carol Mossman, has been inspiring. Their creativity is reflected in many parts of this novel. Thank you, colleagues!

Along the way as this story was coming together, a number of people generously offered one or another kind of assistance. I'm grateful to: Kay Beisse, Lisa Birman, Barbara Carle, Larry Colagiovanni, Erin Cusick, Shireen Day, Jamie Flowers, Louisa Hollman, Sonora Jha, Arnie and Joan Kerzner, Sue Lerner, Susan Meyers, Peter Mountford, Peter Riva, Pedro Seidemann, Murry Sidlin, Kevin Sturmer, and Ted Teather.

Many thanks to Deb and Phil Harris, owners of All Things That Matter Press, for the care they took with each stage of the book's publication.

Cheryl Richey has looked over my shoulder at many times during this writing trek. Her ideas inevitably opened my eyes to potential twists and turns in the plot. Her painting titled Facing West is the cover art for this book. One of the joys for each of us, now that we are retired from academic life, is cheering one another on in this phase of our lives.

Dedicated to the Defiant Requiem Foundation

"By honoring the defiance and bravery of the prisoners in the Theresienstadt Concentration Camp (Terezín) during World War II, performances by The Defiant Requiem Foundation show the role that music and art play in confronting contemporary challenges of increased Holocaust ignorance, Holocaust denial, and antisemitism."

~From the mission statement of the Foundation

Prologue

Taste of an Apple

May 1, 1944

I don't know if I will ever again see light in the world. As I look out through the grimy windows of the room that I share with eleven other women, I wonder. If by some miracle we are liberated, will living as we once did even be possible?

No, I think it more likely that what is being done to us will forever darken the lenses through which we view all that surrounds us. The execution of nine boys solely for sending news of themselves to their mothers. The emaciated, lame, and dying old people, their bowls in their hands, pleading outside the kitchen for a bit of soup, scraping the cooking tubs, desperately sorting through mounds of rotting potato peelings. The constant fear of transport and rumors of extermination camps. The filth, the epidemics, and the never-ending hunger.

Obsessive thoughts of food pervade my memories. In one I am at my mother's side as she teaches me how to make challah. I can remember only glimpses from that scene, as if a film projector lurched to a stop repeatedly, single frames showing on the cinema screen one after another.

From the corner of my eye, I see the white embroidered apron she's wearing as she stands next to me, and I feel my shoulder brushing her arm. I smell the piney scent of the soap that she had scrubbed the floor with earlier that morning, and my body is warmed by the oven's heat.

"Your fingers will never forget once you've learned this," she says quietly. She sprinkles flour on the cutting board and then rolls the sticky glob out of the wooden dough bowl she always used, separating it into one big and one small mound.

"Kneading dough makes the bread chewy and light, but if we don't do it correctly, it will be flat and tough. Here, you try it."

She places the smaller ball in front of me on my own flour-covered board. "Watch what I do and see if you can follow each step." She pushes down on the mound to make it look like a thick pancake, grasping the side farthest away and folding it in half toward her. Then, placing the heel of one hand above the other, she pushes the mound into itself. Turning the dough, she repeats these actions. Turning and kneading, turning and kneading.

Once the dough has risen, I watch her take a small piece off and say the blessing: "Ba-ruch a-tah A-do-noi Elo-hai-nu me-lech ha-o-lam a-sher kid-sha-nu b'mitz-vo-tav v'tzi-va-nu l'haf-rish chal-lah."

Her hands I remember best. Big knuckled and arthritic, Mother's large fingers move with confident certainty. The fingers on my dimpled hand are thin and uncoordinated, hints of Mother's polish still visible on my fingernails. She pushes a strand of hair away from my eyes, leaving a spot of flour on my cheek, quickly dispensed with by a swipe of her apron.

I hear her gentle "Ts … ts … ts" as I get impatient, struggling unsuccessfully in working my dough, my fingers covered in a pasty glop. "One day your hands will take charge, and you won't even have to think."

She was right, of course. My hands do remember.

It is mid-evening now. There is just enough light coming through the window for me to finish writing a recipe for Shabbat challah and complete this entry in my journal. But I am once again out of writing materials. Ljuba, the woman in the bunk next to me, trades a stub of a pencil and two pieces of scrap paper for half of my food ration for the next two days.

Tomorrow I'll share my challah recipe with Iva and Bohumila. Iva said she'd recite the recipe for her hamantaschen, and Bohumila promised to talk about how she makes apple strudel.

It's not as if any one of us doesn't know by heart each of these recipes or would change how she cooks. No, it's really all about bringing others into a memory, the rest of us listening while one tells her story, picturing herself in her kitchen, her thoughts immersed in the feel of that place. Keeping those memories of better times alive.

Apples. I realize that I can't remember what an apple tastes like. Is it really possible to have forgotten this? I feel a lump in my throat just from the thought of holding an egg. A shiver courses through my body. I feel as if I'm slowly disappearing, a heavy mist having descended between me and the life I once lived.

Then, when I anticipate our conversation, it brings a smile. We'll bicker, in a good-natured way of course, about just which ingredients and cooking steps are correct. And our tears—always our tears as these memories flood our souls—will push us into one another's arms for comfort.

Moments of reminiscing, sharing recipes with my friends, and, of course, the precious hour or two when I can see Tomas or be with Milena some evenings sustain me when despair looms. I will hold on until that day when this horror has ended.

Two and a half years ago, we were forced from our home. Some other child or adult sleeps in the bed where I tucked in my daughter. Someone else slips between the bedsheets that Tomas's mother had embroidered for Milena. The goose-down pillows that my child plumped up before I read her a story have been given to someone else, as if we had never existed.

I look back to the months before that and think, if only we'd known what was coming. Milena returning home from school with a note saying that beginning the following week, Jewish children would no longer be permitted to attend classes there. The day I sewed yellow stars on our coats. The owner of the haberdashery two streets over from our apartment building blocking the door when I tried to enter. If only we'd been able to see what lay ahead.

Increasingly, we were scorned by our non-Jewish neighbors, our children's teachers, the people we had done business with all of our lives, and even strangers on the street. Such hateful looks on their faces. Hitler's saying Jews were filth who threatened the master race somehow gave people permission, even encouragement, to treat us with brutality.

One day, Chaim was running his pharmacy, serving Jews and gentiles alike with wisdom and respect. The next day, he was spat upon while opening his door in the morning. And the following week, a thrown brick destroyed the store's front window. He trembled when he told me these things.

It wasn't only the broken windows. It was watching our people disappear, being erased from society. One of Milena's best friends said her parents told her they could no longer play together. Tomas's boss told him his pay would be cut. Then, when someone else was ready to take over as supervisor of his department, Tomas would be let go.

And Sara. At one time, we had walked together in the park with our babies in strollers, sharing stories about our families and giving one another advice about teething, and baby foods, and runny noses. Then came the day I saw her cross to the other side of the street rather than face me.

In late 1941 the transports were announced. We had to inventory all of our property. I made that list: my mother's wedding ring, the silver candlesticks that had been hers, and the piano that Tomas was teaching Milena to play. Each possession became simply an item on a sheet of paper.

I thank God for our Christian neighbors across the hall. When Magda realized what we were having to do, she showed me a space deep under the eaves in their bedroom.

"Put your family photographs in there," she said as she quickly emptied a small suitcase and handed it to me. "Your ketubah, the letters you've saved, your recipes, and any legal papers should also go in there." She looked me in the eyes and held me by my shoulders. "This abomination will end, and you will return. We will keep this suitcase safe for you. It will be waiting as will we." I had no words.

With three days of notice, we were taken to the Trade Fair Palace, where we were treated as if we were cattle. For several days, each of us was restricted to two square meters of space on the cold concrete floor. The stench from unwashed bodies and overflowing latrines added to our dread. Tomas's head was shaved. Then, under the gaze of the Aryans, in pouring rain, we were marched through the streets to the train station. Most bystanders looked away, as if by not directly watching what was happening, they could feel absolved of any responsibility, even to acknowledge the inhumanity taking place before them.

It was only the children who looked. In their innocence, they could not possibly have understood what was unfolding.

If only we had known.

And my sweet niece, Kamila, whose loss I can hardly bear to acknowledge. She was a prodigy with the violin, and we'd been thrilled at her prospects as a performer. Dead from starvation and pneumonia at twenty-seven. My dear God.

The bleakness of our lives each day magnifies our despair. For me there is but one exception. It is singing.

More than a year ago, Rafael Schaechter, a composer and conductor before being imprisoned, secretly formed a choral group of 150 singers to learn Verdi's Requiem. He had smuggled in a single copy of the score. We practiced in the basement of block L410.

Why had he chosen that piece? After all, it was written for a Catholic mass for the dead. He explained that we would have our own interpretation of the libretto. "We will be resisting," he said. "We will be crying out for our salvation. We will be defiant."

Performing this complex work has been nourishment for our ears and solace for our souls as we sing the lyrics of this enduring music with a yearning for liberty in our hearts. It reminds all of us of man's best, even in this place of man's worst.

"When I sing," my friend Martina said to me, "I am not here. I feel no hunger, and I am cloaked in beautiful garments instead of these rags. There are no walls. There are no oppressors. When I sing, I am in Prague. I am home."

I feel the same way. Through Verdi's music, we are all carried back to a world we so dearly miss.

In the past year, the camp commandant began permitting prisoners to hold classes, perform plays and concerts, and produce art. We have been allowed to perform the Requiem fifteen times. However, because many of our singers have been transported, Rafi has had to reconstitute our choral group three times. Now, just sixty of us remain.

Two days ago, Rafi told us what he had learned from the head of the Jewish Council of Elders. The commandant has ordered that we perform one more time. The audience this time will be a visiting International Red Cross delegation accompanied by a group of high-ranking Nazi SS officers.

Rafi was angry. It is evident we are going to be used by the Nazis as part of a charade.

In recent weeks, we have all watched as they hastily created a sham village out of this wretched place. Terezín is to be a showcase of their largess.

Houses are being painted, flower boxes are being mounted outside the windows, and shops and cafés, even a bank, are being opened. Overnight, a playground and a library have come into existence.

And then the transport of the elderly and the ill, eight thousand of them. They would have tarnished the shine on the theatrical obscenity the Nazis are creating for this inspection visit, so they are being sent east.

To complete the deception, our chorus will perform the Verdi. "No, we will not," Rafi at first insisted, storming back and forth in our basement rehearsal room. Then, at the urging of two members of the council, he was convinced to change his mind. Their argument was that refusal would most certainly result in severe reprisals, not only for him, but likely for every one of us in the chorus.

More important, from Rafi's changed perspective, performing for these visitors will give us an opportunity to telegraph the truth.

"We will sing to them what we cannot say to them," Rafi told us. "If just one person in the delegation of Red Cross visitors understands the meaning we are giving to the lyrics, realizes why we are performing the Requiem, perhaps our cry of condemnation will be heard far outside of these camp walls. Rather than a performance, it will be a statement."

"As we sing," he said, "we will pray for the many in our chorus who have been transported."

I think of Radka, a woman from Brno who stood on one side of me, and Zdenka, from Bratislava, who stood on the other, both now gone. In my hand, I clutch a mezuzah Zdenka gave to me on the morning her transport departed, tearfully asking that if I survive, I light a yahrzeit candle in remembrance of her.

It is less than two months until the sixteenth performance. I dearly hope that with my voice I can be heard by the Red Cross visitors. Resisting. Defying. Crying out.

But over these coming weeks, there will undoubtedly be more transports. Will I still be here?

Will I be alive?

1 ~ Red Line

This morning, as Elliott walked down to the lobby, the scene that was about to play out caught him by surprise. Stepping off the stairwell's bottom tread, it was as if he were splitting— one persona remaining on stage while the other took a front-row seat in the audience. Except this wasn't theater; there was no performance under way, no stage, and no spectators. Instead, it was a Monday in early July, shortly after nine, and he was about to leave for his office. Routine. His first client was at ten.

In an instant he became an observer. An actor, assuredly his doppelganger, stood there gazing at the mail bowl, listening for the sounds of someone in the hallway, and peeking through the front door window to see if anyone was coming. The actor was suspended in indecision, the tension palpable. Elliott held his breath.

Since meeting Milena after he moved into the apartment next door to her two months earlier, Elliott had been obsessed. It was those letters he couldn't stop thinking about, the ones she placed in the outgoing mail bowl in their lobby every Monday morning.

A client's suicide had shattered his self-confidence, his wife had asked for a divorce, and he'd alienated his twenty-seven-year-old son. Elliott hungered to discard the deeply scratched lenses through which he now saw his life.

If only Milena were writing to him. But, her letters were for her daughter, a journalist who covered war crimes and cartels and lived in despair for the victims of mankind's insatiable greed, so many of them children. Her life must not go on as usual, Anneka insisted, as long as these inhumanities continued.

Eighty-seven and a survivor of the Holocaust, Milena wrote about her choices, the decisions she'd made to intentionally live life with optimism. She hoped her example would illuminate a path, set out guideposts for her daughter on how to avoid dwelling helplessly in the darkest of thoughts.

She's so different from his mother, Elliott reflected. After his brother Todd was killed in Vietnam when Elliott was nine, the blinds in their home were drawn day and night. His mother insisted that her husband install security doors and bars on the windows. "Stay home, Elliott," she admonished him when he wanted to ride his bike. "Keep me company," when he asked if he could play football with neighborhood kids. "I can't breathe when I'm worrying about you. Stay home." Elliott did as she asked. The years passed and a scrim descended, obscuring his mother's ability to discern any beauty in life. Milena, in contrast, was so full of vitality. She had an eager enthusiasm for new adventures and that inspired him.

In a flash, the actor snapped up the letter and slipped it into his briefcase. When Elliott walked out onto the street, the split closed. His heart pounded and he half expected someone would shout, "Thief. Bring that letter back here; it's not yours." The adrenaline rush propelled him, his pace to the bus stop almost a jog. And with each step, what the actor had done became more and more irrevocable. Yet, when Elliott's bus pulled away from the curb, he had a smile on his face.

Every seat was occupied. He stood in the aisle for the twelve-block ride. Glancing around at the other passengers, he felt heat rising in his neck and perspiration running down his back. A teenage boy three rows toward the rear of the bus was smirking, and when their eyes momentarily met, Elliott had the thought that he was cheering him on. "Dude, you got away with it." Elliott looked away.

Then it was his stop and, hyperconscious that he might be being observed, he carefully measured his pace as he stepped onto the sidewalk and strode the block and a half to his office building. Too impatient to wait for the elevator, he climbed the four flights to his floor. His hand was shaking as he tried to unlock the door, and after several unsuccessful tries to get the key into the lock, he dropped it, the jangling sound ramping up his anxiety even more. He looked furtively down the corridor, first one way and then the other. *Did anyone see that? Might someone think I'm trying to break in?*

Finally, he was able to control his hand enough to unlock and open the door, and he quickly slipped inside and closed and locked it behind him. He wanted no interruptions.

He held the envelope, feeling its weight and estimating the number of sheets of paper it contained. He carefully felt along each of the seams, looking for enclosures and finding no evidence of any. Next, he tilted his desk lamp so that the light was shining directly in his face and held the envelope close to the bulb. He couldn't see any writing and suspected that meant there was more than one page. The rapid rhythm of his pulse edged him on in anticipation.

And then he sat there. He could still call a halt to this. There was a red line yet in front of him that he could choose not to cross. Never once in his life, including his decades of practice as a psychologist, had he been this close to committing a serious illegal act.

His mother intruded, her shrill voice bordering on panic. "You'll destroy me, Elliott. Don't."

He heard himself whispering a shout, "I'm a man now. Leave me alone."

Just then there was a knock on the door. He jumped. His heart was racing with eagerness to read Milena's letter, and the thought of enduring an hour-long delay while he saw his client was excruciating. Maybe he'd ignore his knock. "I suddenly became ill," he'd tell him later. Quickly dismissing that idea, he slipped the envelope into a desk drawer and unlocked the door.

Bill nodded almost imperceptibly in greeting, his gaze held mostly toward the ground. Elliott was relieved. Surely, Bill would realize something was wrong if he really looked him in the eye. But he was distracted. Walking quickly with a slouch, he took a seat on the recliner and pushed back. Before any words were exchanged, his body language broadcast his continuing despair. Bill's wife had died six months earlier when her car was broadsided at a train crossing. Even worse, she had been drunk. The accident was her fault.

Bill was a tall, thin guy. His copper-brown hair was neatly combed, cut short, shaved closely in the back, and his sideburns were trimmed. With a pronounced part on the left, every hair on his head was in place. He wore cordovan loafers, dark-charcoal dress pants with cuffs, a starched light-blue button-down shirt, and a maroon tie with thin yellow stripes. *Tight.*

In their first three sessions, Bill had repeatedly dwelled on his anger at his wife. He'd also complained that Kate, his twelve-year-old daughter, had become sullen, raging at him at the slightest perceived provocation. A mid-thirties law professor, he saw himself in limbo, pessimistic that he'd ever again feel a zest for living. He was having suicidal thoughts but insisted he wouldn't kill himself because of Kate.

Elliott expected they'd cover the same ground today, and that's precisely what happened over fifty agonizingly slow minutes. He felt a pulsating knot in the pit of his stomach and, remembering there was a pack of Tums in his desk, struggled to stop himself from getting up and walking over to get it. The letter was in the same drawer. Elliott swiped his handkerchief over his forehead. *Calm.*

"Nothing I say is okay with her. Kate explodes without any warning, and it's not as if I've been critical of her." He was picking at a cuticle. "Or told her that she couldn't do something." He looked up at the ceiling. "She even said she hated me when I brought home a book I thought she might like. 'You don't know anything about me, Dad. Nothing.'"

"Do you think time will heal, Bill?" Elliott asked. "That it will heal both of you?"

"I don't think so," he said. "Not for us. No amount of time will fill the void left when we lost Jan."

Elliott's mind repeatedly diverted from Bill to that unopened envelope. Twice it somehow escaped Bill's notice when Elliott realized he'd taken in nothing he'd just said, covering his inattention with a therapist-sounding "Mm-hmm."

Finally, the session ended. But because of an unsettling awareness that struck him moments before Bill left, he was now in a quandary. He stood next to his desk, looking at the untouched envelope sitting in its upper right hand drawer.

Three Months Earlier

2 ~ The Fog Comes

Milá Anneko—

Today is your birthday. My apartment is filled this morning with a yeasty warm aroma: your grandmother's challah recipe. I've just taken it from the oven and wish so much that you were here to enjoy it with me.

I tried to phone you earlier and will try again. I won't be surprised, though, if my call is unanswered. I know you tire of hearing me nag at you, urging you to pick a less dangerous job. Yet week after week goes by without any word from you, and there are no replies to my letters. I'm hesitant to say this. Please don't misunderstand. I'm eighty-seven years old, Anneko, and we can never know just how much time we have left.

When you worked in war zones, of course I worried constantly for your safety. It's even worse now because of the ruthlessness of the cartels. Where you are, journalists who write about them are specifically targeted. So, my daughter, if you must remain there, at least find a way to regularly let me know you're okay.

Your baby album is open on the dining room table in front of me. I'm looking at the dozens of photos your father took on the first few days of your life. As if it were yesterday, I remember our frantic race to Providence Hospital on that rainy Sunday night exactly fifty-four years ago today. We barely made it through the door before you made your own entrance. Your father, ordinarily such a proper man in the clothes he chose, was so flustered when my water broke that he forgot to put on his socks. I can still see him there, wearing the paint-stained corduroys he so loved and hopping expectantly from foot to foot!

Such mayhem greeted us on the ward, people darting in and out of the corridor as I was wheeled into the delivery room. A nurse hovered over me, instructing me how to breathe. Then the doctor came to my side. "Now push," he said, and I remember what it felt like for my body to protest and protest until suddenly, gratefully, you slid into the world. I felt exhilaration like I had never known before, when, finally, I felt your miraculous body on my chest. And your hands, Anneko, your hands were grasping for me. My child, it feels as if it happened yesterday.

I'm back. I stopped writing for a moment to put a recording on the stereo. It's Dvořák's Minuet no. 1 in A-flat Major, a piece I learned decades ago. It gave me such pleasure when my instructor invited me to perform it at a recital put on by her students at St. James Cathedral the year I turned forty-three. You and your father were in the audience that day. Do you remember? I do. You wore a dress with a swirling yellow-rose fabric that I had sewn for your tenth birthday. You loved picking out the mother-of-pearl buttons for that dress, and we agreed your outfit should have shiny white patent leather shoes and a matching belt with a gold buckle. I caught a glimpse of you in the audience as I sat down to play and can still see your beaming face when I finished and stood for the applause.

I wonder if I still have the sheet music. I should find it and relearn the piece. Whenever I hear it, I feel close to you.

I can't share the Dvořák with you in this letter, but I can include a poem, one of my favorites that I reread just this morning. It was written by Carl Sandburg.

The fog comes
on little cat feet.
It sits looking
over harbor and city
on silent haunches
and then moves on.

To me this poem has such elegant simplicity. The fog chooses to visit, gliding in, observing all that's happening below, and then sauntering away. Isn't this remarkable imagery? Might a blizzard gallop in on the haunches of Clydesdales, or a summer shower flitter in on the wings of a hummingbird?

Poets have such an extraordinary gift. They see the world as it is, but they can also open our eyes to see it as it might be. If only, I think to myself. If only I could write poems that would open your eyes.

I haven't the imagination of a poet. I am only able to stand on the sidelines and applaud the literary parade. But, if I had that kind of vision, I'd write for you, my daughter. I'd harness metaphors and allegories and images to illuminate possibilities in your own life. I would erect signposts to show you avenues you've not taken, perhaps because you've never known they existed.

For such a long time now, it seems as if you've been enveloped in your very own fog, Anneko. What you witnessed in Nigeria two years ago has led you to have an even darker view of the world, and it is blinding you from seeing the good in people. You are haunted by inhumanity. I am proud of you for the values you hold dear and for your courage. You are right that we must make our voices heard when we see suffering inflicted in the name of tribal hatred. But you put yourself in such dangerous places, as if self-sacrifice could possibly make all such evil disappear.

Unlike the fog that sits looking over harbor and city and then moves on silently, this fog that now hovers over you has not moved on. I fear, my daughter, you are holding on to it, clutching it, giving it free rein to blot out the sun and snuff out the air. It is keeping you from growing and thriving.

We will never be able to erase our memories, and of course we must not. They are as indelible as the numbers tattooed on my arm. But our memories do not define us. As I try to do every day, you must try to live your life as fully as you can.

In each of my letters, I'm trying to point the way. I hope that they will open your thoughts to how you might come to terms with the horrors you've witnessed and make other choices about your professional life.

Well, I'm babbling, and I guess it's my way of easing myself into a message I hope you'll be able to hear. You're a beautiful woman, my child, and you've a heritage of strength and courage that can carry you through this dark time in your life. You have a choice.

By the way, after twenty-three years living in the apartment next door to me, the Rosenthals have moved. Because of their health problems, they needed to be in assisted living. I'm so curious about who my new neighbors will be. Of course, you know me. I'll invite them over for coffee and koláčky so they'll feel welcomed.

Love—

Tvoje máma

3 ~ Too Volatile and Fragile

A few minutes after four in the morning, Anneka gave in to the inevitable. Sleep would not return. Staring at the white stucco walls, she had lain there half-awake for the past three hours, her head throbbing and the acid in her gut just shy of triggering yet another bout of expulsive vomiting. She pushed the duvet aside, cautiously maneuvering herself upright, and swung her legs to the terra-cotta tile floor, her feet searching in the dark for her slippers. Turning on the bedside lamp, she spotted her mother's latest letter crumpled up on the nightstand. She couldn't go on like this. Then, a spasm of fear.

She shuffled to the bathroom, splashed water on her face, put on a navy cardigan and, over that, her brown hooded terry-cloth bathrobe. Grateful for the mindless distraction that the next few minutes would bring, she walked into the kitchen, half filled the electric teakettle, and set it to boil. She reached for the glass jar of *poleo* infusion, scooped a tablespoon into a tea ball, and set it in her blue ceramic pot, waiting for the water to heat. After throwing the two empty wine bottles into the trash, she leaned against the counter for a few moments, her eyes closed, losing the fight to keep her mother's pleading message from breeching the periphery of her thoughts.

A toilet flushed. The building's squeaky front door opened and closed. She glanced at her clock. The policeman who lived on the floor below her must have the early shift this month. In two hours most all of the eight apartments would be empty, giving back the daytime quiet that her writing required.

Carrying her tea, she walked out to the tiny balcony, catching the swinging door with her left elbow to prevent it from slamming shut. She eased herself into the green wrought-iron chair, placing her mug on the deck. Pulling up her hood and tightly wrapping her robe around her to ward off the pre-dawn chill, she breathed in deeply, grateful for the air's cleanliness. That time of day afforded a relief from the stink of factory pollution and the exhaust of delivery trucks clogging the narrow alley that was shared with children walking to *la escuela secundaria* a block away. Dirty air had become far more of an irritation than she had expected when, a month earlier, she moved into this third-floor walk-up apartment on the city's outskirts.

In choosing her austerely furnished apartment in this neighborhood, she had intended to simplify her life, paring away material fixation and widely skirting the image-driven artiness in other more touristy parts of the town. The living room had a faded-green leather couch, a scratched bridge table along with three folding chairs, and two brass floor lamps on the worn terra-cotta tile floor. Neither artwork nor plants brought color to her surroundings.

At times, covering combat had required she live out of a knapsack, sometimes sleeping in the back of a jeep or taking shelter in a bombed-out building. It was not always that way, but it happened often enough to make her aware of a key difference. When she had to cope with her own discomfort while also facing the perils of being close to, if not in the middle of, battle, her writing was far more edgy. Edginess sold, she learned, and the four prestigious journalism awards she'd won thus far attested to her penetrating authority in the gut-wrenching portrayals she wrote of warfare's bowels.

Her editor at the *New York Times* was well accustomed to their sparring about assignments. More often than not, he'd been able to hold his ground for only so long before her doggedness prevailed.

Several years earlier, they'd argued over her request to be sent to Nigeria. It was mid-2013. She'd wanted to cover the militant Islamist Boko Haram. The previous year had seen just under eight hundred people killed in bombings and other attacks by this group, many of them targeting Christians. The name Boko Haram meant "Western education is sinful." Anneka wanted to know how Nigerian children and their teachers were affected and write about what she learned.

Her editor responded with a flat-out rejection. While he respected Anneka's experience as a war correspondent, the death toll, particularly of civilians, had been rising precipitously in the three years since the insurgency had begun in 2009. Boko Haram's leader had vowed to continue targeting anyone who supported democracy or Western values. Reporters, particularly Americans, would most certainly be in the militants' crosshairs. The newspaper would continue covering the story, but by reporters based outside of the country.

Anneka was relentless in her campaign to convince him. He held firm. Then, in the coming months, the atrocities increased. Forty-two killed in a Yobe State secondary school, fifty-six in a Maiduguri mosque, more than forty students massacred in Gujba College.

She implored him. What was happening in the schools simply had to be covered firsthand by the *New York Times*. He gave in.

In early February 2014, she visited a boarding school for eleven- to eighteen-year-olds in the town of Buni Yadi. The first child Anneka met was a twelve-year-old boy.

The principal suggested that she talk with the boy on a bench in the schoolyard. She thought she'd begin by asking him to tell her about himself. Almost immediately, it was evident that Gbadebo had a very different plan. Grabbing her by her hand, he excitedly took her to meet each of his teachers, introducing her as his new friend from America and beaming with pride as she stood beside him. "Mrs. Anneka needs me to teach her about our school."

In one classroom, he opened a cabinet and took out two drawings that he had completed. He explained each in detail. "This is my little sister feeding the chickens. Can you see how hungry they are?" Another was of a helicopter. "The soldiers fly all over the world. Someday I will be a pilot." And then they were off to another classroom, where he took her over to a map hanging on the wall. "Here is Nigeria, and way over here is America. I will come and visit you in America."

Gbadebo was crestfallen when the principal came to tell him it was time to return to class. When she thanked him and said she'd write to him from America, he grinned and hugged her before running off.

After interviewing three teachers and speaking for a second time with the principal, Anneka moved on to another school thirty kilometers away. The next morning, while drafting a piece in her hotel room, she learned on the internet what had happened in Buni Yadi just hours after she had left.

As children at the boarding school had slept in their dormitory, Boko Haram militants had set fire to the building. Dozens of boys, fifty-nine all told, were either burned alive or shot as they tried to escape, Gbadebo among them.

Anneka rushed back to Buni Yadi and surveyed the now completely destroyed school campus. Distraught family members were kept behind barriers while men in white coveralls removed the boys' remains. Her intention to interview both family members and officials was cut short when the enormity of the devastation propelled her into a state of shock.

Could it have been her fault? She was haunted by the possibility that the insurgents had targeted that school specifically because she had been granted permission to visit.

Her editor insisted that she leave Nigeria immediately. She complied reluctantly, and, once back in her office, the trauma she'd experienced in Nigeria was compounded.

She requested that the atrocity in which those Buni Yadi boys had been killed be reported in a three-part series, one part of which would specifically focus on Gbadebo. Her editor rejected it. "We're giving that goddamn conflict more than enough space as it is," he said. "You need to move on."

As the days and weeks passed, Anneka couldn't move on. She ruminated about Gbadebo's being burned to death. Gruesome images scrolled through her mind. And in the coming months, the killings multiplied. Thousands more Nigerian children were murdered in January of 2015, their bodies strewn in the bush, and UNICEF reported that a quarter million children were starving in regions controlled by the terrorists.

Anneka's mood darkened. Simply put, in a world where vicious acts so often were the first and only response to disputes, children were expendable. Even in the newsroom, it appeared. They needed to be seen.

And there were so many young victims of atrocities in many disparate regions of the world: terrorism, invading armies, ethnic cleansing, millions displaced, and the insidious consequences of rampant greed and tribal hatred. She knew that "never again" was an empty and futile promise. Genocide and all manner of inhumanities were thriving. Children's lives simply didn't matter, and their loss was barely a footnote.

Remaining in New York and writing about a world far distant from the safety of her Manhattan apartment were untenable. Once again, she pleaded for a frontline assignment covering children ravaged by war. Her editor wouldn't budge. "Anneka, you are way too volatile and fragile about this issue and, if I do what you ask, that makes you a serious liability to the paper."

For the next two months, her job future, at least in her mind, was up in the air. She wrestled with the thought of resigning. Maybe she could be successful in raising funds privately to support her traveling back to Nigeria. She'd propose writing a book, telling the story of what was really happening, unencumbered by arbitrary word limits for a piece in a daily newspaper. Surely there'd be a receptive readership.

As she thought seriously about it, she was drawn more and more to the idea of working on a book. Perhaps doing so would give her much more latitude in not simply reporting the horrendous acts being perpetrated. In a book she'd be able to give voice to resistance. Her resistance.

In short order, she hit the wall. Receptive readers? Maybe, but finding a deep pocket funder was another matter entirely. As it became inescapable that turning away from her employment income would be an act of virtual suicide, she found herself musing about a plan B. The book to be written didn't have to be in Nigeria.

The cartels. In Mexico, thousands were dying—one hundred thousand in the past decade—as the drug cartels eliminated competitors, law enforcement officers, crusading politicians, and even journalists who covered the carnage. That obscene number, however, paled alongside the tallies of the consumers of heroin and meth, so many of them children and adolescents, whose lives were lost.

When she proposed a cartels assignment in Mexico, omitting the part about writing a book, her editor was amenable. Without telling him, she'd make this more than a reporting assignment.

She would write a novel. It could have been set in any number of diverse venues where atrocities were commonplace. But this assignment in Mexico lent itself to her agenda. The thriving world of the drug trade would be the book's focus.

The series of news stories she'd file for the *New York Times* would lift the veil to expose the cartel bureaucracy. She'd detail government corruption, the violence, and the massive amounts of money passing hands. She'd interview ordinary people to learn how their lives had been changed. Her day job would tell what was happening.

Not so her night job. Vicariously, in the pages of her novel and through the personal war that her protagonist would wage, she'd do far more than tell. In those pages she would fight back. She, in the person of her lead character, would retaliate.

***

In the first glimmer of daylight, Anneka watched an old man, his neck wrapped in a thick scarf, pushing a cart filled with vegetables down the alley on his way to the nearby street market. The rumble of the cart's wheels seemed to shatter what remained of the nighttime stillness as several pedestrians walked past her building chatting loudly, and a light appeared in the window of the apartment across the way. A church bell rang five times in the distance.

Returning inside, she retrieved the crumpled letter and reread it while sitting on the bed. Rapidly skipping over the first two pages, she again came to the part that had led her to crush the letter in her fist.

I tried to phone you earlier and will try again. I won't be surprised, though, if my call is unanswered. I know you tire of hearing me nag at you, urging you to pick a less dangerous job. Yet week after week goes by without any word from you, and there are no replies to my letters. I'm hesitant to say this. Please don't misunderstand. I'm eighty-seven years old, Anneko, and we can never know just how much time we have left.

Her temples throbbed. Then she remembered a fairy-tale remedy for feeling anxious. Rummaging in a cabinet above the sink, she found her bottle of soap bubble solution along with its plastic wand. She returned to the balcony. Standing at the rail, she softly blew bubbles into the alley.

Two children passing by stopped at the sight, one jumping to try to catch a bubble before it hit the street, the other pointing up to her balcony, both laughing with delight at the game they'd stumbled upon.

Accidentally entertaining an audience disconcerted her. That was not her intention.

With the bottle in her left hand and the plastic wand in her right, she shifted into an emotional place where she felt protected. At a young age, she had first learned of this psychological refuge from her mother, who also had been taught it as a child. An uncharacteristically kind Terezín female guard had demonstrated how to blow bubbles. But there was more. The guard told the story of a beautiful princess who was held prisoner in a tower by an evil king. "You see, by blowing bubbles, the princess could imagine herself living in a world of pretty flowers, puppies and kittens, and a merry-go-round. You can be that princess, Milena," the guard had said.

"You can be that princess, Anneko," her mother had said.

Standing on her balcony, looking out from the tower that held her captive, her fear abated, one bursting bubble at a time.

Then, she slept.

***

Early that afternoon she walked down the steep hill toward the center of town, carefully dodging deep potholes where cobbles were missing. Determined to shake off the gloom, at least for the next hour or two, she reminded herself to take in beauty when it was in front of her.

At the gated cerulean-walled entrance of a large hacienda on her left, she paused to glance at a resplendence of bougainvillea vines and bushes—magenta, purple, red, and white splotches radiant in the sunshine. On her right, she passed a small dark tienda with racks of Bimbo bakery snacks and a display cooler filled with beer standing next to a bin of dried beans. Three dogs raced back and forth, happily trading roles of pursuer and pursued.

She stopped at an intersection, looking westward at the distant purple hills. A glimmering lake was visible on the horizon, and the domes and spires of churches dotted the countryside. Continuing on to the city's *centro,* her destination was a flagstone square shaded by towering Indian laurels.

She needed to be among people that afternoon, hearing the *ranchera*, the music of love performed by the silver-studded costumed mariachis. She wanted to be reminded of lives lived with exuberance. She needed an antidote, at least for a few hours, to the frighteningly dark patina of perspective in which she'd been held for so long.

The plaza was bustling: expats who'd retired here in droves, local families filling the wrought-iron benches, and teenagers eyeing one another, furtively masking their interest with studied indifference. The spires and intricate domes of the massive apricot-colored *parroquia* offered a vivid backdrop to this scene, and the aroma of *elote*, a mouth-watering corn-on-the-cob concoction slathered with mayonnaise and sprinkled with grated cheese, wafted in the air.

Finding an unoccupied bench in a corner of the square, she opened her well-worn blue cloth carry bag to fish out a yellow-lined pad and a pen. She sat quietly for several moments, clearing her mind. An orange tree, replete with aromatic flowers, shaded her bench. She willed the sweet scent that she inhaled so deeply to reveal insights that were eluding her.

Glancing at one of the *parroquia*'s domes, she began to sketch its form on her pad. The act of drawing often offered her an oblique vantage point when generating plot or conceiving the complexities of character. A straight-on process to these phases of writing, sitting at her computer and waiting for inspiration, too often prompted the quicksand of writer's block.

She added shading between the inked lines of her sketch of the church dome. As she drew, she thought about the protagonist in the story she'd been developing. His name would be Enrique Cardona.

He was going to be sixty-eight years old. He'd have turned away from his once stellar career as a journalist and would now be solely devoted to an entirely clandestine mission of ensuring that justice was meted out. He would be haunted by the memory of the angelic expression on his grandson's face, frozen in death, now and forevermore the one compelling motive for Enrique's existence. Enrique Cardona would be plagued by his grandson having perished from a heroin overdose.

Deeply immersed in thinking about plot, she was startled when her mental image of Enrique, tall and athletic, a full shock of white hair, sitting on a park bench and drinking from a coffee thermos, abruptly transposed to an image of her father sitting in that same spot, drinking from that same thermos. In that moment, she felt a shudder of dread, seeing her father's eyes, blank, empty, and unfocused.

Turning to face her, her father had whispered something, but she couldn't hear what he'd said. There had to have been meaning in that vision, yet she couldn't fathom what it might be, her thoughts muddled by the sandstorm of intense fear that it elicited. Of this she was certain, her father had been haunted.

With no warning, remaining on the bench suddenly became impossible for her. Her pulse raced, and she felt a stab of foreboding. She had to move away from that spot. The apparition of her father while picturing Enrique brought on a sense of looming dread. She felt her heart pounding in her chest.

She needed to take a detour and turn her mind away from the sudden recall of how her mother had ended that most recent letter: "You're a beautiful woman, my child, and you've a heritage of strength and courage that can carry you through this dark time in your life. You have a choice." Half walking and half running, she headed north of the plaza, dismissing the nagging warnings that blared in her head. *Don't. Not again. Stop!*

She had to find relief.

4 ~ Life in Full Stall Mode

Rosalie was dead. As he drove east from Seattle, Mozart played on the radio, but it was the sound of her voice that echoed in Elliott's thoughts.

He stopped at the Mount Baker–Snoqualmie Ranger Station to check out conditions at Barlow Pass and purchase a parking permit. Just after nine, he exited the Mountain Loop Highway and parked his 4Runner in a space adjacent to the trailhead. There were still piles of snow off to the side of the nearly empty lot.

Opening the rear cargo door, he reached for his pack, strapped it on, and secured the car. For late April, the forty-two-degree temperature was normal, although experience taught that he needed to come prepared for below-freezing weather.

The hike he'd selected for this weekend, one he'd not taken before, was rated as very strenuous. Because its demands would undoubtedly require intense focus, he hoped the hours ahead would mute the persistent thoughts about Rosalie that had been plaguing him.

In the wilderness he pushed and tested himself. It was there, perhaps only there, that he still knew who he was.

Elliott was six years old when his dad and older brother had first taken him backpacking to Mountain Lake on Orcas Island in the San Juans north of Seattle. In the decades that followed, his love for being in the backwoods grew. He even became a volunteer instructor for the Mountaineers, where he taught courses on lightweight gear, food planning, first aid, and navigation. He calculated that this excursion would be his sixty-second.

A week earlier, he'd been writing in his journal at a nearby Starbucks and, returning from the restroom, came across a business card someone had left next to his coffee cup. The company name was Prime of Life Photography and a note was penciled on the back side: "We do lots of photo work for outdoors and sports magazines. You'd be perfect. Call if interested."

Elliott Sterling was a very fit fifty-five years old, with broad shoulders and a lean waist. His neatly trimmed hair had turned silver gray in his early forties.

Theo, Elliott's friend from their high school days, was beside himself. "Dude, you're still a hunk. Go for it." Elliott had ripped up the card yet was secretly pleased.

The first four miles of his hike would take him to the ghost town of Monte Cristo, once a prosperous mining community, where about a dozen structures, all in various stages of dilapidation, still stood. The guidebook warned that at about one mile, a washout at Twin Bridges would require him to either ford the South Fork Sauk or find a log crossing. It noted that this early in the season, making it to the other bank could be dicey. Luck eluded him as there were no logs in sight spanning the rapidly moving river.

Needing a pole, he dug out his pack ax, found a downed tree limb, and hacked away the stubs and branches until he was satisfied with its sturdiness. Then, pulling on his waders and assuring himself that his pack was secure, he used the pole to test the water's depth and found what looked to be a shallower spot fifteen yards upstream.

Elliott stepped in. At about a third of the way across, as he put his weight down on his right foot, he felt himself starting to slide on the mossy bottom. His body then tilted to the right and the weight of his shifting pack added to his imbalance. Jabbing his pole into the water, he attempted unsuccessfully to gain purchase on the river bottom. As he tried to anticipate the exact spot where he was about to fall, he let go of the pole and raised his arms in front of him. He toppled into the swiftly flowing water, went under, and swallowed a mouthful. He flailed while trying to regain his footing and fought being pushed downstream by the current. Succeeding on his third attempt to stand, he slowly made his way to the opposite bank, where he collapsed on the grass, panting raggedly.

As he lay there, an image intruded. It was Rosalie who was thrashing and gasping for air. Her arms were waving desperately, reaching for help. Elliott trembled. His eyes closed and he waited while his breathing slowly returned to normal.

He momentarily thought of abandoning his plans and returning to Seattle but rejected the idea. Too much of his life was in full stall mode. That couldn't happen this weekend. Even so, he could hear Sandra's admonition: "You always have to do things the hard way."

He dumped and then repacked his gear to drain out as much water as possible. On his way again, he soon passed the Monte Cristo Campground, entered the empty town, and, rechecking his guidebook, picked up the trail to Twin Lakes. Another four and a half miles of hiking lay ahead, some of it described as steep, increasingly difficult, and so narrow on one rugged ridge that hikers faced the risk of falling into a gulch.

Taking on physical hazards, as he thought of it, served as counterpoints to demands he faced with his more troubled clients. Whether in the mountains or in a treatment session, he had to accurately read the lay of the land, the topography of the physical and of the emotional worlds. He had to be accurate when sizing up the pitfalls that lay ahead. He had to have a solid confidence in his skills. That confidence had been shaken two months earlier, so he took to the wilderness as he'd always done.

Forest groves of old hemlocks and yellow cedars lay ahead on his way to Poodle Dog Pass. He climbed steadily. When he worked his way up a small gully and reached the junction, he was rewarded with an expansive meadow filled with shrubs of flowering huckleberry. He spotted Silver Lake from a nearby knoll before climbing steeper slopes and easing his way along granite ledges. After crossing a field of flowers, he came to a notch at a pass where he was able to see the sparkling Twin Lakes seven hundred feet below.

Maneuvering across the scree on the descending path was precarious, and he slid repeatedly. Each time, he managed to avoid falling, but as he struggled to stay on his feet, again he saw an apparition. It was Rosalie, her long auburn hair tied in a red bandanna. She was screaming for his help, falling face-first on the steep slope, her skin flayed by the avalanche of razor-edged gravel that carried her down the mountain.

Forcing himself to shrug off those thoughts, he passed through groves of mountain hemlock, finally arriving at the larger of the Twin

Lakes in a boulder-filled basin. Columbia Peak, glacier-capped, towered over this area. He continued for another half mile and arrived at a tree-covered knoll next to a waterfall where he'd camp. The morning's overcast had burned off, and the sunlit snow on the towering peak of Spire Mountain sparkled in the distance.

Setting up his two-person ultralight tent, footprint, and rainfly took just a few minutes. After emptying his pack and laying out its contents to dry, he rolled out his sleeping bag and pad and set up the propane-fueled camp stove. He scavenged the area for rocks to make a fire pit and then dragged over a dozen downed branches and chopped them into burnable chunks.

His campsite ready, he put on his waders, grabbed his fishing gear, walked fifty yards to the shoreline, and eased into the water. For these conditions and at this time of day, lake fly lures would do the trick. Within an hour, he'd caught four rainbow trout, keeping two that were about fourteen inches. Back at his camp, he cleaned the fish. At dusk, he lit a fire in the pit and, near the flames, propped up clothes that were still wet on stakes. He then fried the cornstarch-dusted trout in butter on the camp stove. The skies had darkened.

Setting his plate aside, he sipped scotch from a flask. His thoughts turned to his son. It had been years since the last time they had hiked together, years since Elliott had taken joy from watching Peter eagerly learn how to backpack, to fish, and to gain a building trust in his self-reliance. Sparks from the crackling logs flew into the darkness while Elliott, filled with fear, peered into the fire.

Peter was obsessed. Testing himself in extreme sports, the bar relentlessly raised, had become his primary reason for existing and took him entirely too close to the edge. To Elliott's consternation, his son crowed about the adrenaline rush he thrived on from his near-death exploits. This topic had become increasingly contentious during their Skype calls.

Would Peter horribly injure himself? Would he even survive?

The fire reduced to burning embers. Elliott undressed and climbed into his sleeping bag. He slept fitfully, a troubling dream intruding, and woke just as the sun was rising.

After pulling on his clothes, he opened his journal and grabbed a pen. He noticed his hand was shaking.

***

It was that same nightmare, the one I first had two months ago.

The dream always begins the same way. There's a heavy rainstorm and I'm barely able to see the road. A fierce wind buffets the car, making it a struggle to steer.

As I approach the Aurora Bridge, I'm anxious about the risk of being sideswiped by a truck or bus because of the narrow lanes. My windshield wipers are on high.

Once on the bridge, a car comes toward me with its high beams on, momentarily blinding me. I briefly swerve into another lane before correcting myself. I'm sweating.

I see a solitary figure standing mid-span at the bridge railing. I slow down. As I come closer, I see it's a woman. She removes her coat and drops it onto the sidewalk.

I pull over. No one else is stopping. I run toward her. She's climbing the eight-foot suicide-prevention fence.

Just as I reach her and make a grab for her foot, she kicks at me. I can't hold on. Pushing herself over the top, she looks back at me with a pleading look of terror on her face. "Help me," I hear her scream as she falls the 180 feet into the dark water below.

The woman is Rosalie. She's my client.

***

Closing his journal, Elliott built a fire and set water to boil. He stripped and jogged down to the shoreline. Without a moment's hesitation, he dove into the frigid water, swimming briskly thirty yards out, then back to shore. He raced back to his tent, dried off, and dressed.

After making coffee and powdered scrambled eggs, he packed up his gear and set out for the spot where he'd left his car. When he got to the South Fork Sauk, he hiked upstream from where he had fallen and took a half hour to reconnoiter for the safest place to cross. He came to a bend in the river where there was a sandbar midstream offering a waypoint. Chopping two branches for poles, he took the time to plan each step and made it safely across.

Back at the trailhead, after he stashed his gear in the car, he pulled out of the parking lot and reflexively turned on the radio. But then he changed his mind, wanting the silence. He relived his fall into the surging river. As the miles passed, he pictured what could have happened. Had he not been able to regain his footing, he'd have drowned. He'd have been alone, so far from his home. No goodbyes or I love you.

He pictured Sandra learning that he'd died, her hands moving to cover her mouth, her eyes pinched shut, and her insistently shaking her head. He could hear the rhythm of her grief, the blurted words of pleading there'd been a mistake and then the rolling sobs. Of course, she'd grieve his loss. But there would be something else. She'd feel both dejected and incensed about his never having unlocked the filters behind which he hid his feelings.

"You're not letting me in, Elliott," she'd often complained. "You write in your journal the emotions that you can't or won't share with me." Each time they'd faced one another, Sandra's hope newly rekindled that he'd finally commit to being open with her, he'd inevitably close down, locked into a chamber of numbness.

The question of whether he couldn't or wouldn't surface his feelings was not new, having first arisen early in their relationship. Over the years they'd mostly set the issue aside, ignored except when some spark set Sandra off yet again and the dance of how each of them dealt with this gulf between them was once again performed.

And then Rosalie killed herself and the bottom fell out. Could Peter ever be that vulnerable? "No," he abruptly muttered, rolling down his window and turning on the radio.

Arriving home, he found a note from Sandra next to the espresso machine. "I'll be back by five. We need to talk."

5 ~ His Journal Contained Him

"Elliott," Sandra said, "we've walked on the same path for most of our marriage, but that's not where we've been in the last few years. It's as if your road and mine somehow moved onto separate maps in different countries."

They were sitting in the solarium. The late afternoon sun illuminated the potted cacti on four glass shelves in the large bay window. There was no rancor or anger in her words.

It could as easily have been him broaching this subject. They had married when he was twenty-four and she was twenty-two. Both led professional lives, his as a psychologist and hers as a surgeon. With a growing disparity in the rhythms of their worlds, a once bright flame had dimmed, sputtered, and extinguished.

She looked to him much as she had before the chasm opened. Sandra was thin and athletic, with olive-toned Mediterranean skin and dark eyes. Her formerly shoulder-length black hair had a salt-and-pepper coloring now and was cut in a bob. She appeared decidedly younger and happier than she had in a long time, he thought.

She paused. For a few moments they sat in silence. Then the neighbors' dog began barking. A squirrel, he guessed, and stopped himself from going to the window. He realized how much he'd rather be on a run along the Lake Washington waterfront not far from their home, a detour from this moment.

She stood and walked over to a Christmas cactus on a pedestal in front of the bay window. Pinching off some dead blooms, she tested the soil with her fingers. The light streaming in put her in profile, obscuring her facial features.

"In the past few months since Rosalie's death, you've been living an inward life. It's as if serenity fuels you somehow. It's become your life force. I need to continue growing, Elliott."

An inward life. She focused on his weekends by himself in the wilderness and his absorption with journaling, the hours he now spent at it. She told him she'd grown frightened.

He heard the urgency in her words and recognized the accuracy of her portrayal of how life had become for him. His client's suicide had indeed thrown him. With few exceptions, he'd closed himself off from nearly everyone.

"I will always love you," she whispered. She continued, her voice both pained and determined. "But, the truth of the matter, Elliott, is that what we once had is long gone."

He nodded. Cupping his chin in his left hand, he looked at the floor. It had been long gone for him as well. Yet over these past months, he'd been satisfied with coasting, knowing it wouldn't last much longer. It couldn't. Still, he wished the timing were better.

"Look, Sandra, I get it. Going our separate ways is right for us. But I've been hoping we'd first see Peter find his footing."

Twenty-seven years old, Peter currently lived in Colorado. Since childhood, he'd had a passion for challenging himself with increasingly demanding physical feats. When he saw *Maltese Flamingo*, a 1980s film about extreme skiing, he became fixated on making and breaking records on the slopes. After leaving school, he waited tables, guided river-rafting expeditions, taught novice skiing, and pulled together whatever gigs necessary to keep perfecting his skills.

"He's resilient," she said, "and strong in so many ways."

"Is he?" His voice rising with a hint of antagonism that even surprised him, Elliott said, "What if Peter's world starts crumbling? He repeatedly flirts with disaster and I can't help but wonder if his putting himself way out on a limb is somehow self-destructive. How much more can happen before that limb cracks and he crashes to the ground?"

"Elliott, stop. We'll help him get through—"

"Now listen. I think you're being Pollyannaish." Wary of being overcome with anger, he closed his eyes, waiting for several moments and calming his breathing before continuing. "Peter puts up a good front about how cool his life is, skiing all over the world with his buddies. But the cold hard truth is that without your sending him cash, Peter would be living on the street." He saw the look of surprise on her face. "Yeah, of course I knew. Didn't you think I'd figure it out when I saw the monthly withdrawals? But it's not just about his depending on you financially. Seeing his family come unraveled is going to hit him hard."

Sandra was quiet.

"There's another thing. He's stoned much of the time and I wonder how that will affect his reaction to our breaking-up. Maybe it'll give him comfort, but what if it magnifies his unhappiness?"

"He'll understand what has happened to us," she said. "And we'll do whatever he needs us to do to help him get through it."

"And if he doesn't get through it?"

She walked over to sit next to him on the wicker love seat and placed her hand on his arm. "We'll do this together." He began to pull away, but she held on. "He'll understand and he'll cope with it. He'll figure out what he needs in life, and he'll go for it. I'm confident in him."

Elliott sat quietly.

"Why now, Sandra? I mean, if we wait a while, maybe just a matter of months, perhaps he'll turn a corner and start growing up. Is there a reason to hurry?"

Avoiding eye contact, she twisted the wedding ring on her finger. He watched and then, all of a sudden, knew the answer.

"Elliott, there's someone …." She didn't finish the sentence.

She looked directly at him, a pained expression of pleading on her face. Then she took the ring off and handed it to him.

"It's still only a possibility, but I don't want to be deceptive with you."

As the truth of what Sandra was telling him sank in, he stood and walked to the bay window gazing out as the day's shadows lengthened. Minutes passed and neither of them spoke.

He then turned and faced her, a sadness-tinged smile on his face. "I appreciate your honesty."

She nodded.

"But I don't want Peter to know about Rosalie," he said.

"Wouldn't it help him to realize what you're worried he might—"

"Sandra, I need you to keep what happened to her between us. Don't tell him." His voice was insistent. "Do you agree?"

"All right, I won't. I don't get why, but I agree."

He started to respond, but then stopped himself.

***

Three days later, he needed to be at the beach. The weather was unseasonably warm for early May in Seattle. He left his shirt, shoes, and socks in the car. After dabbing sunscreen on his nose and bald spot, he rolled up his pant legs and set off. The sun warmed his back, and he stepped gingerly. Pebbles and crab shells stung tender spots on his bare feet.

High-pitched staccato chirps caught his attention. Two crows were dive-bombing a bald eagle. Was this a territorial dispute, he wondered, a nest being protected, or might it have been a daily ritual, friendly sparring among neighbors? In a moment, they flew out of sight.

The current was flowing swiftly, the water forming swirling eddies as it ricocheted off a train trestle's concrete pilings thirty yards further on. Sitting on a seawall, he rummaged around in his pack to find his journal and a black ultra-fine-point Sharpie pen, and then drew an image of the timber-supporting frames. His pen strokes were meticulous as he attempted to create a precise rendering of the trestle structure.

As he sketched, three short blasts and one long blast of the southbound Amtrak's horn warned of its approach. The larger boughs of two Douglas fir trees bobbed up and down in the wind, as if in response to an appreciative audience's applause.

The drawing completed, he tossed his journal and pen into his backpack, threw it over his shoulder, and continued his walk. Glancing at his watch, he committed to being out there for no less than an hour.

He'd given the same advice to hundreds of clients over the years. When you're at loose ends, don't wait for inspiration. The wait will be endless. Just go dip your toes in the ocean, go to the zoo, find out what's on exhibit at the Asian Art Museum, or rent a bike. But, for God's sake, get out and *do* something.

Standing at the waterline, he bent down to examine an onyx-colored stone about the size of his fist. Its streaks of white and black were striking in the sunlight. Nine wooden pilings, gray with age, stood at attention in two rows of even intervals just ahead. Once supports for a pier, these rotting poles, with thick coatings of droppings, were now well-used perches for gulls and terns. Detritus from an earlier time had been transposed, much like the rusty gasworks factory on the shore of Seattle's Lake Union, now useless as an instrument of energy, but treasured as a massive art icon.

Again, he opened his journal and quickly captured the highlights of this scene in pen and ink, a reminder that he was here. He'd written in a journal every day since his sixteenth birthday. On that day, his dad had finished writing a memoir and given him a bound copy. When Todd, Elliott's older brother, joined the army, their dad had started his first journal. The memoir was based on his stack of notebooks. The book was a project his father had taken on after learning his time was short. Within six months he was gone, the treatments for pancreatic cancer having run their course.

He'd reread his father's book periodically and often felt surprised to come across passages he hadn't remembered being there. It was as if his dad were continually updating the manuscript from the spirit world, adding new meanings when he believed Elliott was ready for them. He wondered if his own notebooks would eventually morph into a memoir that his son would read. Might Peter discover new facets of just who his father was? Might he come to know of the compassion Elliott felt for him, even while they suffered through the many firestorms?

Elliott had realized long ago that the practice of journaling contained him. Its pages had architecture and formed the floor, walls, ceiling, doors, and windows of the space in which he thought and felt. In between the covers of his journal, he was at home with himself. Filling its pages was akin to taking a sighting with a virtual sextant, assuring him that he knew where he was. Since Rosalie's suicide, his journal was all the more a refuge.

His spiral notebook had a black cover and unlined pages. Currently, he was writing in volume forty, and he had one just like it for each previous year. He had a tradition of beginning each new volume by taping a photograph onto the first page. One decade, the first page photos all were of whales. For another, he chose various breeds of dogs. Yet another included wildlife found on the Serengeti. It was always some creature, and this tradition was a reminder of a time in his childhood when books about nature had given him safe haven.

He remembered the question that Peter had asked when ten years old. "Daddy, why would it matter knowing what you were thinking on a Thursday morning twenty years ago?" At first, that question was surprisingly difficult to answer, at least in a way that would make sense to his young son's mind. But when Elliott read the passage written on the day of Peter's birth, his expressions of wonderment at the baby that he and Sandra had created seemed to make Peter understand. Maybe, when his son had more life experience, Elliott thought, he'd appreciate what all these words had meant to his father. Then again, maybe he wouldn't. A wave of sadness came over him at the thought that he and Peter might never regain the tight bond that they had once had.

He'd been out on the beach for just over an hour, his get-himself-moving goal achieved for the day. The uplift in mood it was intended to prompt, however, felt as ephemeral as the fading horn blast from the freight train that moments ago had crossed the trestle, heading north.

***

Finally, after two weeks of searching, he found a promising apartment: one of four in a two-story brick building in Seattle's Capitol Hill neighborhood. A massive western red cedar stood in a courtyard just to the right of the building's flagstone walkway. The tree looked timeless, a sanctuary for generations of squirrels and birds, with a canopy shading two wrought-iron benches that faced one another on the lawn to the left of the path.

An oriental rug lay on the highly waxed dark oak floor in the building lobby. A crystal chandelier hung from the ceiling, and a stained-glass window was visible above the staircase landing. For outgoing mail, a vintage hand-carved wooden dough bowl rested on a mahogany antique Victorian side table that stood just to the left of the entrance door.

That morning, Sandra had gone with him to take a look. He'd winced when realizing he'd never seen the sapphire pendant necklace she was wearing. "Well," she'd said, standing by the living room window, "you'd be on the second floor, so you wouldn't get as much noise from the street." She turned away from the window. "And you'd have more privacy," she'd added, almost as an afterthought. "Okay, I've run out of time and have to get back to the hospital. Good luck in making a decision."

He walked once again through the rooms, returning several times to gaze at the tree. This seemed like the right place. Yet he thought he'd better look at one more listing later in the day.

Then, just before walking down the stairs, he became convinced. It was the sweet aroma of freshly baked bread coming from the next-door apartment.

He'd move in the following week.

6 ~ Thinking I'm Done

"I don't believe it! You were sold after seeing the cedar tree and smelling baking bread?" She chuckled. "You can't be serious." Sandra turned from the stove to face him.

He slapped his hands in a done deal gesture. "Signed the lease without giving it a scintilla of additional thought."

"Well, you get points for passion. I have to say that the condition of the appliances and the amount of storage space would have been higher on my priority list." She rechecked the recipe. "Oh, and I'm going to need three egg yolks and a half cup of melted butter."

Elliott rolled up the sleeves of his Huskies sweatshirt. After putting the butter into a small pot that he set on the burner, he took three eggs from the refrigerator.

She opened a bottle of pinot grigio and filled their glasses. She raised hers in a toast.

"To the future." He looked closely at her expression, seeing warmth in her smile.

"To whatever different directions it takes us," he replied, lifting his glass. "What kind of sauce are we making?"

"Bearnaise." Sandra drizzled the asparagus with olive oil before sprinkling on salt and pepper. She then slid the baking sheet into the oven. "We're also having poached salmon garnished with sliced cucumber and lemon wedges." Elliott watched as she took a platter from the refrigerator, removed the plastic wrap, and placed it on the dining room table.

"I wonder how many couples, two weeks after they've decided to break up, not only are speaking with one another, but are breaking bread with such gusto," he said.

She laughed. "More likely they're breaking dishes at this point."

Sandra took the baking sheet from the oven and plated the asparagus. Elliott brought the sauce to the table.

For the next several minutes, they sat and ate without speaking.

Sandra set her utensils aside and turned to him. "Elliott, months have gone by. What in God's name is going on with you? I want to understand."

"Get in line." He shook his head with a wistful look. "It's as if I'm in some bizarre state of limbo. Finding a way out is eluding me," he said, wiping his mouth with his napkin. "You've also had some rough patches, haven't you? I remember a time early on when you were tempted to quit. Has it happened again?"

"Quit surgery forever?"

"Yes."

"Yeah, well, you know about the first time."

Elliott nodded. He recalled the bitterness in her voice when she told him, about four months into her training, that she'd been dressed down by the senior resident who'd grilled her about an article he'd recommended. It had just been published. She wasn't the only one who hadn't read it yet, but the other residents were all males. He singled her out for a scathing lecture. Budding surgeons get used to having their faces rubbed in it. But that day Sandra was so exhausted from the long hours and lack of sleep, in part because Peter was colicky. She just couldn't brush off what that son of a bitch had said and drafted a letter of withdrawal.

Elliott had drawn a hot bath for her. Afterward, he made them a very late dinner. While they ate, he listened to her rant about arrogant males. "Even on my off days, I'm as good as any of the male residents," she'd said. "But being twice as good? I'm so damned pissed that two hundred percent has to be my normal to stay afloat in this profession."

"Yes, I thought of quitting. But the next day I was back, and that crisis was history."

"How'd you get back?"

She smiled. "That time, I caught some sleep and decided there was no way I'd give that bastard the satisfaction of seeing me drop out."

"Spitefulness?"

She laughed. "Hell, no. Self-preservation. I thought at the time that if I wasn't vigilant, surgery would make a man out of me in the worst sense."

"Was there another time you nearly quit?"

"Yes, and again it was about the blatant disparities in my field. I learned that female surgeons were paid something like sixty-two percent of what their male counterparts made. That made me angry. But, I also had a lot of guilt about work-life balance and was feeling I just couldn't win. On the one hand, I wasn't a good enough surgeon when I prioritized time to be with you and Peter. On the other, I wasn't a good enough wife and mother when I spent such long hours at the hospital."

Shaking his head, he said, "The dice were really stacked against women in medicine."

"It really hasn't changed all that much." She took another sip of her wine. "Why are you asking about this?"

He stood and walked over to the bay window. "I'm thinking I'm done."

"Elliott?" she said, her voice raised with an edge of disbelief.

"Maybe I'll increase my teaching load at Antioch or possibly apply for a full-time position at Seattle U or the U-Dub. I'm really unsure . . ."

"Your clinical career down the drain?" She held up her hands, a disbelieving look on her face. "God, Elliott."

"Rosalie wasn't your first suicide. You managed to get through it okay the first time. I remember one of your former professors helped you grieve."

He returned to the table and sat. "That's not the issue this time. At least, I don't think it's grieving. It's a mystery and I just can't see how I'll get my mojo back."

"Speaking of getting back on your feet, you did just that when you slipped crossing that river and went under." She held his gaze. "I mean, you're an expert at wilderness survival. You even teach courses about it. If someone is going to fracture a bone while far from a medical facility, you're the one they'd want to have by their side."

He shook his head. "That's just the point. Out in the boondocks, I'm solid. I know what I'm doing."

"I don't get it. What's the point?"

"The point is that my skills in the boonies aren't worth a crap when it comes to sitting in an office with a client across from me."

"You've been practicing for thirty years. How can all of that experience suddenly dry up?" He heard exasperation in her voice. "You've helped so many people." She waved her fork at him.

"You need to deal with this, Elliott, and soon. Maybe see a therapist and get some help about needing that journal so much."

He began to object, but she cut him off. "Never mind. Forget I said that." She pushed back from the table and began taking the dishes to the kitchen. "As I see it, your clients deserve you to be fully committed, all in. It just won't do for you to be self-doubting because of the rotten hand you've been dealt. The same goes for surgeons. No more. No less."

He picked up the cutlery and wineglasses. "Fish or cut bait?"

"Something like that." She set down the plates and leaned against the counter, her arms crossed. "If quitting your practice is what you need to do, get on with it. Don't make your clients have to deal with a practitioner who's drifting, only partly in the room. Make the decision and do it," she said. "If I could see myself through uncertainty about my professional life, so can you. And there's another reason why you need to get past this. Peter needs you."

"Peter's not in the least bit interested in what I'm—"

"Wait a minute, Elliott. You're wanting him to make a huge change in his life. I think you've got to show him the way. You can't be a no-show."

He shrugged, continuing to load the dishwasher. He didn't reply. Minutes passed.

He heard her sigh. "I've got some paperwork to do," she said as she went into her study, closing the door.

He finished cleaning up. Then, putting on his jacket, he headed out for a walk. Before leaving, however, he grabbed his journal and a pen.

Two Months Earlier

7 ~ It's Okay to Bark

Peering out of the window in his living room, he watched the furniture-delivery truck pull away from the curb and was aware this was the moment marking a chapter's ending. He was alone, their separation no longer an abstraction.

The truck reached the end of the street, turned left, and he watched until it disappeared from sight. The silence became heavy. Hours passed and he remained sitting at that window, his thoughts lost in the limbs of the western red cedar in the courtyard.

A few days earlier, while walking the aisles of a home-furnishing rental store, he chose Danish modern. Lots of teak, a clean and simple design. His choice didn't come from a sense of the aesthetics, but rather as the path of least resistance. After spending just a few minutes with the saleswoman, getting the impression that she was working her way into an in-depth discussion of at least four decor variations, he wanted and needed to cut that experience short.

"Yes," she assured him, "the delivery can be scheduled for Wednesday." He signed an unread four-page contract. The furniture was his for six months.

He slowly moved through the rooms. The kitchen, bedroom, and bathroom were to the right as he walked into the living room from the hallway. It shared a common wall with the other apartment on the floor. He mentally inventoried the tasks that lay ahead.

The living room furniture—a brown suede couch, a black leather chair with ottoman, two bookcases, a desk and chair, end tables with lamps—seemed adequate. Stacked boxes containing: clothing and books, his computer and sound systems, and three paintings, each protected with thick layers of bubble wrap, lined one wall in that room. Newly purchased bedding and towels, cooking utensils, four place settings, a shower curtain, and a rug for the bathroom sat in unopened packages in the bedroom.

Making the bed would be the right way to begin, the first task Sandra would take on. "It's logical," she'd have said, her list of numbered tasks in hand, but he started with his books. Unpacking the first carton, he came to the biographies and autobiographies and placed them where they'd always been, on the top shelves of the bookcase to the left. He sorted them in alphabetical order by author. When he came to Ron Chernow's *Alexander Hamilton*, still unread, he set it on his night table.

Partway through the first stack of cartons, he had a sinking feeling when he came to a box containing client charts. Rosalie's was among them. He'd read and reread his clinical notes, searching for something, anything that might answer the question that troubled him. Why did she surrender? Nothing had turned up, leaving him in a quandary. What had he missed?

The first day she had come to his office, she very nearly hadn't. At the time of her appointment, he had walked into the waiting room only to see a slender young woman, in her mid-twenties he guessed, on her way out the door. She looked back at him with such a frightened expression on her face, yet she stood there, half in and half out, her hand gripping the doorknob. For a moment, neither of them said anything. Then he noticed the words on her sleeveless gray T-shirt, "Oh, won't you stay with me, 'cause you're all I need," and instantly thought of the irony. She'd called to ask for an appointment yet was fleeing before they'd even met. So, he took a risk. "I'm Dr. Sterling. I like Sam Smith's music, too. How about staying with me for just a little while this morning?" She stood there for a moment longer, her eyes closed, and then turned and briskly walked past him into his office without making eye contact.

He motioned to one of the two brown leather recliners that faced one another, but she ignored him. Instead, she walked over to the window behind his desk and, placing both of her hands on the glass, looked down at the street four floors below.

"I'm glad you're here," he said as he took his seat. She didn't reply. Rosalie then began walking slowly around his office, first standing in front of his framed license, diplomas, and certificates, looking as if she were carefully reading each one. Minutes passed as he watched her. Her shoulder-length auburn hair was gathered behind her ears, and rectangular, red-framed sunglasses were perched on her head. She wore blue denim shorts, threadbare in places, and black ankle-length suede boots with black-and-white-striped socks. A chunk of turquoise was suspended on her thin silver chain necklace. She had a deep tan, maybe even a bit of sunburn on her shoulders. Something about her eyes reminded him of a young Sally Field.

"I'm glad I'm here, too," she said softly as she continued to look around, stopping next in front of a framed print of Miró's *Dog Barking at the Moon* that hung above the tan corduroy couch. She remained there, her arms folded across her chest.

"I sometimes feel like that dog," he said. "The painting reminds me it's okay to bark."

His saying that seemed to make a difference because she turned from the painting, walked over to the recliner, and sat down. "I don't want to have to keep feeling so depressed. Can you help me?"

And so, they started. Over the coming weeks, he learned that she'd been in a series of short-lived relationships in the past several years, none of them particularly memorable. After graduating from the Evergreen State College, she'd worked as a writer at her mother's public relations firm, not really liking the products she'd had to produce but apparently being quite successful at it. In the middle of their sixth session, she told him she needed to apologize for not being truthful when she'd answered several of the questions that he'd asked in their first two meetings. While she'd been honest about alcohol, she'd lied about pot. In fact, she'd been getting high a half dozen times every day for the past six months. And it was not true that she'd never been abused. When she was twelve, she'd been seduced by her father's brother, and that relationship continued for nearly a year while he lived with her family. "He didn't force me," she'd said.

After these disclosures, her progress accelerated. Believing that her pot use was getting in the way, Rosalie made the decision to quit. Their conversations went deeper as her trust in him and in herself grew stronger. In one particularly difficult session, she used the word *rape* when talking about what her uncle had done. She knew there was much about the impact that it had had on her life that needed to be brought to light. It frightened her, but she thought she was ready for that work.

But then he read a two-paragraph article in the local news section of the *Seattle Times*. She had killed herself. In the days that followed her death, he'd obsessed about not knowing what he had missed that he ought to have tuned into. His distress had been compounded when her father came up to him as Rosalie's funeral was about to begin and quietly asked him to leave the church. "She trusted you, Dr. Sterling, but I don't. I want you to let us grieve without your presence here."

He could've protected her, but he didn't. How could he have been so out of touch?

Derailed from unpacking, on impulse he moved aside two cartons, looking for his journals. Opening that box, he selected one randomly: a photo of brilliant orange-and-black monarch butterflies pasted on its first page. He'd written in it thirty-six years earlier. He grabbed his keys and walked downstairs to the front yard, where, gratefully, the benches were unoccupied. He flipped spontaneously to the middle and read.

Thursday, April 22, 1982

Todd. Today's anniversary has hit me like a ton of bricks. I woke in a cold sweat this morning, remembering that day ten years ago when two army officers, one a chaplain, came to our house, no words needing to be spoken for the horrible truth to be known, just their presence at our front door. From my bedroom I watched them park, get out of their government van, and come up the walkway. I heard Mom scream for my dad and saw Mr. Meyer across the street hold his sobbing wife as they looked on.

I cringe with shame at the memory of the awful things I did later that night when my parents had finally gone to bed. My God.

The phone is unplugged, the drapes closed, and all of the lights are off. Screw the classes I'm supposed to attend. Today, I don't want to be awake.

***

Feeling his pulse quicken, he quickly closed the cover. No. Just now, looking back at that day was not what he needed to do. He ran up the stairs and dropped that notebook back in the storage box.

Just to get through this first day, he thought about what he had to do. He'd set up the Bose Wave radio, line up three CDs—Beethoven, then Mendelssohn, then Shankar. Once the music started, he'd make the bed, then work on the bathroom, and then go out for a walk. Dinner? He'd decide while walking, maybe eating out, picking up a few groceries—juice, milk, coffee, bananas, cereal—for tomorrow morning.

The plan calmed him, a glimmer of order in the midst of chaos. In a few minutes, after taking in the made-up bed, the lit lamp on the nightstand along with his Hamilton biography and the digital clock set to the accurate time, he hung the shower curtain and moved on to putting away some of his clothes.

Heading down the stairs to begin his walk and find some food, he hummed the Shankar tune he'd just heard. The sense of desperation he had felt a short time earlier had lifted.

8 ~ An Octogenarian

Dear new neighbors:

A very warm welcome to you! I'm the woman who makes her domicile across the hall, an octogenarian, I might add, so you needn't fear being blasted with what seems to masquerade as music these days, middle-of-the-night pizza deliveries, doors being slammed, floors jarred, or the wafting pungent aroma of pot. Well, I just might someday reconsider the latter now that it's legal!

You may, however, hear me practicing piano, generally for several hours beginning mid to late morning. Chopin's études are my current preoccupation. Please tell me if it ever disturbs you, and I'll make the appropriate adjustment to my schedule.

Leaving a note taped to your door is hardly a sufficient greeting, so if you've time tomorrow evening, please join me for coffee and a taste of pastries at 7:00. I very much look forward to meeting you.

Very sincerely,
Milena Hodrová

9 ~ A Quinquagenarian

Dear Ms. Hodrová—

Your note left me feeling warmly welcomed and greatly reassured about the cultural norms here on the second floor of our building.

However, I have noticed a motorcycle parked on the street out front. Might it be yours? I am slightly alarmed by the one misery that you didn't rule out, that is you revving the engine at 2:00 in the morning.

With that nagging fear weighing heavily on my mind, I look forward to our meeting tomorrow evening. It's just me, a quinquagenarian by the way.

Your new neighbor,
Elliott Sterling

10 ~ Caught in a Closing Vice

Milena first ground the coffee beans and then spooned several measures into a French press before turning on the burner under her kettle. He made a mental note of her appearance so he could describe her in his journal. She was about five foot seven, had regal posture, and was wearing a navy skirt, an almond-colored blouse fringed with lace, and a loosely fitted matching cardigan. Her white hair, parted in the middle, was gathered in a twist and secured with a mother-of-pearl comb.

Then there were her eyes. What could he write about them? The first thing that came to mind was how thoroughly accepting they seemed. He felt seen by her, seen and understood and valued.

While she worked, he sensed her glancing at him as he walked around the room. On the wall opposite the windows looking out onto the courtyard where the western red cedar cast early evening shadows, five framed photographs were hung. Three of them, lined up horizontally, were black and white, an orange/yellow tint hinting at their vintage, and portrayed family groupings, all posed quite formally with the men and boys in suits and the women in dresses that hid their necks.

He moved to look more closely at a work of art hanging on the wall just to the right of her baby grand piano. It was an oil painting of a Gothic cathedral's dark interior. Visible in the foreground to the left in this scene was a statue of a kneeling man, adorned in religious vestments, his hands clasped and resting on a prayer rail. An ornate vaulted ceiling with a sunlit nave was visible in the background, and three curtained confessionals stood to the right.

As he continued studying the scene for several more minutes, Milena said, "I don't think any of my visitors have ever been so interested in that painting." She set a tray of porcelain cups and saucers, white with green ivy vines, along with a plate of apricot-filled cookies on the coffee table in front of the divan and then came to stand next to him. "It's the Saint Vitus Cathedral in Prague," she said. "It dates back to the fourteenth century."

"This painting is mesmerizing, Milena. I feel drawn in, as if while standing here I'm being pulled into the cathedral."

She touched him on the shoulder. "Ten years ago, when I finally stood in the spot where the artist must have been when he captured this image, I cried. It was as if I had returned home after a very, very long time in another world."

They stood there silently for a few more moments before moving to the sitting area. She said, "I have the same experience you had when I look at that painting. But I've never heard anyone else say that it affected them that way. I'm moved by your reaction."

"Prague was your home?" he asked.

Milena poured coffee for each of them and didn't immediately answer his question. He wondered, as she stared off into the distance, if she might have been weighing whether or not to respond. He ate one of the cookies and sipped his coffee.

Then, turning to him, she said, "Yes, I was born in Prague. And my father was the artist of this work, Elliott. When I sit at my piano and gaze into this scene, the music I play is for him and for my mother. I imagine myself standing in his footsteps inside that cathedral, but in my mind's eye, I'm an adult, and my parents . . .," a pensive look on her face, "and my parents, still in the full vitality of their early years in marriage, are on either side of me."

"I'd like to know about your father and mother. May I ask?"

Milena walked over to the piano, sat on the bench, and began to play softly. His gaze moved to the long, flowing pastel-colored drapes moving gently with the breeze. Unlike his apartment with its dark hardwood floors and moldings, Milena's design motif was airy and light throughout.

"This is Chopin's Étude in E Major," she told him. And as she played, she began to answer him. It seemed as if the telling of her past, what he learned was a childhood marked by unspeakable tragedy, required that she be cradled by the music.

"I was twelve years old, Elliott. We were living in Prague when the ground fell out from under our feet." She wasn't looking at him as she spoke, but rather at the painting—or perhaps through the canvas into some infinite distance. "I have memories of our earlier lives, merely wisps. In one, my father is playing a piano. In another, my mother is lighting candles and covering her eyes while praying." She stopped speaking for several moments but continued playing, as if to prepare herself for what she was about to say.

"Then, we, the Jewish people I mean, were caught in a closing vise as, step-by-step, our place in society was eradicated. At first, we told ourselves that Hitler would only go so far. We'd adjust." She looked up at him. "That's really what also happened as the people throughout Europe watched the Nazis devour one region after another, one country after another. 'He'll only go so far,' people said. 'We'll adjust.'"

The ethereal beauty of the composition she was performing, a favorite Chopin piece that in ordinary circumstances sang to his soul, felt altogether too innocent when heard as backdrop to Milena's Holocaust memories.

"Once we arrived in the camp, a stranger led me away. For a few months, I saw my mother in the evenings but only sporadically saw my father. We'd never again see our home; we'd never again live together. The days turned into weeks, and then months, and then years. We heard rumors of transports that would take us east, and other rumors that in the east there were extermination camps."

For a few more minutes, Milena continued to play, neither of them speaking. He sat listening, immersed in the scenes she was creating about that time in her life.

Gazing at the painting, Milena asked, "Can you imagine the terror that those children experienced? Can you imagine what their parents must have felt?" He realized her questions were rhetorical. How could he possibly answer her?

He was startled when Milena's questions transposed to his nightmare, that moment when Rosalie, begging for his help and beyond his reach, fell to her death. He'd been powerless to stop his client from committing suicide. What had been done to Milena and her parents had rendered them completely powerless.

How had she been able to go on with her life, to stand on her feet after being so brutally beaten down?

Milena finished playing, and together they wordlessly carried the dishes into her kitchen. Walking to the door, he turned to her. "I doubt anyone who was not there can really understand what you or your parents felt."

Standing next to him, she looked him in the eye and slowly nodded.

"Good night, Milena."

Returning to his apartment, he struggled to breathe normally. In a few moments, he reflexively reached for his journal as he turned on the desk lamp, but it was too soon.

He turned the light off and sat in the darkness.

One Month Earlier

11 ~ Looking Always

Elliott was annoyed. They'd been friends for decades, but today he was irritated by Theo's relentless hovering. Three voicemails and a barrage of emails, all in the past ten days, reminding him of this evening's poetry slam and urging him to come. Theo had worn him down, and he'd just run out of excuses.

Forty years earlier they'd met in high school. Theo was one grade ahead. Throughout that time, when one of them struggled while navigating some particularly tricky twist on the road his life traversed, the other was consistently in his friend's corner.

Theo came out at the age of twenty. Neither of them flinched in figuring out how gay and straight guys could remain close friends.

That same year, the tenth anniversary of Elliott's brother's death in Vietnam occurred. On that date and with no warning, Elliott puzzlingly fell into a depressive slump. For days, Theo's near constant presence, mostly just hanging out, provided him a safety net. Then, late in the second week, the gloom mercifully lifted. Each year since, that anniversary had caused Elliott to tumble yet again into a similarly intense but brief period of immobilizing melancholy. Repeatedly, Theo had been right at his side. He was again there for Elliott when his client killed herself.

Elliott owed him. So he surrendered.

At the bookstore, two large bookcases built on rollers to make space for events like this had been moved aside. It looked as if about twenty-five people were in the audience. Elliott found a seat in the last row.

Three or four poets read their work. Staring off into space, his thoughts were elsewhere. Their poems blurred until, suddenly, without understanding why, he heard these words:

i have crossed another
ocean to arrive at
this counting / looking always
for what might be mine

Quickly opening his journal before he forgot the line, Elliott jotted it down. *Looking always for what might be mine.* It told him about the poet's having traveled across an ocean while on a search.

But looking for what? What was it that he wanted to make his own?

For Elliott, looking had become a constant. He longed for a path to regaining a sense of who he was, imploded since Rosalie's suicide.

Looking always for what might be mine. Is that what I'm doing?

After introducing the next poet, Theo walked back toward the entrance and, seeing his friend in the audience, flung his arms in the air in mock surprise. With a nod of his head, Theo signaled for Elliott to follow.

In his mid-fifties, Theo was just over six feet tall and bald, but he had the athletic body of a guy in his thirties. He enjoyed flaunting his tight abs as well as being out and proud. That day's form-fitting T-shirt sported a large paw print and the words "Woof Woof."

"My man, your presence is telling," Theo whispered. "I now know the formula."

"What're you talking about?"

"I got the formula for how to move your sorry butt out of that lonely apartment. Don't think I'm going to be hesitant in using it." Theo beamed with smug satisfaction.

"Bugger that, buddy. You'll need an Enigma machine because the formula changes after every transmission." He aimed a noogie at Theo's left shoulder, but his friend ducked out of the way.

"I've got to introduce the next poet, but here's a little surprise." Theo took a piece of paper from the shelf under his cash register and handed it to Elliott. "I printed out a copy of one of your poems. How about doing a reading? I'll work you in right after Melanie."

Feeling cornered, Elliott reached over and snatched the poem from his friend's hand. "Damn it, Theo." He stepped over to his chair and grabbed his coat.

Having overheard, two people sitting closest to where they were standing glanced at them with alarmed looks. Elliott ignored them.

"Okay, okay, not one of my best ideas." Theo held his hands up in a gesture of apology. "But hang out a while longer. Let me do this next introduction and I'll come back. No pressure, I promise. There's something I want to ask you. Okay? Will you stay?"

Elliott grudgingly agreed and returned to his seat. When the next poet began speaking, Theo headed to the back row.

"I'm sorry I pounced on you like that, but I've got an idea. This time it's a good one." Theo's face was animated as he laid out his plan. "There's a weekend booksellers' convention in San Francisco at the end of the month. How about flying down there together? I'll only need to spend a few hours at the meeting. We can take in some galleries, check out Berkeley and Oakland, and maybe go to a play. What do you say?"

Elliott could tell Theo was frustrated with him. Shaking his head, Elliott said, "Not now. I don't know when, but just not now." Elliott looked him in the eyes as he spoke. His voice was firm but not hostile.

"Will you please take a look in the mirror?" Theo said, exasperation in his voice. "See what you're doing to yourself? You've stopped taking new clients. You're ignoring your friends and saying no has become your rapid default whenever I suggest something new." Theo grabbed Elliott's arm. "You did everything anyone possibly could have done for Rosalie. Can't you accept that? Do you really think it's a good idea to live life as a hermit?"

Elliott yanked his arm away. "Will you please let up?"

The two onlookers waved their hands to be noticed. They both loudly whispered, "Shhh."

Staring each other down, the two men stood there. Moments passed. Elliott then bolted for the door.

Theo told his assistant he had to leave and ran after his friend. "Wait!" Catching up, Theo pleaded, "Can't we at least talk this out?"

Elliott continued walking, saying nothing.

"Please, stop. The Witness Bar is on the next block. Just one drink?"

Elliott kept walking.

Theo ran in front of him. "For Christ's sake, Elliott."

Elliott halted. He stood there momentarily, weighing his options with his eyes closed, his arms stiffly at his sides. Agree to talk with Theo about an issue he'd hardly been able to sort out for himself?

"Please?"

Elliott made up his mind and walked in, leading them to a table near the back. When the waitress came over, Theo ordered a Careless Whisper and Elliott chose a Son of a Preacher Man.

Theo began. "Look, take your time, however much time you need. But don't you think it might help you pull out of the quicksand you're in if you nudged yourself just a little? I mean, do you really want me to leave you festering?"

"I'm not festering," Elliott muttered, averting Theo's gaze. "I'm not depressed either, in case that's what you're thinking."

"What's going on with you, then?" Theo asked, his voice tinged with desperation.

For several minutes, neither of them spoke. The waitress brought over their drinks and placed them on coasters. Theo took thirty dollars from his wallet and paid. Each took a sip.

"All I know," Elliott quietly said, "is that I was Dr. Sterling, who had some competence in helping his clients, even those who thought ending it all was their only answer." He was looking down at his hands. "Once upon a time I was Peter's dad and Sandra's husband. I taught a little boy how to ride his bike and camp in the wilderness. My best friend and I created that little boy and loved figuring out how to be his parents as he went through each new stage in his life." His voice cracked as he spoke those words.

Theo began to say something, but then stopped himself.

Looking up at Theo, Elliott said, "It's all slipped away from me. It's slipped away, and I don't know what's left of who I thought I was. Or even what value I have as a therapist, husband, or dad." Finishing his drink, he said, "I'm not depressed. I just don't fit in any of these roles any longer. I feel as if I've lost any purpose I once had in my life."

The two of them looked at each other for several moments.

"There are answers," Theo said. "There have to be. If you've lost your purpose, we're going to need to go searching for it."

They headed to the door. Elliott nodded, shrugged his shoulders, turned, and walked away.

He left Theo standing there mute.

12 ~ He Turns into an Asshole

It would be Peter's last run and he'd be alone. The blizzard was an anomaly this late in the ski season. Three of his stalwart buddies said he'd be crazy if he didn't call it quits. But, hyped at having the mountain all to himself, even if he was bone weary at that point, he rode the lift a final time, swaying empty chairs lined up ahead of him on ghostly parade. Reaching the top, he fought the pressure of a howling squall that vacuum-sealed his butt to the seat, and finally broke free by tucking his head between his knees and pushing for all he was worth. Turbulent gusts of snow blurred the horizon, veiling the craggy peaks of the San Juan range, and the wind pummeled the wobbling and barely visible bamboo fence line. Trusting in muscle memory to navigate the storm-shaped, nearly opaque shadows on that mile-long run, he set off.

Picturing what lay ahead, he reminded himself that the hill first panned left, followed by a quick dogleg to the right. He swiped at his goggles' kaleidoscopic glaze of ice, and his adrenaline pumped at the trepidation of what came next, the possibly obscured terrain he'd be traversing for the next forty or fifty seconds before reaching the gentle glide at the bottom. In an instant, engulfed in a complete whiteout, he was airborne, neither the ground nor the sky visible through the swirling morass, his internal gyroscope disabled, and an eternity of endless falling producing a metallic taste of panic in his mouth.

Upright? Would he land safely? When? Bracing for an impact, his skis abruptly slammed the ground. His body folded like fireplace bellows as he raced forward, his legs straining to keep the skis parallel, and he shouted "Yes," when he realized he'd beaten the odds.

Then, without warning, he was airborne again, his body flipping and suspended in weightlessness. Seconds passed, and his head snapped back as his skis again found the slope, his thighs and calves burning, his ski poles gaining merciful purchase in fending off a spiraling fall, and then, finally, the lodge was in sight, just a bunny hill away from his triumphant run's end. No one was there to hear it, his roaring laughter. "I'm a god," he shouted, his arms raised in victory, swirling to his right in a celebratory snow-spraying hockey stop.

"Your dad phoned again," a voice called out as he walked in the door of the one-bedroom basement apartment he shared with five others. Lying on the floor in his sleeping bag next to their blue Formica kitchen table, his head resting on his pack, Tat was reading a three-month-old *Powder* magazine. The ink covering both of his arms, every spot on his torso, and circling his neck offered an easy clue about his handle. No one was officially recognized as a bona fide ski bum without one; they all had handles.

Peter's was Pan, Peter Pan to his mom, her mischievous boy who'd never grow up. Pan to his friends, god of the wild and companion of the nymphs. Peter was muscular, with a gymnast's physique and a shaved head. His eyes were a piercing blue.

He popped open a Bud and handed one to Tat, who wordlessly raised his can in a toast. "Why aren't you calling back? Got a beef with him?"

Peter pulled up a folding chair and yanked off his wool socks. Spotting a jar of Vaseline that one of the girls had left on the counter, he carefully ministered to his blisters and bruises, collateral damage from thrift-shop ski boots half a size too small.

"I'll tell you why I don't call him back. When we talk, he turns into an asshole."

Tat set the magazine aside, sat up, and took a swig. "What's his problem?"

"He just doesn't get it, Tat. Shit, I don't understand what's going on with him," Peter said. "There was a time when he and I were cool. Now, he gets pissed that my life isn't a mirror image of his. Rigid. Routine. Safe.

"When I was a kid, he taught me how to live fully in the moment. He got off on testing himself in the face of danger. He talked about each of us needing to find his relationship with nature." Peter spotted a pair of someone's flip-flops and slipped them on. "I mean, he was my hero.

"Some of the greatest times we spent together were hiking and camping. He wanted me to learn I could survive, so we'd leave our fishing gear at home. We'd make do with a hatchet and some branches. I remember we made a gaff out of a bent nail that we strapped to a chunk of tree branch with some bark. And now . . ." he popped open another can, "now, I think he feels my life is somehow an assault on him and his values. Yeah, he's obsessed about my taking too many risks. That the way I live my life is too hazardous." Peter stood and tossed the empty can into the trash. "Hell, I don't know, maybe he has no choice."

"He hasn't got a choice about his own life?"

Peter felt a lump in his throat. "I don't know what happened to him, but it had to have been a big fucking deal. Sometimes I think of him as a prisoner. It gives me another way of seeing him, so different from the angry accuser always making demands: 'Why don't you?' 'Why can't you?' and 'Stop tossing your life away.' But, man, it's so easy to get hooked by his disapproval."

For a few minutes they sat quietly, and Peter mulled over this impasse with his father. He watched Tat take a packet of hemp rolling papers, his grinder, and a fat bud of OG Kush from his pack. After rolling and lighting a joint, Tat took a deep drag and passed it over.

Peter made up his mind. He'd ask Nureyev if he could borrow his computer. It was time to try again. He'd have a Skype call with his dad.

Tat nailed what Peter was thinking. "Pan, maybe your dad needs to find a way out of his personal prison before he can hear you talk about your freedom."

Peter took another drag.

"But I got to tell you, man," Tat said, "maybe he has a point. If there's a limit to be pushed, for you pushing is never enough. You got to demolish it."

13 ~ I Just Wish You Could See Me

As Elliott finished drying the dishes, he thought about his neighbor. Milena had survived and was now eighty-seven years old. From the photos on her grand piano, it appeared she'd been married and had a daughter. Now she was living alone. Was her husband still in her life? Her daughter? She was an accomplished pianist. Did she perform professionally? Perhaps as a soloist or a member of an orchestra? Who was she?

He poured a second cup of coffee and glanced at his watch. At a few minutes before nine, as he and Peter had agreed in an email exchange, he logged on to Skype, ran a sound test, and waited for the call. Peter and he hadn't had any contact for over a month. Their usual routine of checking in weekly had deteriorated. They'd fallen into an all-too-frequent pattern in which the father provoked the son's resentment. Their talks these days were rarely free from painful edginess.

Colorado was an hour ahead of Seattle, and Peter might be getting ready for work, whatever job he'd managed to land to keep him in the mountains. When they last talked, he had been running river rafts. It was Wednesday, so Elliott was not scheduled to see clients.

The familiar Skype tune announced that Peter was calling. "How's my old man doing?"

Elliott chuckled, relieved by the lightness in his son's voice. Peter seemed genuinely happy to see him. He also felt disarmed when he saw his smile. He was wearing an orange-and-white-striped soccer jersey and sipping from a carton of orange juice. His head was still shaved, and he sported a trendy several-days' stubble of beard.

Elliott realized he'd been tense with anticipation that this call would start off badly. More to the point, he worried that he'd lose control, come out of the gate swinging, and Peter would have no choice but to clam up or join the fray.

"Peter, I'm missing you terribly, kiddo. How about a tour? Let me show you my new digs." He lifted the notebook computer and aimed its webcam to scan the living room, beginning with the bookshelves.

"Nice, Dad," Peter said. "I worried you might be living a spartan life in some dark and dingy one-room studio. I can see you've got lots of space, and—oh, just a minute, go back and show me the couch." Peter groaned when Elliott pointed the computer to that side of the room. "Not sure that couch is going to be very comfortable if I crash at your place, but it's cool seeing you've not forgotten us."

He realized that Peter was looking at the framed photograph on the end table. The three of them were sitting on lawn chairs in the backyard, one of his rarely successful efforts to have all of them ready just at the moment when the time-delay shutter on his camera opened. He felt a pang of loss in hearing Peter talk of "us," as if they remained a family unit. That image had fractured for Elliott, but it was one that he desperately wanted to stay steady for his son.

Walking through the apartment, Elliott narrated the scenery. The tour ended with a shot of the western red cedar in the building's front courtyard.

Elliott savored talking with his son when they were simply being with one another, no contentiousness or rancor poisoning the well. *Can we sustain this?*

"Dad, I want to know how you're doing—I mean how you're really doing. Can I ask? How's life for you with this huge change?"

He looked at Peter's face. Remnants of childhood were still visible in his dimples, the cluster of freckles on his nose, the boy's innocent sincerity in his eyes.

"You know, it's not easy," Elliott said. "The decision your mom and I made was the right one, but it's such an enormous adjustment after so many years. Who knew what a roller-coaster ride learning to live alone could be? I mean, as simple a task as unpacking a box of books or even suddenly remembering that I'd need to buy a vacuum cleaner can set off a powerful urge to go for a hike or take a nap—anything to escape the moment. There was someone alongside me for more than thirty years, someone whose opinion I'd always hear. Losing that voice leaves an ear-splitting silence."

He was aware that he was leaning on his son's shoulder. Peter was listening and was holding back whatever advice might be scrolling through his mind, all of that despite the acrimony that had made their recent conversations so toxic.

Elliott laughed with a sudden realization and relished the chance to say something positive for a change about his son's life. "I have to tell you that I'm seeing you from a new vantage point. Here I am whining about adapting to a new apartment, and you—you travel the world, so adventurous and curious. Your passion for skiing, for meeting people, the excitement you feel while peering into strange cultures, and your ability to go with the flow, couch surfing, and carrying all your worldly belongings in your backpack. I have to tell you how much I wish right now that I had your resilience. Can you bottle some of it up and put it in the mail to me?"

A sadness unexpectedly welled up in Elliott. Intermixed with his admiration was anger for his son's ever-more-daring thrill seeking. Someday, Peter's over-the-top zeal for death-defying record breaking could lead to a tragic outcome.

He knew he had to be careful. He didn't want to subject either of them to where their conversation could be headed.

"Enough about that. Listen, my neighbor has just begun her piano practice, a Brahms piece, I think. Let me hold the computer close to the wall. Can you hear it?"

They were both quiet for a few moments. "Yeah, it's beautiful. Have you met her?"

"Just a few days ago, Peter, and only for a short visit. Such an intriguing person. She's Jewish and was born in Prague, survived the Holocaust, lost both parents, and—God only knows how—lives her life with enthusiasm and an incredibly positive outlook. She's in her late eighties."

He stood at the wall for a moment longer, and they listened to Milena play. When she ended the piece, he again put the computer on his desk and sat.

"After she described the day when she and her parents were forced from their home, and then her memories of the concentration camp, she asked if I could imagine the terror they felt." Elliott looked away, slowly shaking his head and biting his lip.

"My God, Dad. I wish we could be having this conversation in person instead of by Skype. I don't know that I'd have anything much to offer, but maybe just hanging out together . . ." Peter paused, and then his caring smile tipped the scales for Elliott.

"Son, I'd love hanging out with you. It's been too long, and I've been wary of asking how much longer it will be. Helping your old man get through this psychological storm, I just . . . I just love you for the thought. But I . . ."

Precipitously, he felt the electricity, a warning. *Leave it for another time. Just leave it.*

A silence suspended between them as they examined one another's eyes. Unmistakably, the unspoken question each of them was asking was, *Can we step back from the precipice?*

Can I? Elliott's heart was racing and his breathing faster. He felt propelled by the spiking tension in his body. "Peter, I have to . . ."

This can wait. Don't poison this moment.

But he recognized what was now inevitable. He plowed ahead. "But what would be even more important to me is seeing you put an end to these horrifying risks you've been—"

"Dad, please don't—"

"Wait. I know this isn't a comfortable topic, but I'm suddenly aware of why it's so important to me. Please, please listen to me."

Peter's eyes were closed.

"My neighbor suffered horrible losses. Your uncle's death in combat in Vietnam, your grandfather's dying of cancer, your grandmother's mind depleted by the ravages of Alzheimer's, and your mom and I coming to the end of our road—all of these losses are real, overwhelmingly real, and all of them together are making me feel acutely worried about the possibility of losing you."

Peter was slowly shaking his head. "Okay, Dad, say what you need to say." His arms were crossed.

Elliott stopped, took a breath, gauging whether the cause was lost. "All right, I guess I'm in it with both feet. Let me just say that whatever else you ultimately decide about your life, please stop chancing that you'll have some awful accident. I just don't get what you're trying to prove over and over again by these extremely hazardous stunts."

Peter sighed. He opened his eyes and moved closer to the webcam. "Dad, if only you'd try to take in my experience. I feel it in every pore in my body that the mountain can take me at a whim and that death is at hand if I make one wrong move. When I'm being tested—my will, my faith, my strength, and even my ingenuity—I'm not just surviving danger, I'm thriving in it."

Elliott began to speak, but Peter continued.

"The life I'm living is as authentic as it can be. I work my ass off so I can be on the slopes as much as possible. You worry about an awful disaster. I get that. But for me, I yearn for each God moment when the magic of having defied death is pure ecstasy. If you were with me, you'd hear me howl. Dad, I—"

"What about getting stoned all the time, Peter? Aren't you actually doubling your risks when you're ripped while having these God moments?"

Did I have to say something about his drug use? It's as if I'm hanging on a precipice and on the edge of losing it.

Elliott watched Peter roll his eyes and clench his jaw. What felt like minutes passed without either of them saying anything. Elliott had an impulse to apologize and change the subject. He didn't do that.

Soon it was too late, and the sarcasm in Peter's voice was unmistakable. "You need to understand that I plan to the tiniest detail every step I take, every maneuver, and every bit of the topography. I'm constantly practicing and studying. None of what I do is simply an impulsive act."

His volume was louder with each phrase.

"You believe that because I could get blown off a mountain, slam into a tree, or fall into a massive crevasse in the ice, I should live my life differently. There's no way I'll agree to that."

"But Peter—"

"It's my life, Dad." His eyes were blazing. "Will you please get off my fucking back?"

Elliott's foundation cracked and collapsed. He had an impulse to pick up the computer and hurl it out the window. He exploded. "Okay, let's take a close look at the actual scenarios if we're going to play this game." He heard the drip of venom in the sound of his words. "What if some unexpected glitch suddenly pops up that you can't practice for? Isn't that a reality that every extreme athlete faces?"

He didn't wait for a reply. "Your Facebook posting this past weekend is a good example. You stood at the edge of a cliff and did a back flip. I saw that you landed just where you had been standing. But what if a strong gust of wind had come up? Or what if the ground had given way? Or you twisted your ankle and fell over?"

Elliott moved closer to the screen, his eyes unblinking. "I'm talking, by the way, about your self-indulgence. You've told me what you get out of these stunts. But do you ever think about what it would be like for your mother or for me if you died?"

He felt trepidation in the fragments of thought that were coming together as he ranted. "What about finding yourself at a point when you run out of escape strategies?" His nightmare about Rosalie's death was ripping into his consciousness. "What if there's nothing you can do to save yourself? What about that scenario? You just can't …"

He choked, fearing that he was about to vomit.

Peter was holding his head in his hands. After several moments he glanced up, the bitter countenance on his face slowly morphing, his fiery rage cooling. And then, as Elliott watched, his son's expression became one of compassion. Peter sat there staring at his computer and saying nothing.

"Oh, Peter, I didn't mean to … I wish I hadn't—"

"Dad, what happened to you?"

Elliott looked away from the monitor.

Peter continued speaking, but in a low volume, carefully measuring each word. "Where's the man who taught me to trust in what I know and in the survival skills he taught me? How did you make such a one-hundred-eighty-degree change? And, for God's sake, why?"

"Peter, you were a kid then. Don't you see the difference?" Elliott said, a plaintive tone in his voice.

Peter continued as if he hadn't heard. "Don't you remember? We'd hike for twenty miles, find a place to camp, catch fish, maybe shoot some game, and live off the land for weeks." He paused and thought of something else. "And what about your teaching me to find my way, reading the moss on the trees or using a compass to get oriented? Wasn't the point to help me if I got lost? You're at home in the wilderness, and you taught me to be. So how can you suddenly be so terrified by my choice to walk off the beaten path?"

Elliott cringed and shook his head. "The beaten path? Are you serious?" His tone was acerbic. "Look, Peter, reading a compass was vital to knowing where you were headed, but you're at a time in your life when finding your way in the woods isn't the issue. It's finding your way in life. Can't you see that?"

"Dad, I am finding my way. It's just not your way. And I've got my own compass, and I know exactly where I am." He looked down and said quietly, "I just wish you could see me, the person I am, not the person you so badly want me to be. I just wish you could trust me."

Elliott heard the sadness in his son's voice and felt torn. Those memories from Peter's childhood reminded him of the pride he once felt. Now, however, his fears were hammering in his brain. *I'm losing him.*

"The deep and cold crevasse you're frightened of my falling into? That's your desperation, and you're projecting it onto me. I'm not like you, Dad. I don't hide in the pages of a notebook because I'm too frightened to live my life." Elliott watched Peter grimace and quickly shake his head. "I didn't mean that. I ... Dad, let's talk again soon."

And the connection broke.

14 ~ Open Your Eyes

"He's pissed at me," Elliott said. "Actually disconnected us when we were talking on Skype."

"No surprise. Peter's been pissed at you for a while," Theo replied. "Anything different this time?"

Just before seven, they were standing in a crowd at the take-out window at Ivar's Salmon House. They'd both ordered Alaska halibut fish and chips.

Elliott went up to the counter when their number was called. As they walked to the car, Elliott said, "Before our Skype call, I made up my mind that I wasn't going to bug him, but—"

"But you blew it," Theo said, an edge of sarcasm in his tone, as he slid into the driver's seat.

"Afraid so. Hold on. I'll tell you more when we get to the park."

From there they drove a half mile to Gas Works Park, overlooking Seattle's Lake Union. Climbing to the top of Kite Hill, they spread out a blanket. It was a sunny day in the upper sixties, and they noticed at least a dozen other picnic spreads dotting the park's expansive lawn.

"This is my favorite spot in the city," Theo said. He took a thermos filled with sauvignon blanc from his backpack, filled two cups, and handed one to Elliott.

Three amphibious landing craft, emblazoned with Ride the Ducks, were ferrying tourists around the lake, and at the south end, a race with a dozen daysailer boats was under way. A Kenmore Air seaplane glided over the Fremont Bridge before touching down and heading toward the terminal in the shadow of the Space Needle.

"I wonder how those planes avoid crashing into the boats," Elliott said, opening the paper sack and handing Theo his fries and fish. "Hundreds of them out there."

For several minutes they ate quietly.

Elliott laughed. Pointing to a small raft, about the size of a king-size bed, Elliott said, "Now that's class, man." The raft was being towed to a spot about fifty yards offshore. Shortly, the tow boat left. On the raft, two people were dining at a cloth-covered table, complete with lit candles in a candelabra and champagne in an ice bucket. The guy was wearing a tux, the woman a gown.

"Wonder if someone's going to propose," Theo said.

"The answer had better be yes. It'd be a damn cold swim to shore," Elliott said as he gathered up their garbage and took it to a trash can. He returned to sit on the blanket.

"So, you lost it? What happened?" Theo asked.

Elliott slowly shook his head. "He undoubtedly thinks I'm a broken record, but I have to keep trying to get through to him. The way he's going, it's only a matter of time before he ends up—"

"Ends up how?"

Elliott's lips were pursed. "Dead, Theo. Fucking dead," he shouted. Elliott crossed his arms, looking at his friend directly, and then lowered his voice. "I told him I fear that he'll end up dead. He has to keep raising the bar. People have to gasp and heap praise on him for executing what's unbelievable. So it's never good enough to just dazzle people. It's as if he needs to terrify them and maybe himself as well."

"Terrify? Is that what happens to you?"

"Of course it is." He stood and looked out at the skyline. "He tries to assure me that he never attempts something new until he's thought through every detail and practiced every step. Yet the concept of something unexpected and out of his control happening doesn't seem to occur to him."

"What else did you say?" Theo had a stern look.

Elliott realized he was feeling apprehensive. Theo was waiting to jump all over him.

Elliott turned back to face Theo and quietly said, "I told him I feared his self-indulgence would someday trap him and that he'd run out of escape strategies."

Theo threw up his hands. "Self-indulgence? Seriously, Elliott?"

"He's twenty-seven years old, for Christ's sake," Elliott said, clenching his fists. "It's way past time for him to grow up and—"

"Yeah, I get it. You want him to make the decisions you'd make. But, dude, is all the pressure you're putting on him working?"

"Not yet, but what choice do I have? I need him to—"

"Bullshit." Theo pointed his finger at him. "Here's the deal, my friend. Peter worships you."

Elliott sat again on the blanket. "Maybe at one time, but now he's ready to disown me."

"Just listen. When he was a kid, those wilderness trips were the highlights of his life. He gobbled up all of the survival skills you taught him. And, more than anything else, he wanted your approval."

"And he got it. I always encouraged him, gave him lots of praise, and we were buddies. There's no way he didn't know I approved of him."

"Until you didn't, and he damn sure knew when that changed."

Elliott, bit his lip and looked at his watch. "You want me to approve of his risking his life again and again?" he said, his voice raised. "And by the way, living as if there's no need for a profession? A career?"

Theo started to say something, but Elliott cut him off.

"What about sponging off his mother so he can be a ski bum? Being stoned all the time? Fuck it, maybe even being a dealer to support his habit? Should I approve of all that?"

"I'm telling you, buddy," Theo said, "I feel a chill listening to you. When I was in my twenties, I had no idea where I was going to land for a career. I was into some crazy shit, and I smoked way more than my share."

"You're different."

"Am I really? Or did you have a hell of a lot more faith in me when we were his age than you have in your own son?"

"Back off," Elliott said, slamming his palm on the ground next to him. "Don't shovel that crap at me. My faith in him won't protect him from a fatal accident. And it's because I have so much faith in him that I worry he's tossing away any possibility of meeting his potential."

"Don't you think it's up to him to decide?"

"No, I don't. A day will come, assuming he survives, when he'll realize how much he's screwed himself. I need to do whatever I can to keep him from getting permanently stuck in a dead end."

Dusk was falling rapidly.

"Do you seriously think he'll overestimate what he can safely do?" Theo asked.

"Sounds crazy? What if the real tragedy was my not giving that possibility any thought? How would I feel? For that matter, how would you feel if he died and we never saw it coming?

"Elliott, I'm no shrink, but I gotta tell you, I think you're letting Rosalie's suicide blind you to who your son is, particularly his ability to find his way through the forest. Christ, you taught him that."

"That's crap. She's got nothing to do with what I think about Peter."

"Buddy, open your eyes."

"Okay, Theo." He stood up. "I'm heading out. I'll walk home." Elliott started to stride away, but then stopped and turned. "I know you're trying to help. I know it. But I'm going to ask you to leave it alone."

Muttering a reply that Elliott couldn't hear, Theo lay down on the blanket, rested his head on his hands, and closed his eyes.

As Elliott strode down the concrete path from Kite Hill, office lights in the downtown buildings were coming on, the skyline animated by the twinkling illumination.

Two Weeks Earlier

15 ~ Sweet Millions Tomatoes

Dear Elliott—

I knocked on your door, hoping to invite you to join me for supper on Friday. We'll talk of other things, far more pleasant. Come and let me introduce you to Sweet Millions tomatoes!

Milena

16 ~ Wishing Dearly That He Believed It

Walking south on Broadway, he headed to the Pike Place Market. After reading Milena's Post-it note, his mission was to buy a bottle of wine at Pike and Western. It would take just under an hour. Maybe a bit longer if he dawdled.

Elliott was in a funk and knew he was being absurd, stubbornly so. As he walked along, he collected an inventory of complaints to add even more fuel to his dark mood. He watched a driver parking an SUV that was sure to block the car behind him. Elliott contemplated pointing it out but didn't.

A few minutes earlier, he had passed two waiters who were scrubbing off anti-Muslim graffiti sprayed on the plate-glass window of Julia's. A defacing of both the restaurant and Seattle's proudly worn progressive cloak. His annoyance festered.

The previous night, he'd had that damned nightmare yet again. Coupled with the angry Skype call he'd just had with Peter, it all but ensured he'd begin his day seeing through emotionally scratched lenses. He described the dream in his journal.

Inexplicably, this time I'm driving a van I actually sold at least ten years ago. Blustery winds rock the vehicle, making staying within the narrow lanes of the highway nearly impossible.

As a bus passes, my van swerves into it, metal scraping violently against metal. My side-view mirror is ripped from its holder. Out of desperation, I overcorrect and drive up onto the sidewalk, slamming into a mailbox and knocking it over.

There is no Aurora Bridge in this version. Instead, I'm somewhere in South Seattle on a poorly lit street in the industrial area. Because the driver's side door is crushed, I climb over to the passenger seat to escape from the van, which is rapidly filling with smoke.

In the next moment, the exploding gas tank fills the vehicle's interior with flames. Scorching heat from the blast knocks me off my feet. And then, the impossible. The tormented face of a man is peering out from inside the van's back seat, imploring me to save him.

It's my brother. It's Todd.

Remnants from that nightmare reverberated as he continued walking. Then, in front of Bartell Drugs, a panhandler, reeking of alcohol, grabbed his sleeve. "God bless you, sir." The man waved a cracked plastic cup in his face. Elliott had a handful of change. Usually, he'd empty his pockets. Not this morning.

His jaw clenched.

He watched himself descend even deeper into a cynical place and yet did nothing to stop the slide. It was almost as if he were willing himself to be there.

No, forget the *almost*.

It occurred to him that if one of his clients were in an emotional state such as this, Elliott would have questions. "Anything bothering you from earlier that day?" "Did you think about at least giving equal time to noticing more upbeat happenings around you?"

Giving equal time was not on Elliott's agenda that morning. Not even a glimmer of possibility. What made it all the more absurd, he recognized, was his being keenly aware of the choices he was making.

He chose to make no room for taking in the sunshine, or the warmth of the day, or the smile on the face of the excited kid for whom a balloon seller had just finished making a giraffe hat. Or the high-school-age girl in a white apron outside a bakery, offering warm donut samples to passersby. No letting loose while going by a vintage clothing shop where Tina Turner's *Better Be Good to Me* was blaring from an outside speaker. He loved that song.

Not today. He was wound much too tight for any of that. Ticking.

He grasped the curious enigma to this psychological state of mind. It was apparently of no importance which interaction he was having or recalling, which conversation he was in or replaying, or which event he was remembering or anticipating. His dark rumination was steady and unwavering. It was undisturbed by any awareness that the lens through which he was looking might be distorted, a skewed interpretation not to be trusted.

Peter's insistence that Elliott was projecting his demons grated on him. So did Theo's unrelenting cheerfulness campaign.

Crossing First Avenue, he glanced up at the illuminated "Public Market Center" sign and clock on the rooftop. Even at a few minutes before nine thirty, the crowds were considerable. The vendors were busy opening their stalls. He browsed among the magazines displayed in the international newsstand with its "Read All about It" banner. Just in front of the Pike Place Fish Market, a father boosted his daughter onto the back of the life-size bronze pig. Phones and cameras were being held up by dozens of tourists. They were taking photos of the fishmongers tossing whole fish to a packager whenever a new sale was made. "*Albacore—albacore ... eeeeey yaaaaa!*" An older woman dressed all in black and navigating with a walker was scowling as she moved through the crowd. He noticed himself scowling back at her. Had she seen him?

About ten people were waiting in the buffet line just outside Lowell's. He headed upstairs for table service. Young waiters carried heavy food platters up the steep staircases. One of them pointed him toward a table next to the window overlooking Elliott Bay. He passed on the Dungeness crab omelet, that day's special, and ordered eggs benedict on rosemary bread. A cup of black coffee and a little pitcher of milk appeared without his being asked. The coffee wasn't hot enough, and he was impatient for the waiter to come back.

The giant Ferris wheel on the waterfront was turning. He remembered riding it with Sandra and Theo a few months after it opened. A ferry, one of the four-hundred-foot megaboats, was just leaving the terminal. A seagull flew by just a few feet from the window. One of the two women sitting at the next table asked the waiter which of the Bloody Marys on the menu was his favorite.

He'd ordinarily savor this collage of Seattle scene fragments, but he was stuck in a state of perfect gray. The absurdity of his funk was all too apparent to him as he sat there, his arms folded across his chest. Was he broadcasting his dark mood? Might someone sitting nearby wonder what was going on with that angry guy over there?

The waiter delivered the eggs benedict, and he picked at the food, wishing he'd chosen the crab omelet. After paying, he crossed Pike Place and passed the ever-crowded French bakery, Le Panier. Sometimes he thought that the wafting aroma of freshly baked bread from its kitchen put passersby into a trance, involuntarily drawing them in the door in a slow, mesmerized shuffle.

On the next corner, a guy with a scraggly beard and wild white hair was playing a piano out on the sidewalk. There was a kind of a paradox, Elliott thought, between the beauty of his music and his zany appearance. His CDs were lined up next to his tip jar. "Please tip for a photo," his sign said.

Dropping into the wine shop, he began perusing the shelves. When a clerk asked if he could help, Elliott answered that he wanted a top-tier red. He accepted the man's first suggestion and stuffed the bottle into his backpack.

Back across the street in the floral section of the market, he leaned against a dumpster to get out of the way of the moving crowd. A woman working in a flower stall handed two huge bouquets to a customer. Were these women Hmong? He remembered an article about their having been farmers in the mountains of Laos and Cambodia before coming to Seattle as refugees in the 1970s and early 1980s.

One of them, he guessed the oldest, was selecting flowers one by one from plastic buckets and putting them into arrangements. Her skin was deeply creased, and she was wearing a blue knit hat with red and green stripes. The other two women tended to the steady stream of customers while she continued making bouquets. Elliott watched her hands as she expertly created another floral combination and, at least for the time being, observing her was all he had the energy to do.

His gaze shifted to the tiles lining the floor. Each was engraved with the name of a donor to the market's preservation fund. He wasn't sure how much time had passed when he became aware that the old woman's hands had stopped working. She was looking right at him. He quickly turned away, but after a moment peered back.

She was still looking at him. This time, he didn't look away. Her blank expression gently morphed into a look of confusion. It was as if she were wordlessly questioning him. Seconds passed.

Then, with the fingers of her right hand, she beckoned him to come close. He walked forward. When he stood in front of her, her face slowly broke into a smile. Compassion radiated from her wizened eyes. They stood there silently.

He watched as she took a half dozen bright-yellow daffodils from a bucket. She added a few pieces of greenery and wrapped them in white paper. She leaned toward him and said quietly, "Tomorrow will be better," and tapped his arm lightly as she handed him the flowers. Pausing to again peer into his eyes, she nodded and then returned to her work.

A bolt of anxiety coursed through him. His muscles coiled, his hands tight in fists. For several moments it seemed as if the cacophony of voices from the milling crowds was muted while the flower vendor's words replayed in his mind.

Tomorrow will be better. Tomorrow will be better.

He realized her gesture was intended to crack the shield of armor he'd been wearing with such mulishness for the past several hours. But it was having the opposite effect.

Her gift had propelled him back to that day in the living room of his childhood home. It had been crowded with uniformed army soldiers and women wearing black. Dozens of floral arrangements covered the tables, and their sickly-sweet aroma was making him ill. They had buried his brother that morning.

He stood there for several more moments, struggling with indecision. He looked back at the Hmong woman, but she stayed steadily focused on her work. Holding the flowers, badly wanting to toss them in the trash, he turned and retraced his steps back through the market.

Three teenage girls were standing next to the huge bronze pig. One of them wore a crimson Harvard University sweatshirt.

"Would you please take our photo?"

He mumbled an apology that he was in a hurry, thrust the bouquet into one of the girl's hands, and dashed away, almost knocking over the all-in-black grumpy woman with a walker. "Piss on you," she hissed at him.

He had to get back to his apartment, get back to writing in his journal. When he reached Broadway on his way home, he spotted the panhandler sitting on the sidewalk near the crowded Dick's Drive-In. All around the man, people were coming and going, and he was invisible.

No more "God bless you, sirs." He was just seated there with a dazed look, a bottle in a soiled paper bag lying on the concrete next to his leg. Was he even conscious?

He's trapped, Elliott thought. There might not be visible jail bars, but the truth of the matter was that this panhandler was imprisoned in a set of dead-end circumstances. Likely there was no way out. Would it be a life sentence for this guy? Maybe even a death sentence?

Then another thought. *Is Peter facing a death sentence, with it just being a matter of time before it's carried out?*

These images were just too troubling. He had to do something to fight back. Anything. He had an idea.

He got in line. When it was his turn at the window, he ordered a deluxe burger, fries, and two cups of coffee.

Easing himself down next to the man sitting on the sidewalk, he held out the bag of food and one of the cups. For a moment, there was a wary look on the man's face, but that quickly passed as he took both and dove into the food.

Neither of them said a word. Elliott was aware of disapproving glances from a few of the people walking by, but he ignored them.

I see you. You're not invisible. I see you and I hear you.

Elliott put a twenty-dollar bill into the cracked cup. He looked the man in the eyes, and the man looked back with an expression of what Elliott interpreted to be such a profound sadness.

"Tomorrow will be better," Elliott said aloud, wishing dearly that he believed it.

17 ~ Adrift

"A malbec? A wonderful choice for tonight's dinner. Thank you." Moving away from her doorway and motioning Elliott to follow, she took the bottle and closely read the label. "Oh my, it's a 2006 Catena Zapata. Superb! You know, Argentina produces world-class wines, and this 2006 malbec is said to be among the finest." Milena looked up with a questioning glance. "Are you an enologist, per chance?" She cocked her head and smiled.

Elliott hung his brown suede sport jacket in the closet and closed the door. "Milena, to be honest I simply threw some money at a wine merchant and asked him to recommend a great red. Uh, what was that word?"

"It's *ee-nawl-o-gist*, an expert on the science of wine. For this bottle," she held it up in her right hand and pointed to the label, "you must have thrown a boatload of money at him." She removed a crystal decanter from the glass-enclosed mahogany hutch next to her dining table. "I just completed a three-week course on wine basics. Actually, I have a confession to make. I'm addicted to taking classes. Here, look at these." She pointed to a stack of course catalogs resting on the floor next to her overstuffed leather chair. It appeared that they came from at least half a dozen Seattle-area colleges.

Milena handed the bottle and a butterfly corkscrew to Elliott. After he removed the cork, she poured the malbec into her decanter.

"Wine fundamentals was just one of a myriad of esoteric subjects I've studied. I'm remarkably well informed about topics I'll likely never have use for, but what fun it's been going back to school. Come see me, by the way, if you're at all curious about monarch butterflies and, let's see, oh yes, 1920s American jazz, or Robert E. Lee."

He laughed. "My neighbor, the encyclopedia." He leafed through one of the catalogs and saw a listing she had circled. "Children's operas?"

"Yes, perhaps there's a story to tell you about that." She looked at him with an inquisitive glance. "Well, we'll see. Here, take this to the table and I'll be there in a moment." After handing him the wood salad bowl, she slid a broiler pan into the oven and set the timer. "Halibut's on the menu tonight." Milena joined him and served them both. "I'm proud of my tomatoes—Sweet Millions, they're called. There's a community garden just a block from here."

He poured the wine, and they began eating, soon interrupted by the ding of the timer. Milena took the fish from the broiler and returned carrying the platter and a potato casserole side dish. For the next few minutes, they ate silently.

"So, why does children's opera interest you?"

"It's more than just being interested. Actually, it kept me alive at a time when some my age in Terezín were falling into an inertia of despair. I lived in Mädchenheim L410, the dormitory for ten- to seventeen-year-old girls. The adults tried as much as possible to keep us engaged with art, music, and learning so that we'd not be as overwhelmed by the separation from our parents. Learning my part in an opera called *Brundibár* was one of those activities, and we sang it at Terezín many times." She walked over to her bookcase.

"You sang there? In the concentration camp?"

"Yes, and my mother sang in an adult chorus."

"*Brundibár* is the Czech word for bumblebee." Milena took a picture book from a shelf and handed it to him. Its brightly colored cover illustrated a boy and girl running and holding a milk bucket. She said, "If you page through this, you'll get the gist of the story and the main characters. A little girl named Aninku and her brother, Pepicek, sing in a marketplace to earn money. Their mother is ill, their father dead, and the doctor says the mother needs milk to recover. They're chased away, however, by the evil organ grinder, Brundibár. You'll know him from his mustache. The day is saved, however, when the children of the town, along with a sparrow, a cat, and a dog, rout Brundibár so the brother and sister can sing."

Elliott imagined a child in a concentration camp singing the sparrow's part, and that thought brought a lump to his throat. Looking at a drawing of the organ grinder, he said, "This must have been allegorical. Weren't people afraid they'd be punished?"

"To the contrary. The Nazis used the fact that we sang an opera for children as propaganda. They wanted to convince the world that Terezín was a model village where Jews were happily resettled.

"Being in the cast was fun for me. More than that, really. It allowed me to think of things other than missing being with my parents, our home, and my being hungry so much of the time. It allowed me to go on even in the face of large numbers of us, including children, regularly being taken away in transports." She paused, a slight shake of her head, and said, "Then, it was my turn. At Auschwitz, all remnants of light were entirely extinguished."

Elliott surreptitiously glanced at the number on her left arm.

She began collecting their plates and he joined her, carrying the platter and their empty glasses to the kitchen. Putting a kettle of water on the stove and spooning coffee grounds into her French press, Milena said, "Okay, it's your turn. I want to know about you." They moved to the sitting area. "Tell me about yourself. What is your family's history?"

"I know more about my father's family than my mother's. He and his parents were all born in America. Dad's grandparents were originally from England. His grandfather was a pharmacist as was his father. My dad taught high school for years until he retired."

"And on your mother's side?" Milena asked.

"I've often thought that I'd someday look into my mother's background. All I remember hearing was that her parents were Austrian farmers. When she was just a child, they sent my mom to the US to live with relatives when war appeared imminent." Elliott paused, drumming his fingers on the table. "Oh yes, one more thing. A massive storm destroyed their farmhouse and they perished."

"What else can you tell me?"

He felt himself slouching into his chair. Family photographs scrolled through his thoughts: his parents, Todd, and then Sandra and Peter. "My dad and brother are gone, and my mom's in a nursing home with Alzheimer's. And after thirty-one years of marriage and raising my son, Peter, I'm getting a divorce."

She looked at him with a questioning gaze.

"Yeah, you're wondering whose idea that was. Sandra raised the issue first, and, as it turns out, she's seeing another guy, a fellow surgeon at University Hospital. But it was over for me as well."

He walked over to the window. Looking out at the western cedar in the courtyard, he thought of its being a home, a place of safety for birds and squirrels. Milena's home somehow felt that way for him. Without dwelling on whether or not to let it all out, he opened the spigot.

"Life's gone topsy-turvy for me, and I've felt mostly adrift for quite a while." He watched a Steller's jay collecting breadcrumbs someone scattered on the lawn. "I'm a psychologist, and I lost a client to suicide. I was blindsided."

Turning from the window, he walked over to her piano, remembering that she played music while telling him about her parents and how they had died. He sat on the bench and glanced at the open sheet music.

"Every year I fall into a slump. Like clockwork, the anniversary of my older brother being killed in Vietnam rolls around, and I lose the battle. A fog takes over. For days, sometimes weeks, I'm caught in it.

"When my client took her life, that fog rolled in again. I failed her. Just at the time that this beautiful young woman had begun to have enough trust in me and in herself to start delving more deeply into the trauma she'd experienced as a child, just when it looked to me as if she were getting stronger, she killed herself."

The kettle's whistling drew Milena back to the kitchen. For several moments, she said nothing as she poured the hot water into the French press.

Returning to the living room, she said, "I'm thinking about what you've described, Elliott. Is it really like a fog? Do your thoughts become obscured?"

"Exactly."

"Do you think you might be punishing yourself? Are you paying a price for something, something that started with your brother's death?" She paused for a second. "Does the fog conceal what you're doing to yourself?"

He felt goose bumps as he heard Milena's words and a pang of anxiety. This possibility absolutely was not something he wanted to think about, particularly when it came to Todd, and he quickly shrugged off the question. Standing up, he picked up one of the framed photos on the piano. He guessed it was Milena's daughter.

"Peter's really my current worry. Twenty-seven years old, and he's obsessed with breaking records by doing insanely dangerous stunts. He's a stoner to boot." Elliott found a photo on his cell phone and showed it to Milena. "He says he's happy. But the truth is that he's living his life dangerously close to the edge. Some people might admire him as a kind of daredevil who's driven to push limits. In my mind, though, it seems as if his flirtation with disaster is like a moth flitting about a flame. Whenever I plead with him to stop, there's a freeze in our conversation."

Milena handed the phone back.

"Sandra's not worried about him and tells me I'm being way too rigid." He shook his head while gazing at the photo. "Of course, my response is that her being laissez-faire is just making things worse."

"Are you able to stay in touch with him?" Milena asked. "He hasn't refused to speak with you?"

He was puzzled that she was surprised by this. "No, we manage to stay civil most of the time. I think we both try to avoid taking it too far." He thought about the Wednesday-morning Skype call that had clearly been an over-the-top exception. "Each of us realizes that the bonds in our family have already been painfully strained because of the divorce. Why were you thinking he wouldn't speak with me?"

She pointed to the framed photograph he had been holding. "Anneka was thirty-five when that was taken. At the time, she was a journalist working for the *San Francisco Chronicle*."

In the photo, her daughter was sitting in a cubicle, every surface of her desk covered with stacks of books and paper. A young Katharine Hepburn came to Elliott's mind. Intently looking at her computer screen, she had a pencil between her teeth, her brunette hair was pinned up in a pile on top of her head, and her oversize, rounded eyeglasses teetered at the end of her nose. She wore what appeared to be a beige-colored fisherman's vest with rows of pockets.

"She turned fifty-four recently. She won't take my calls and rarely replies to my letters." With a wistful look, she said, "I envy you."

"Why doesn't she—"

"The reason? If I fully understood what's haunting my daughter, I think I'd feel less distressed. What I do know is that while covering the militant insurgency in Nigeria, a young boy she'd met and become fond of was killed. She's told me that it's untenable for her to go on with her life as long as genocide destroys children's lives anywhere in the world." She bit her lower lip, glancing at the oil painting of the Prague cathedral hanging near the piano. "Her father fought the same kind of despair. He was in the army during the Korean War, and his unit did some despicable things that obsessed him. When Anneka was thirteen, he killed himself.

"I think there's more to this, though. Something must have happened to her. Sometimes I wonder if she doesn't want to frighten me." She shook her head slowly, her arms folded across her chest. "I also wonder if she understands what's underlying her being in such a very dark place. More than that, I sense that this beautiful woman, so full of reverence for life, has become terribly fixated on vengeance. Might she have the delusion that she must become judge and jury? I dread the thought of her taking such enormous risks in the stories she covers."

"What is she doing now? Where is she living?"

"She's living in Mexico for three months and writing about one of the major drug cartels for the *New York Times*. She's also writing a book. She said that it's a story that's obsessed her for years, and now is the time when it must be written. The central character is a hero who goes after the cartel leaders. That's as much as I know."

"You write to her?"

"Every Monday, and they're long letters, full of road maps as I think of it, ideas about how people whose souls have been injured manage to go on with their lives. One I recently sent shared some of Elie Wiesel's wisdom. Sometimes I quote some poetry, and I often mention some tidbits about my day. I even told her about you.

"Oh, by the way, have you noticed the wooden bowl in our lobby? It's where we put outgoing mail."

Elliott nodded.

"I purchased it in an antique shop. It's very much like the wooden dough bowl my mother used when I was a child. I bought it for our building because I wanted my letters to Anneka to first be held in a vessel that carries her family's heritage, its wisdom, and its strength."

"Actually, I want that for all of my letters. You'll see piles of them in that bowl. I regularly write to people who came to this country as immigrants. I helped them learn about our ways and have kept in touch for years."

Milena returned to the kitchen and brought two mugs of coffee and a small plate of brownies to the coffee table. Leafing through the opera storybook, he asked, "Are happy endings only the stuff of storybooks?"

Handing him his coffee, she said, "Our Aninku and Pepicek need to find their own paths through the forest, Elliott. Perhaps you and I are the sparrows in their lives, hovering over their shoulders and chirping encouragement in their ears."

**

He guessed that Milena's plot at the community garden was roughly one hundred square feet. It was still light out after they had finished dinner, and she invited him to go for a walk to see it.

Just half a block from her front door, Milena suddenly stopped. A teenage girl walking a German shepherd was coming toward them. The dog's aggressive-looking posture and low growl raised Elliott's hackles. Fortunately, the girl and dog crossed to the other side of the street before they got much closer. The danger had passed, yet Milena was standing there trembling. She held his arm tightly. Moments passed.

"I'll be okay. Just give me a moment. It was the camps," she said. "There were times when the guards' dogs did terrible violence. Just horrible. And the guards encouraged it."

He felt her shudder.

"I don't want to think of that," she said. "Let's continue our walk."

When they reached her plot, she seemed to be over the scare. She pointed out sections where several varieties of tomatoes and squash, lettuce, chard, radishes, and carrots were growing. She told him the lifting and carrying were a bit much for her these days, but happily there were always people eager to help. She said she returned the favor with Czech pastries.

She picked a ripe tomato and handed it to him, pointing to a water faucet two plots over from hers. As she knelt down to pull some weeds, he thought about her enthusiasm for life, growing her own vegetables, all of those short courses she took, and her forever practicing new pieces for the piano. And then there were all of those letters. He suspected there were even more unexpected ways her lifestyle fueled this amazing woman's vitality.

Watching her tend her garden, he pictured her as a child singing a part in an opera. The Nazis' propaganda purpose was clearly an obscenity, yet what she did along with the other children carved an emotional haven from the chasm of barbarism that surrounded them. A thought came to mind. Had Milena thrived because she had tilled every field she'd encountered, even when dry, weed-laden, strewn with rocks, and left abandoned?

That Day

18 ~ No longer Any Ambiguity

Gazing at that still unopened letter, a punch-in-the-gut insight from just before Bill's hour ended was heavy on Elliott's mind. Because the date for their next session fell on a national holiday, Elliott had gone to his appointment book to look for an alternate slot. When Bill came over and stood next to him, Elliott felt the hairs on his arms stand up. His journal was lying there, its covers open, and the words he had written about doubting his competence were clearly visible.

Pivoting his body, he herded Bill toward the door saying he'd follow up in an email with several possible days and times. His heart was pounding and with that lapse came an uncomfortable revelation.

Her privacy was no less important than his. The confidentiality he'd assumed was inviolable in his journal could easily have been breached a moment earlier. Those pages were the repository for his thoughts about the most intimate of matters in his life. Now, looking at Milena's letter, his immediate thought was that there was no acceptable justification for reading it that would withstand a damning counter argument.

He had an hour before his next session. He'd take the unopened letter out to a mailbox right away.

Elliott stopped in the bathroom and splashed water on his face. Glancing in the mirror, he was startled by an unmistakable sadness in his eyes. Even more troubling were the changes in his face's topography, more creases, and deeper furrows.

Riding the elevator to the ground floor, he held Milena's letter in his hand, remembering the uplift in spirits he'd been so eagerly anticipating. Listening to her speak about the poems she sometimes included and how Anneka could follow her example in reinventing a meaningful life, the opportunity he was about to surrender bore down on his consciousness.

He turned north after exiting the building. The mailbox was two blocks away. As he walked, he began to vacillate. Was he acting too hastily, he asked himself. His pace slowed.

Yes, of course, privacy is of tantamount importance, he thought. But he's a clinical psychologist, not just any man on the street. Anything he learns in sessions with his clients is taken in without judgment. So, if he doesn't judge and never discloses what she's written to anyone, is Milena really harmed by his reading the letter? Or Anneka, for that matter?

He'd already taken the letter from that outgoing mail bowl, he added. It wasn't as if the slate was blank. What he'd done couldn't be undone.

Elliott stopped mid-block, aware that he needn't be in a hurry. He still had time to decide. In the meantime, it wouldn't do any harm to do some preparing. He turned and walked quickly back to his building.

On the web, he googled how to open and reseal an envelope. To his surprise, there was a slew of links. That somehow comforted him. He wasn't the sole wrongdoer who intended to violate someone's privacy. A sudden thought—*He'd need to delete his search history.*

Elliott filled his electric teakettle, assuring himself he was still on the safe side of the line. When the water started to boil and the kettle clicked off, he reviewed the instructions, wanting to know how to avoid it being obvious the letter had been tampered with. The guidance was to try to get an even distribution of the steam across the seal while not holding the envelope too close and getting both it and the letter wrinkled. Once the glue became tacky, it said to use a flat blade to gently pry the flap up. It also warned about protecting one's hand to not get burned.

He held the envelope in both hands. *Do it, just do it,* he chanted to himself. The impulse to open the letter was becoming overwhelming.

There was a dissident voice. *No, if you're that unsure, don't. There'll be another letter in that mail bowl next Monday. Maybe you'll know for sure what to do by then.*

He looked at his watch, surprised that his next client was due in fifteen minutes. Then, with a jolt of impulse, he crab-walked over to the electric kettle, conscious that he was making a decision while not directly acknowledging doing so. He slowly passed the envelope back and forth over the steam. A minute later he began sliding his letter opener under the flap, careful to use just the right amount of pressure.

He was in. The envelope was unsealed. He opened the flap and removed the three sheets of paper.

As eager as he was, he intended to savor this experience, every word and every sentiment, so he slowed down. He picked a section and read one line at a time, stopping before going on to the next.

Do you remember the day you and your father laughed so hard while listening to a recording of Smetena's Má vlast? I think you were maybe eight or nine. When the Vltava section began, your father stood up. "Use your imagination, Anneko," he said. "Imagine how the river sounds." As if he were a ballet performer, he swayed and marched while describing the river's journey, beginning with the burbles of two small streams and later as it flowed placidly through woods and meadows, then widening before swirling into rapids and finally magnificently disappearing into the distance. For your father, music offered a much more effective means than human language for communicating the mysteries of life.

For me, both poetry and music help me survive bouts of sadness. Might they nurture you as well, my daughter?

He closed his eyes, picturing Milena at her dining room table, pen in hand, and classical music playing on her stereo. With each phrase, he inhaled Milena's resilient outlook, determined to prolong the experience. After reading the letter from beginning to end, he sat back in his chair and felt her perspective course through him.

He re-read it several times that evening and planned to put it in a street mailbox in the morning. One thing was now clear, however. There was no ambiguity about what he'd become.

In the Following Months

19 ~ Become One with the Mountain

Nureyev pulled up in his rusty '64 VW camper, rolled down the driver's side window, and shouted, "Food truck." In a flash, all three of them made a run for the van door. Tat reached in for the stuffed plastic bag in the back seat and handed each a white Styrofoam take-out container as they walked back to the fire pit to sit on the surrounding tree stumps.

The first snow of the season was falling in cotton-ball clumps, but they were protected by a tarp-covered lean-to they'd constructed a month earlier out of scrounged lumber, a discarded ten-foot irrigation pipe, and a few large tree branches. For several minutes they sat quietly, devouring the fried chicken and listening to the crackling fire. The tarp flapped whenever it was hit with a sudden burst of wind.

After removing the bones, Harpo fed three pieces to No Name, a brown-fur mutt with a white bib and muzzle. The dog had adopted him at the recycling station where Harpo worked.

"Not bad pickings, dude," Peter said. He reached into the cooler and tossed Nureyev a Bud Light.

"Yeah, Pan, dipping chicken into a fryer for eight hours is a shit job, but one benefit is the manager looking the other way when our shifts end," Nureyev replied. "Hell, you wouldn't believe the stuff he hauls out of that place after the doors are locked. Must be feeding an army."

Harpo, his moniker a tribute to his scruffy reddish afro, poked a stick at the coals to stir them up before tossing a handful of small branches and another log on the fire. "I guess the perk from working at the dump is being there to salvage a perfectly good piece of furniture when some idiot tosses it into the pit. But, man, you gotta move fast before the bulldozer crushes it."

"Gonna have to take out an insurance policy on you, Harp," Tat answered, and they all laughed. "So, for me, being a substitute teacher is just grief, USDA Prime, pure and simple. No perks whatsoever. When a sub walks into a classroom, the kids transform into a primitive tribe of cannibals, pouncing on any poor schmuck who shows the least sign of weakness."

"Wait a minute, Tat. Now hold on. You're forgetting something," Peter said. "Weren't you the poor schmuck who got a commendation and a raise from the school superintendent last month?"

"Baksheesh, my friend. Just goes to show how a little bribery can grease the skids." Tat walked over to the cooler and handed brews around to each of the others. "I suspect she was trying to placate me, kind of an insurance policy against my murdering any of her monsters."

"Hmm," Peter muttered in response. "Note to self. Get an insurance policy for Harpo and set up a bail fund for Tat."

Several of them groaned, and Tat barely missed when he aimed a chicken bone at Peter's head.

"All right, all right, calm down. We can do the food fight later," Peter said. "Right now, your cruise director, Pan, has got some breaking news." He paused purposefully, letting them wait for it. "Now that I've got your attention, anyone up for doing Dragon's Tail Couloir tomorrow?" He looked around and saw the three others looking at him with surprised expressions on their faces, even No Name, whose floppy ears had perked up. "Okay, get this. It's been coming down at an inch an hour, and the forecast is saying there'll be a thirty-two-inch fresh stash tomorrow morning at Flattop." Peter stood and began pacing excitedly, his arms waving as he laid out his mental picture of the scene. "Dragon's Tail will be a totally rowdy run, and we'll rip the hell out of it."

"Not much snow the last time I skied there," Tat answered. "The crux and rock outcroppings were a royal pain. You had to hopscotch the run in sections, some of them tiny. Almost wasn't worth it."

Nureyev was nodding, clearly having had a similar experience. "But thirty-two inches of fresh powder?" he said. "Damn, I'm stoked."

Harpo asked, "What's the deal? I've never been there."

"My man," Peter replied, "picture your coolest-ever day skiing backcountry. Compared to that, Dragon's Tail's going to make it seem like a bunny hill. Totally rad. We'll need an early start because it'll probably take two hours to drive to the Bear Lake parking lot. We'll trek for two miles, passing two more lakes before getting to Emerald and the southern base. Then, it'll be another couple of hours getting to the ridge where the Dragon's Tail Couloir tops out. It's about an eighteen-hundred-foot climb, but man, what an incredible mind-blowing descent."

Nureyev, nodding enthusiastically, held his right hand on a downward slant. "Picture a fifty-degree drop at the beginning of the jump off, Harp, and then slaloming from one near-vertical chute to another, and it keeps getting better and better."

"Wait a minute, guys," Tat interjected. "Did you check the forecast, Pan? That terrain can be ripe for some serious slides."

"No worries, no worries. The bulletin says the risk is high, but that's to warn away the novices. It's never stopped us before. My read on it," Peter said, "is that we're way good enough. Hell, we've all been in some pretty hairy flows and kept ourselves moving. C'mon, Tat, we're mountain gods."

Peter good-naturedly punched Tat on the shoulder, who looked at the enthused expressions on all of the others' faces before replying with a shrug, his hands raised in mock surrender.

***

Suddenly, mercifully, it stopped.

Peter lay on his back under the surface, encased in a cocoon, his head downslope from his legs. "Try to swim," he'd remembered learning from an avalanche-safety course, and while tumbling in the forty-mile-per-hour maelstrom of snow and ice, he'd stretched his arms forward and stroked down forcefully, arching his head and shoulders up. Then, just before the flow halted, he cupped his mouth with his left hand, creating a balloon-size air pocket in front of his face.

Snow and ice chunks had gone everywhere, ripping away his gloves, goggles, and ski cap, packing into his thermal underwear, top and bottom. There was just a glimmer of light, an ice-blue laser-thin ray of color visible to him as he blinked away bits of snow that had caught in his eyelashes. *Can't be too far from the surface,* he thought, but he was unable to move his arms, and both legs felt as if they were enclosed in casts of cement.

Was his beacon working? Before setting out that morning from their apartment at four, Tat had insisted that each of the four of them replace their batteries. *Tat ... oh God!* His body shuddered as he recalled, just after they'd partnered up and both had begun the run, watching Tat five seconds ahead of him, getting swept into an explosive cloud of swirling snow as a slab pulled away from underneath him. Peter's sudden wince caused a shot of stabbing pain in his right shoulder.

The raspy sounds of his breathing and the rapid beating of his heart echoed in the air pocket, now rapidly becoming ice-sheathed due to the moisture in his breath. *Slow. Breathe slow and steady.* He reminded himself that his limited air supply could easily be squandered. *What've I got, maybe ten, twenty minutes?* The numbers were terrifying, the chance of survival after forty-five minutes just thirty percent. He knew that if it took longer, he might still be resuscitated, but the risk of brain damage would be considerable. The concentration of carbon dioxide in the air he was now breathing was quickly building.

Nureyev and Harpo! He abruptly remembered that the two others had hung back at the start of the run while Harpo worked on his bindings. *Maybe they're okay. Maybe they're looking for me.*

Fuck it, he thought. He bellowed a shout, and then another, "*Aaahhh ... aaahhh,*" his voice cracking as he felt overcome by desperation. Several minutes passed as he listened for any sound of digging. He began to sob as the ominous truth set in. He was going to die. It was going to happen very soon, and it was going to happen right here.

He replayed the terrible things he'd said in one of their Skype calls when his father nagged him about extreme stunts. He pictured the abject fear on his father's face. "I'm not lost, Dad," Peter had replied. Now the reality he faced was that he almost certainly was lost. He grimaced. *Wait, no, I need time to tell him ...*

Scene after scene in a slideshow of images faded in and out: his high school English literature teacher commending him for writing a top-notch paper on Elizabeth Barrett Browning; spotting an alligator while on an airboat ride during the family trip to the Everglades when he was eight; and the look on her face and sound of his mother's laughter when he brought home a stray solid-black cat, tearfully pleading that they keep her.

His thinking became sluggish. His breaths were more drawn out, but he didn't fight it.

All at once a wave of euphoria began to flow through him when, with surprise, he sensed his friend lying next to him. *But that can't be,* he thought. Peter tried to turn so that he could see Tat but he couldn't move. The snow held his head in a vise.

"Become one with the mountain, buddy," Tat whispered, his favorite mantra about the Zen of skiing. Peter felt joyful to no longer be alone. "Give in to it, Pan, follow me." Peter's eyelids fluttered and then closed. He was so incredibly tired.

His consciousness silently slipped away.

***

"What've we got?"

"He's been in and out," Harpo replied, an anxious look on his face. "Took us about twenty minutes to find him. He wasn't breathing, so we did CPR." Harpo pointed to a spot fifty yards away. "Our friend Tat is still buried out there."

"What's this guy's name?"

"Pan. Uh, no, I mean Peter, Peter Sterling."

"Age?"

"Twenty-seven."

Harpo watched as one of the medics from the Flight for Life helicopter removed his backpack and kneeled beside Peter. The other guy began radioing in a report.

"Team Bravo Eleven at Flattop: north four-zero degrees, one-eight minutes, four-three-decimal-nine-nine seconds, by west one-zero-five degrees, four-zero minutes, one-seven-decimal-two-five seconds. Male subject, twenty-seven years old, buried by avalanche. Dug out after twenty minutes. Second skier still buried. Need search and rescue."

"Peter, my name is Larry, and I'm an EMT."

Peter, shivering uncontrollably, stuttered an answer through gritted teeth, "P-p-please help m-m-me. Cold ... so cold."

"You're going to be okay, Peter. Just bear with me while I give you a quick check-over," the EMT said. "Kevin, let them know patient is voice responsive. Breathing labored. Moderately hypothermic. Respiration seventeen." Larry placed a green oxygen bottle next to

Peter's head. "This is going to help you feel more comfortable." He strapped the mask over Peter's nose and mouth.

"Can I go help look for Tat?" Harpo urgently asked. Nureyev and two other EMTs from the helicopter were digging where Tat's beacon was sounding.

"Slope's too dangerous," Kevin said. "They'll find him. Besides, we need you here."

"Peter, I know you're really cold, but I need to loosen your clothes so I can check for bleeding or injuries. I'll be quick, and then we'll get you warmed up. Let me know if anything I do is painful." Larry ran his hands under Peter's shirt, beginning at his waist. When he reached his right shoulder, Peter cried out. "Okay, buddy, I'll ease up." Larry motioned for Kevin to take a look. Pushing gently against his collarbone caused another shout of pain from Peter. "Clavicle, do you think?" A nod from his colleague resolved the question, and Larry continued his physical exam.

"What? Tat?" Peter whispered, trying to raise himself up. "Please … Tat? Is he …"

"Hold on, Peter, you're going to injure yourself. Lie still." Larry eased Peter back down. "We'll find out as soon as we can, but right now we've got to warm you up."

Kevin and Larry slid a Cascade litter alongside Peter and opened the tarp. On Kevin's signal, they lifted him into a sleeping bag lying open on the tarp. Peter screamed in pain.

Larry then removed a bag with chemical instant heat packs, activated them one by one, and placed one in each of Peter's hands, alongside his neck, under each armpit, in his groin, and up against the sole of each foot. Then they strapped him in.

"Base, patient is packaged, and we're ready to transport. Suspect clavicle fracture."

"Harpo, we'll need your help getting the litter to the chopper." The three men stood and, with two taking the lead and the other one holding the rear litter straps, began moving toward the waiting helicopter.

None of them heard Peter whimpering almost imperceptibly: "Tat …"

***

"Bye, Peter. You're in good hands now."

"On my signal, lift."

"Mr. Sterling, can you tell me what year this is?"

"I'm going to take your blood pressure again."

"Body temp is ninety-five-point-two."

"Yes, I'll ask about your friend and let you know."

"Peter, I'm Dr. Sanchez."

As if in a blur, he recalled glimpses of trees as his litter was being pulled, the sound of the rotors as the helicopter lifted, and the hospital emergency room nurses who cut away his clothing. When asked, he'd been able to count backwards from one hundred by nines. He lay quietly in an intensive care cubical, wrapped in heated blankets, and slept.

An hour later, he opened his eyes. Three men were standing next to his bed. As he looked first at Harpo and then at Nureyev, both seemed to have such sad expressions on their faces.

"Where's Tat?" Peter asked.

He didn't know the third man, much older than his friends. He was wearing a black suit and a clerical collar.

Peter was confused. "Tat. Did he make it?"

20 ~ The Swamp

Draining her glass, Anneka set aside her spiral-bound drawing pad and came in from the balcony. Her last hour had been devoted to sketching the curlicues on the rusted security door to the bakery's delivery entrance across the alley from her apartment building. She parked the bite-pocked pencil behind her right ear, a long-standing habit.

Opening one of several notepads in which she'd recorded interviews about the cartels, she reviewed quotes from two reporters, an assistant to the mayor, and a prosecutor. Still pending was her request to speak with a prominent real estate broker reputed to be involved with Los Zetas; some were saying he was a high-level leader.

A frenzied ping-pong of cascading ideas about her protagonist, Enrique Cardona, forced her to get up and move. Pacing around the room, she ran through a mental checklist of his key biographical features. His family would have emigrated from Mexico to the States when he was twenty—no, seventeen years old.

He would now be sixty-eight. Check.

Before recently reemerging from retirement, he'd have had a stellar career. For that matter, by the time he clocked out on his final day, he'd earned quite a few more accolades than most of his peers in journalism. He'd nabbed a coveted Peabody for his four-part series on Mexican drug cartels. Check.

He'd have made his home in an upscale Queen Anne condo with a spectacular view of the boat traffic on Seattle's Elliott Bay. He and his wife, a mystery writer who taught at Hugo House, would have been together for thirty-nine years, and they'd have two children, thirty-eight-year-old Enrique Jr., and Alexa, twenty-nine.

He'd be a member of the elite Washington Athletic Club, where, until recently, he played racquetball twice a week, routinely followed by lunch at Torchy's with the *Seattle Times'* sports editor and two retired cops, one a former deputy chief. Check, check.

Anneka sat at the bridge table where her computer was set up and opened the file with notes about Enrique. She typed in the character development possibilities she'd just come up with and then, refilling her wineglass, returned to the balcony.

Two quick swallows and she put her glass down, again picking up her drawing pad. Pencil in hand, she finished detailing the door and began outlining the graffiti-covered green steel trash container just to the right. The church's bells began chiming, the call to prayer. It was 6:00 p.m.

Bow ties. She'd say that he always wore bow ties and was known for being fastidious about his appearance, his thick head of neatly coiffed hair, silver not gray, and his much-admired collection of brightly colored silk vests. A dapper guy. For all intents and purposes, she'd write, Enrique had been living a stellar life, highly regarded in his profession. More than that, she'd say that he and his wife were consistently on the A-list in their celebrity studded social circle. *PPP,* she thought to herself: *picture-postcard perfect.*

But Enrique would have a secret—a very dark secret, indeed. For, in heeding his self-invented post-retirement calling, he had become an assassin.

She planned to have him suffer, burdened by a depth of agony that would tear into his soul. Much like the persistent ache radiating from his arthritically gnarled knuckles, Enrique's seething rage about his grandson's death six months earlier would drive him to put it on the line. All of it, despite the risk of a violent ungluing of the mosaic of his good life. All of it, despite the injury, perhaps fatal, he was inflicting on his moral core.

Back at her computer, she opened the most recent chapter file and began to write.

***

"Six months?" Selena threw her typed lecture notes onto the table. "In Mexico?" She glared at him. "Maybe longer? By yourself?" Moving out of her chair, she loomed over him. Consternation darkened her face. "To write a book? What are you talking about, Enrique?" she said, her voice rising. She yanked the belt of her robe tighter. "You're nearly seventy years old, for God's sake."

He watched her wringing her hands.

"And you're depressed. How are you going to take care of yourself? I can't believe ...." She slowly shook her head.

Her arms folded across her chest, she walked over to the floor-to-ceiling window in their condo living room. He heard her sigh.

She looked up into the clouds. He knew that gesture all too well. This was how she punctuated her dismay, an unspoken concession.

And he'd do what he'd decided. None of her rational arguments would sway him.

Truth be told, every one of her points had merit. But this mission was going to be completed.

He'd been ruminating about it since the day they'd buried Adrian, his only grandchild.

"Just a baby." His whispered words had immediately set off a clutch in his throat. "Oh God."

Had she any idea of the true reason for this trip, Selena would have pulled out all the stops to try to prevent it.

But she didn't have a clue.

It had been adolescent inquisitiveness; that was all. Just the second damned time! Some junkies needed to blot out the anguish of a seemingly disposable life. Not Adrian.

For God's sake, medical school had been in his future. His grades had been solid. Now he was dead. At sixteen.

His heart and lungs had been silenced. The unexpectedly super-potent dose of heroin he'd mainlined far exceeded his novice level of tolerance.

He'd just been curious.

***

Anneka was on a roll. In the next seven days of his life, as Enrique prepares for the trip, she'd have him ruminating about what he must do and whom he needs to contact in order to get the gear he requires. He'd ask himself again and again whether his son and daughter-in-law could possibly have done anything to prevent this tragedy, anything more than sending Adrian to top-ranked private schools and providing the culture-rich upbringing with family trips to much of Europe and Asia. He'd conclude that the decision he made was not only right, but unequivocally righteous, no matter the cost.

She flipped the switch on the kettle, took down the jar of tea from a shelf, grabbed a handful of raisins, and paced back and forth as plot and character questions raced through her mind. How intensely committed would Enrique Cardona be? She pitched another handful of raisins into her mouth. Giving a used coffee mug a quick rinse, she poured out what was left in the wine bottle, glancing at the shelf to assure herself that two unopened bottles remained. The tea was forgotten.

***

He had stashed his 2014 Lexus LS 600h in Seattle. Abandoned his identity there, too.

In Nuevo Laredo you had to know who to ask. If you had the cash, doctored paperwork could be obtained. No questions asked. No trails.

With three hundred bucks, and an extra fifty thrown in for stolen plates, he bought a rusted 1971 Datsun pickup.

This border town had seen better days, much better.

Three years earlier a drug kingpin known as "El Coss" had been jailed. In retaliation, a message had been sent.

Nine of them. Hanging from a Nuevo Laredo bridge the next morning were the tortured and murdered bodies of four cops, three police cadets in training, a newspaper editor who'd championed the arrest, and an anti-drug citizen activist.

Want a war against organized crime? Be careful what you wish for. Blood will run in the streets.

Enrique decided he'd be a peasant. Scratch the bow ties. He'd wear well-worn but clean manual labor attire—work pants, shirts, and boots.

Scratch shaving. Scratch his silver hair. The medium-dark-brown coloring would wash out in about three weeks. He brought along enough to carry him over for several months. It'd probably take that long, he told himself.

Either he'd meet a yet-to-be-determined quota or, at some point along the way, he'd be taken down.

Finally, the finishing touch: a limp. A bike accident when he was in his twenties gave him the needed muscle memory. His left leg had fractured, and he had worn a cast for six weeks.

His disguise had to work. It was a matter of survival. He couldn't risk being made by someone he'd met when researching cartels ten years earlier.

He'd be targeted.

Now, he needed to blend in while he observed Los Zetas foot soldiers. They were the entirely expendable battalions of worker ants. Many were teens, some as young as ten or eleven.

If there was any question about who he was or why he was there, the cartel security wouldn't take the chance. Killing him would be just business.

He waited until ten thirty at night. The action would just be getting rolling. His rooming house owners were more than happy when he offered to take their pug to a park for a walk.

He parked his truck in a dark corner of a lot, kitty corner to the Green Door. He'd hung out in that disco years earlier.

Lighting a cigarette, with the dog on a leash, he walked slowly down the opposite side of the street. He concentrated on his limp and scanned to see who might be taking note of his presence.

The heavy beat of reggaetón was slamming the neighborhood. Three flashy Hummers driven by bodyguards were idling out in front.

Scores of patrons, most of them in their twenties, were mingling at the entrance. Mercedes, Beamers, and Jags, none more than a year or two old, filled the parking lot.

Could've been a fashion show. Guys sporting white suits, gold chains at their necks, and ten grand watches. Elle cover women adorned in slinky metallic dresses and deadly stiletto heels.

A wealth tsunami derived from the drug trade. Money, unimaginable amounts of disposable cash, thrown around as if the faucet would never shut off.

These kids, and that's really what they were, he thought, were rolling in the spoils of the illegal market.

They were narcos. Apprentices, yes, but hauling in cash by the fistfuls. They were the couriers, transporting cocaine, heroin, pot, and meth across regions and borders.

But they were also the thugs. They carried out orders to rough up and sometimes snuff competitors, uncooperative cops and politicians, and journalists asking the wrong questions.

Even with all this gaudy pretentiousness, he knew these kids were close to the bottom of the cartel hierarchy. The wealth amassed by those above them on this food chain made the pricey cars, get-ups, and jewelry he was looking at pale in comparison.

He thought of his grandson. His jaws clenched. These were the people whose greed and egregious immorality had taken Adrian from him.

Just then one of the drivers got out of his Hummer. Slowly walking up to Enrique, the man gestured for him to wait.

The bald-headed and beefy bodyguard, an unmistakable bulge in the left armpit of his black suit coat, casually asked, "¿Porqué estás aqui?" What are you doing here?

The man's voice was calm, but his steely eyes were all business.

"Nothing much," Enrique replied while pointing to the dog and shrugging. "Just hoping my friend here does his thing soon so we can both go to bed."

Without waiting for any more questions, Enrique limped down the street, pulling the dog along, hoping he'd put on a convincing show of being harmless. To his relief, the driver returned to his Hummer.

Not bad for a first night of reconnoitering.

There'd be many such nights ahead of him. He'd spend hours observing from the shadows. He'd watch for patterns, who came and who went, and where the action happened in Nuevo Laredo. He'd take the time.

Then it would begin.

**

Anneka was sweating, and her head was pounding. Moving out onto the balcony, she glanced at the drawing pad. She really should slow herself down and do some more sketching, she thought. Enrique needed to be more than a one-dimensional cutout. She should let his complexity develop, see him struggling with the profound ethical questions.

Back in her apartment, she marched in a circle in the space between her computer and the bathroom. She grabbed her wine on the second pass.

No. Slowing down was the last thing she wanted to do. No other path to justice for these murderous cartel members was working. She needed him to be there. She needed him to shoot those bullets. She was hooked by her protagonist's audacity, despite her visceral revulsion for taking a human life.

But if she were in Enrique's shoes, and the weapon were in her hands as she stood facing a cartel leader, would she pull the trigger?

**

A tarp partially covered him as he lay in the bed of his truck. The tailgate was down. It gave him a clear view of the two-story house's front entrance.

Three sandbags supported the muzzle of his SIG Sauer MPX-S. He relaxed his breathing to maintain a steady sighting. It was 11:50 p.m.

They had a routine. The courier would arrive at midnight. He'd watched them doing this for three weeks.

A city police commander lived there. So did his wife and three school-age children. Enrique had read an interview in which this man pledged his department's commitment to protecting citizens' safety.

Alongside the article was a photo of a headless body hanging from its feet on a lamppost. A banner was pinned to the body. It read "We'll kill you, too, if you interfere."

The head had been found on the steps of city hall. It was an unmistakable threat to the newly elected mayor who had campaigned with a promise to clean up crime.

Enrique's temples throbbed as he thought of the police commander's righteousness. Staunchly law-and-order while on the take from the Zetas. What'd he pull in? Enrique wondered. Fifty grand a week? Twice that?

The drug trade required corrupt cops. This guy had a senior rank in his department. He probably recruited many other cops to be on the cartel's payroll.

But could Enrique do this? He had time. He could still back out, return home to Selena and the more-than-comfortable life they had in Seattle. No one had to know what he had so meticulously planned. No one would learn how close he had come to carrying it out.

No. Backing out was just not going to happen. He forced thoughts of this man's wife and children from his mind.

A car pulled up and stopped. The driver turned off the lights and left the engine running. Carrying a backpack up to the front door, he knocked quietly.

The door opened almost immediately. No greeting, no words spoken. The courier handed the backpack to the commander and turned to leave.

In quick succession, Enrique shot the courier first and then the commander, each squarely in his temple.

Tap, tap.

As their bodies slumped to the ground, he viewed each man's head through his night scope. He shot again to assure himself they were dead.

The silencer on his gun had done its job. Not even a dog bark disturbed the quiet neighborhood's calm.

Enrique climbed from the back of his truck and quickly drove away. He made it two blocks before swerving to the curb, throwing open the truck door, and vomiting.

Adrian's death would be avenged. He wiped his mouth on his sleeve and took a deep breath.

This was just the first installment.

**

She was halfway through another bottle of wine, and the staccato energy that had fueled her inventiveness was now morphing into a sluggishness in which her thoughts had begun to blur. Still, she pushed on, not wanting to interrupt the flow, bubbles in a cauldron rising to the surface in a rapid boil. Moving quickly back and forth from the balcony to her computer, more of the story plot emerged.

Walking into the bathroom, she splashed her face with water, patted it dry, and examined herself in the mirror. Her eyes looked tired and bloodshot, and her hair, neglected for days, was greasy and straggly. She thought about stopping to take a shower but shrugged it off. She needed to continue this, to take it further.

She typed quickly, eager not to omit any of the plot points. Then, a bolt of reality broke through. There really wasn't any hope of redemption. Her protagonist would eliminate cartel members, a dozen or two, maybe more, but—as she'd been learning from her interviews, particularly the one with the prosecutor—they'd quickly be replaced. Their grieving wives and children would simply be collateral damage, detritus of the grinding echoes of a massive machine fueled by expendable lives.

And then there were the children, the parents, the husbands, or wives of all those injured or shattered by drug consumption. Even her dapper, charming journalist, Enrique Cardona. His soul's destruction, if not his body's, was preordained now that he had begun committing these assassinations. There would be no opening of the clouds, no ray of sunshine proclaiming salvation.

She felt nearly overwhelmed, terrified about the swamp in which she found herself sinking. She had an impulse to delete all her files for this novel and to tear up her scribbled notes, purging herself of a story that was becoming all too, too … she couldn't finish the thought.

She realized that what was making the idea of abandoning this project so compelling was the gray, the shades on the color spectrum between black and white, insistent hues of truth that overpowered her need for absolute certainty.

The story she wanted to write was about a journalist who had gone rogue, carrying out his own sentence of death on mass killers, exacting retribution for the many thousands of people who, like him, grieved for their lost loved ones. A necessary evil, pure and simple. Taking an eye for an eye.

But an insistent voice demanded she make room for the humanity within her. *Barbarism in response to barbarism?* Enrique was entirely certain about the course of retribution he was taking. No haunting self-doubts plagued him. *If only I had the same hundred percent conviction.*

She realized she'd lost her grip on the course that her narrative would traverse. Her thinking had become clouded, and as she walked to her bed and lay down, she thought about a poem her mother liked, something about a fog coming in on little cat feet.

The room was spinning. Moments before unconsciousness encroached, she pictured Enrique sitting on a park bench and drinking from a coffee thermos. Once again, his visage blurred, and an image of her father turned to look at her. With a quiet whisper, he pled, "We're killing the children, Anneko."

21 ~ Safe from My Predator

Milá Anneko—

I practiced a Mozart piece for two hours this morning and then took a long walk, carrying an umbrella because it was raining. We had some thunder and lightning earlier, but by the time I ventured out, the center of the storm had moved on, leaving a summer shower in its wake. The air was rich with the smell of ozone and a hint of chlorine. That's always been for me a sign of rebirth and renewal.

My destination was one of my favorite spots, the dahlia garden in Volunteer Park. Remember how you loved searching for fairies in the tree trunks there? It'll be several months before those stunningly beautiful plants are in full bloom, and then the splendor of that garden will draw crowds. Today, in the rain, I relished having it to myself. Then I laughed when I realized that I was, indeed, not alone. Slugs, snails, earwigs, aphids, and spider mites were lurking there with me unseen, eager to take a very different kind of joy from the garden's bounty.

The sound of the raindrops slipping through the branches of the blue spruce tree that looms over that garden and bouncing off the leaves of the nearby rhododendron plants was musical. No competing chattering voices, barking dogs, or honking delivery trucks. I loved it and, of course, wished you were with me.

As I stood there, Anneko, I thought about the gardeners' challenge in helping those delightful plants to survive. Then, it came to me what I'd write to you today. I would tell you how I survive. I'd tell you how I figuratively keep the slugs, spiders, and snails at bay in my life. Be patient. You'll see where I'm headed.

By now I've helped just under forty immigrants who moved to Seattle and needed help learning their way around. I still correspond with many of them years later. My outgoing mail sometimes includes two, three, or four letters in addition to the one I write to you each week.

Do you remember the Miksyte family? They immigrated to the US from Lithuania in 1994, and I helped them for the first few years after they settled here. When you stayed with me for a few days, they came to dinner, and you told them about a piece you'd written about the architecture in Vilnius. They were thrilled that you'd been to their country and knew so much.

Now, I'm doing the same thing with the Litovchenko family, Stanislav and Tetyana and their two daughters, Hanna and Vira. They arrived from Ukraine last October, and I was asked if I'd help them with the transition. So, once a week I spend a day with them, sometimes in their apartment and sometimes here. Tetyana and I bake, teaching each other our favorite recipes as well as English and Ukrainian words. The twins love watching Sesame Street and are amazing in how quickly they're catching on with English.

Stanislav's another story, and I've taken him on as a special project. He's glum and depressed, overwhelmed, I think, by all the relearning he'll have to do if he ever hopes to again practice as a dentist. But he grudgingly goes along with a game I play with him each time we visit. I tell him he'll get to eat the food that Tetyana and I have cooked only after he goes for a fifteen-minute walk in the neighborhood with me. I point to a tree, or a car, or a dog and say the English word and give him lots of praise when he tries to repeat it. The first time we went for that walk, he threw up his hands in frustration after just a few minutes and hid out in his bedroom when we returned. But it's getting so much better, and every once in a while, I catch him smiling!

Why am I telling you about this? I fear it'll be a trite thing to say, but, truly, I get so much back when I spend time with these families or write to those from years back. By permitting me to become involved in their lives, they are giving me the work I need to take me off of the path of despair. That work keeps me safe from my own predator, the danger of dwelling helplessly in the darkest of memories.

Elie Wiesel wrote about this theme—work that preserves one's sanity. Of course, you know who he was; we've talked about him. He and I were born two years apart and both were in the camps. Like you, he felt called to stand up to atrocities committed against humanity. What an inspiration this man was, a teacher to humankind.

Have you read Day? It's one of his novels. Perhaps you have but let me say a few words about it. Here's the premise: A young man steps off a curb in Times Square, gets hit by a taxi, is in a coma for five days, and then remains hospitalized for many weeks. During that time, he reviews his life.

So, who is this young man? We learn that his name is Eliezer, that he survived Auschwitz as a boy, and that he's now a journalist. All of this, as well as the accident, is taken from the author's actual life.

And the rest of the story? Just how much is true, I don't know. I suspect, however, that while many details might be fiction, what we learn about Elie Wiesel's mind and heart couldn't be more honest. And that's what I will focus on in this letter.

In the opening scene, a woman is with Eliezer. Kathleen is her name. They've left a restaurant and are walking to a theater. The accident occurs, and he's nearly killed by that cab. He's rushed to the hospital and when he comes out of his coma, he has a flashback to the night they first met in Paris some years earlier.

That night she asked him to tell her about himself. His answer was chilling and foreshadowed the story's main theme. He said to Kathleen, "You might end up hating me."

Hate him? Why would he possibly say that to her? Was he some kind of monster? If he were truthful about himself, would he disgust this young woman? Was he a murderer? A thief? A rapist?

He was none of these, but the very fact that he survived the Shoah left him haunted each day of his life by an existential quandary: how to find meaning in life after Auschwitz.

Some may find this puzzling. I don't; I understood it immediately. I also walked on that path after liberation and know it well: the deep ruts of hatred that can trip you; the twists and turns in your thinking that confuse and disorient; and the heavily shaded places, despair really, where you cannot see where you are stepping. More to the point, I found a way to take a detour out of that quagmire, and it saved me.

Perhaps those who know only at some abstract level the unspeakable horrors of the camps won't resonate with Eliezer's dilemma. People who made it out, they might believe, will rejoin their life course, interrupted but not ended. Time will pass. Good health will be regained and family, friendships, work, and play—the warp and woof of life—again will become threads in the fabric of life's meaning.

I suspect Eliezer thought that if Kathleen tried to imagine herself in his place, she might think this way. So, what wouldn't she understand?

It would be his darkness. His immutable darkness.

Wiesel shows us a child challenging his teacher with all manner of questions about the puzzling nature of God's relationship to man. We see this inquisitive boy eagerly immersed in learning. Then, a tragedy of some sort occurs. Maybe his best friend inexplicably rejects him. Or perhaps a thief steals his family's cow. Possibly a fierce storm destroys their crop, or his infant sister suddenly dies. The boy asks, why? Why, Rebbe, would God let this happen?

Likely, the rabbi acknowledges the child's grief, explains that we cannot know God's mind even while we take comfort in His love for us. Perhaps the rabbi will teach the child the words from Psalm 23: "Yea, though I walk through the valley of the shadow of death, I will fear no evil: for thou art with me; thy rod and thy staff they comfort me."

As his knowledge grows, we see that child becoming a person of faith. In his future, all is possible. He believes.

Then, his horizon entirely blackens. Hitler. The spirit, and the hopefulness, and the innocence of this boy's world are muted. Through Wiesel's lens we see him, now as an adult, struggling to find a will to live, questioning deeply his right to exist when so many of those whom he loved perished in the camps. His beloved grandmother gassed to death, her lap once a refuge, the gentle wisdom of her reassurance symbolized in his memories by the black shawl that cloaked her head and shoulders. All now ashes.

And this man's faith? Once the solid pavement upon which he walked, his faith crumbled as he tried unsuccessfully to reconcile God's existence with a world in which an entire people could be systematically exterminated. As he tried to reconcile God's crimes.

Let me return to the fear that Eliezer expressed to Kathleen. Why would knowing these things about him lead her to hate him? In fact, why wouldn't she respond that he was a saint for all that he had endured?

Here, Anneko, we come to Eliezer's brutal truth. He would neither hear nor be changed by words of admiration, encouragement, sympathy, or love expressed by Kathleen or any others. Not while he carried the guilt of having survived, felt the emptiness left by a crushed faith in God, and held with certainty the belief that if he did not die, it was so that he would fulfill a purpose. In living, he would be a messenger of the dead.

He would be a messenger who would perpetually suffer. It would bring him at times perilously close to taking his own life. Knowing that gave rise to another awareness. Any person with whom he became intimate would almost certainly be broken by him. Because there would be no redemption for Eliezer, those who insisted otherwise would come to resent him for their failure to accomplish the impossible, to help him find any other meaning in living. That's why he told Kathleen that if she knew him, really knew, she would hate him.

In her love for him, she'd make a great effort to lift him up. She would fail, ultimately becoming aware that he would exert even more of his spirit in rejecting her attempts.

While he was still in the hospital, one of his close friends visited, a man named Guyla. This man understood Eliezer more than most. Indeed, he knew that what appeared to be an accident that day in Times Square was in actuality an attempt at suicide.

Guyla knew that his friend had committed his life to perpetual suffering as God's messenger, but he had a response. Guyla told Eliezer that the dead are no longer suffering. Only the living can suffer and must think of themselves and those who offer them love.

Guyla's answer is also my answer to you, Anneko.

As the story comes to a close, we see Eliezer taking Guyla's wisdom to heart, searching for a way to unhook himself from the clasp of the dead on his view of his place in the world. I believe the author is telling us that by doing the work of a teacher to humanity, Elie Wiesel found a path away from his own insanity.

Standing at the dahlia garden, I thought about the work the gardeners must do to preserve those beautiful plants from their many natural predators. Without their efforts, the plants would perish. They work at it.

I work at it. I am a gardener when I'm with the Litovchenkos and when I write those letters. And you, my daughter, you, too, have that choice. Can you see it? Might you relieve the burden of distress that you've been carrying by giving to others? I could list any number of ways that you could tend humanity's garden; but in the end, whatever you choose must be what speaks to you, what makes it possible for you to find your way to the light. To be safe from the predator that stalks you.

Okay, enough from the pulpit. I was surprised this morning that it wasn't too early for me to harvest a dozen absolutely gorgeous carrots from my vegetable garden. Normally, they'd need another three weeks in the ground. When Tetyana and her family come by tomorrow, we'll make sweet potato and carrot tzimmes, a dish you used to help me with. I'll save a portion for my new neighbor Elliott, who, I suspect, is struggling to learn how to prepare his own meals. Perhaps you'll meet him some day. I think you'd hit it off.

Before I stop, I want to say that we've not talked for a very long time. It's been months since you last wrote. I wish that you would at the very least find a way to let me know that you're well. Please, my child, won't you call, even if it's just a word or two of reassurance?

Until next week. I love you, sweetheart.

Tvoje máma

22 ~ A Way Out

The digital clock read 2:10, then 2:11, and then 2:12. Elliott plumped up the pillow, rolled onto his right side, closed his eyes, and, recalling a strategy that sometimes worked, conjured up an image. He pictured himself lying on the grass next to a tree-shaded stream on a warm sunny day, the whoosh of the rapidly flowing water lulling him to sleep. He was able to hold on to that scene for only a few moments before an ache in his jaw intruded. *I must be bruxing,* he thought.

It was 2:16. Barely a sliver of light from the streetlamp slipped through the closed blinds, and the room's silence lay in stark contrast with the chatter in his thoughts. He finally gave in and walked to the kitchen, warmed a mug of milk in the microwave, and, despite his ardent dislike for the taste, swallowed it in four gulps along with a melatonin.

Returning to bed, he turned on the lamp and leafed through the latest issue of the *New Yorker,* willing himself to be overtaken by drowsiness. Sometime after noticing that the time was 3:12, he drifted off. At least he thought that must have been the case because he was aware of nothing else until a narrow ray of sunlight was shining on the Mount Rainier painting above his bed and the clock read 7:45.

It had been like this for the last four nights. Lying awake, he pictured Theo sitting on the ground with his back resting against the trunk of his tree. He imagined his friend suffering as his disease progressed and his limbs lost more and more function. At times during this ordeal, he suspected, Theo would be every bit as fragile as when, at the age of fourteen, he first sought refuge in that old-growth park.

Will Theo want it to be where his ashes are spread? Will it be my responsibility? He choked up, and the prospect of losing Theo morphed into another loss, one he could not bear to contemplate.

Peter. More than a month had gone by. Elliott had emailed him at least weekly to schedule their next Skype call. Peter always had other plans. Clearly, he was being evasive. It really was no surprise. *He's gun-shy,* Elliott thought, expecting his dad would lay a trip on him at every opportunity. More than that, Elliott realized his intransigence had achieved nothing, nothing positive, that is, and it had opened a deep chasm between them.

A sudden bolt of inspiration propelled him from the bed. Turning on the computer, he rummaged through the top-right desk drawer to find his pair of off-the-shelf eyeglasses, gave the lenses a quick swipe with his T-shirt, ran a comb through his hair, and logged on to Skype, where, with a grin on his face, he snapped a photo and made it his profile picture. Then, a quick message to Peter. "Hey. Give me a shout."

Will he take the bait? Elliott stayed logged on while filling the teakettle and placing it on a burner, then spooning his favorite blend of Sumatra coffee grounds into his new French press. A few minutes later, just as the coffee finished brewing, the familiar Skype theme music let him know he indeed had a nibble. *Man, that was fast!* He filled his mug and clicked on the green answer icon.

Peter's face appeared in a tight close-up on Elliott's screen. "What's going on? You don't wear glasses."

Elliott chuckled.

"Dad, have you finally lost your marbles, the paltry few you still had?"

An alarm bell sounded for Elliott. It was obvious that Peter hadn't shaved for what must have been at least two weeks, but it also looked as if he had lost weight. There were dark shadows under his eyes, and he was unusually pale.

Is he sick? If I ask he'll get defensive.

Elliott set his concern aside for the moment. First, he needed to break the ice.

"It's a long story."

He paused for a moment, pondering how to begin, and took a sip of coffee. Peter noticed his hesitation.

His son's look of puzzlement dissolved to one of wary skepticism, and Elliott watched Peter fold his arms across his chest. What initially must have come across as a joke apparently was now portending danger.

"Please tell me this isn't just another ploy—"

Elliott hurriedly interrupted him. "No, no. Hold on."

He took off the eyeglasses and held them up to the webcam with one hand while pointing at them with the other.

"For once, this is a conversation about your father's foibles." He put the glasses back on. "I've been such an idiot. Driving a wedge between us was absolutely not what I wanted to do. I really am sorry."

For a few moments neither of them spoke, the only sound on Elliott's end of the call coming from a light brushing of a wind-blown tree limb against his living room window. Elliott noticed the beginning of a tear gleaming in his son's right eye.

"Dad, what's wrong? Has something happened?" Peter's voice seemed tired, the sound of resignation.

He looks terrible.

"No, no, at this point my mental health is fine."

"At this point?"

Elliott nodded. "I've got a tale to tell you. It began three months ago."

Peter had a quizzical expression on his face.

"I moved into this apartment and met my neighbor, Milena Hodrová. You remember, I told you about her, and we listened to her practicing the piano. Ringing a bell?"

"Yeah," Peter slowly said, sounding more like a question.

"Milena's opening my eyes, big-time."

Elliott grappled with how much of what had happened to disclose. Ultimately, it seemed he had little to lose by being candid, and perhaps if he were vulnerable, it might lower the antagonism Peter had felt toward his dad for so long. It was a risk worth taking.

"She's remarkable. I mean, the way she views the world is so inspiring."

"Yeah?"

"She lives a very full life, especially after what was done to her and her family in the Holocaust."

Peter nodded.

"You told me a while ago that you wondered what had happened to me, why I'd changed so much. You were pretty perceptive, Son, but I evaded the issue."

Elliott coughed to clear his throat.

"The fact of the matter is that I took a nosedive. It was when one of my clients took her life."

"I had no idea."

Peter was looking directly into Elliott's eyes, a look of such innocent compassion, Elliott thought. There was no hint of the cloud of acrimony that had hung over them.

"I'm so sorry, but why didn't you tell me?"

Peter can handle this, Elliott thought. He touched his hand to his glasses, reminding himself of the choice Milena's letters had given him. *I, too, can handle this.*

"There was one thing about her that made her death all the more devastating. It was because she was exactly your age. In fact, you were born just four days apart."

"Why did that ...?"

"The truth of the matter," Elliott said, "is it brought me face-to-face with your mortality. I was terrified about the possibility that for whatever cause, you could die. I could lose you, and I'd be unable to prevent it."

He paused, looking down and slowly shaking his head.

"You asked why I didn't tell you. Saying what I was thinking out loud would have been too difficult for me because I knew what would come next."

"I don't" —

"Well, here's how it would have gone. You'd have tried to reassure me how carefully you prepare for each new stunt and that nothing could happen to you."

"Yeah, well that's how I—"

"And I wouldn't have believed a word of it," Elliott interrupted.

They were both quiet, looking into one another's eyes.

"My God, no wonder you were hovering over me," Peter said.

"Rosalie was her name. She was struggling with depression. Heavy pot use seemed to her to be helping, but after a while she realized it wasn't."

As he began telling Peter about this, it felt even more that it was the right thing to do.

"We'd made some good progress in therapy. She'd begun attending Marijuana Anonymous meetings, had stopped getting high, and was really brave in beginning to open up in our sessions about having been sexually abused as a child. We'd talked about her occasional thoughts of suicide. It seemed to me that the probability of her acting on those thoughts was quite low. She thought so as well."

Elliott closed his eyes for a moment. Scenes from that Aurora Bridge nightmare scrolled through his mind.

"I later learned that two days before she died, she started work as a budtender at a medical marijuana dispensary in South Seattle. She didn't mention this in our session. Rosalie apparently relapsed and consumed some very potent edibles."

Peter slowly shook his head. "Jesus."

"Yeah, I suspect she didn't realize how much of an impact it would have on her because she'd been abstinent and lost her tolerance."

"The night she died, her neighbors heard a lot of noise coming from her apartment and called the police. Two cops came to her door. She must have panicked. Before they could stop her, she ran for the window and jumped. I suspect she was psychotic."

"Oh my God. Dad, could anyone have prevented it?"

"That question tormented me for a long time. Eventually, I decided that the care I'd given her was competent."

"Uh-huh."

"I was in a very dark place while trying to sort that out. I believed that I failed her. I thought the same about your death-defying maneuvers. You'd die and I'd have failed you. That's why the terror I felt turned into my ranting at you."

Peter sighed. Elliott knew this must be heavy for his son to hear.

"I realize now that Rosalie's death also triggered something powerful from my childhood. It's about the time when your uncle was killed."

Peter asked, "What do you mean?"

"Your Uncle Todd's death in Vietnam changed me. I was nine years old. The way your grandparents dealt with it upended my world. My mom became hyper-protective, terrified I was in grave danger just in living a kid's normal life, riding my bike, taking a bus, climbing in a tree, or hanging out at a friend's house. Coming late to the dinner table led to a tirade. And . . .," he felt a lump in his throat as he realized where he was headed, "if I talked about painful feelings—being sad, feeling anxious or depressed, missing Todd—any feelings whatsoever other than the one acceptable answer, 'I'm fine,' it threw her into a panic."

Peter remained silent, his slow nod letting Elliott know he was hearing him.

"I learned to follow my dad's example by using journaling as a way—really the only way—of processing thoughts and emotions. And I also learned from my parents that in our family the one assured way each of us could find refuge from danger was by living a life of routine and rigid predictability.

"I recently had an insight. My mom tried to put me in bubble wrap after Todd died. It's beyond me how I could not have seen that after Rosalie's death. I was trying to do to you what my mom did to me."

He reached for his coffee mug and took a sip. A sudden notion led him to laugh.

"Maybe if I'd met Milena Hodrová way back then."

Peter had a puzzled look. "Okay, you really need to spill the beans. What has she done to you and, by the way, what's this transformation all about anyway?"

Taking a deep breath, Elliott braced himself. Disclosing how it all happened and revealing the parts he felt such shame about would be uncomfortable, but he'd manage.

Elliott told Peter about how intrigued he was with her on the first few occasions when they talked. He talked about the fake-eyeglasses gimmick to remind him of the new worldview he'd adopted.

"It's as if you're wearing a disguise. Is that what it feels like?"

"I guess it is a virtual disguise. There's another part of it, though. I'm not proud of what I'm doing."

"Dad, what—"

"Wait. Let me get it all out. Every week Milena writes a long letter to her daughter. She's hoping they'll help lift Anneka out of a state of despair about the many horrific things we humans do to one another, particularly to children. The letters sit in a little wooden bowl in our building lobby until the mail carrier comes. I, uh, I . . ."

Elliott saw Peter's worried expression. But there was no turning back.

"I began taking those letters before the mail carrier got there. I bring them to my office, steam them open, and, after reading them several times, reseal and drop them in a corner mailbox."

Peter was speechless. But Elliott read the meaning of the alarmed look on his face.

"I was drowning, Peter. As wrong as it is for me to steal those letters, they've become my life rings. And as wrong as it is to use that as any kind of a justification, Milena and her daughter will never know."

Peter was looking at the screen with his mouth open. Elliott guessed his son was trying to figure out what to say.

"Let me read something to you. In one of her letters, Milena described her volunteer work with recent immigrants. She helps them deal with all of the difficult aspects of learning to live in a new and strange culture. Here's what she wrote about what she gets out of it."

By permitting me to become involved in their lives, they are giving me the work I need to take me off of the path of despair. That work keeps me safe from my own predator, the danger of dwelling helplessly in the darkest of memories.

"You see, Peter, that's exactly what I'd been doing: dwelling helplessly in dark memories about my brother and my mother's terrors. My fears about you resided in that darkness. Reading Milena's letter showed me a way out."

Elliott rushed ahead and told him how he'd changed. He described his volunteer work doing trail maintenance with the Mountaineers; the community garden plot where he was learning how to grow vegetables; and even the Bread Making 101 course he took at a food co-op in Issaquah. He wanted to go on, to lay it all out, his newfound lightness of being. But he saw there was a heavy expression of sadness in Peter's eyes.

Have I gone much too far?

"God, Dad."

Elliott realized that what he'd hoped would happen—his son feeling enthusiastic for his dad's transformation—was 180 degrees from the apparent gloom that was descending on him at this moment. Elliott braced himself.

Peter closed his eyes, and his facial features crumbled. He rapidly shuddered, as if he were trying to ward off a swell of flooding emotions, and then, his chin quivering, he began to weep.

As Elliott looked on helplessly, hundreds of miles separating them, Peter was no longer the worldly thrill seeker whose way of living, incredibly reckless in his dad's eyes, had prompted Elliott's nagging disapproval. Instead, he saw the fragile five-year-old child who once ran to him for comforting.

"Shhh, it'll be okay," Elliott said quietly, wishing he could hold Peter. "It'll be okay."

Minutes passed. Neither of them made any attempt to intrude.

"Shhh, it'll be okay."

Gradually Peter's tears slowed, and he blew his nose three times. Looking sheepishly up at the screen, there was a glimmer of a smile when he saw his dad's face.

This has nothing to do with stolen letters. It's something else, something far more serious.

"Son, will you tell me what's going on?"

Peter sat there quietly, not saying anything, and not looking at Elliott either. Would he let his dad in on whatever those tears were about?

"Please," Elliott said.

Peter glanced at Elliott's face on his screen, paused for another moment, and then signaled with a nod that he had come to a decision.

"I really didn't mean it when I said that you're lost. I mean, if anything you're doing some awesome stuff, really coming out of your shell. Hearing about it makes me happy for you, and for me, to be honest. It's been so hard to talk with you.

"My life . . . ." His voice cracked. "My life has been coming apart." He stopped momentarily, took a deep breath, and slowly exhaled.

"Peter, what's—"

"Let me tell you the whole thing. It's not going to be easy."

"Of course."

Peter sighed.

"On a Saturday a few weeks ago, we had a bad skiing accident on Flattop Mountain. Four of us did the run. I got caught in an avalanche, and it put me in the hospital for two days."

Elliott gasped.

"I'm okay. Busted my collarbone and it's healing. But that's not all." Peter glanced warily at the screen.

"My best friend, Tat, didn't make it out of there." His voice was gravelly as he pushed ahead. "It took them an hour of digging to find him. He didn't have a chance." He whispered, "It was all my fault. We knew the forecast showed high danger, but I shamed him into it."

Tears again were running down his cheeks, and it seemed that he was struggling to get the words out. "He tried to convince us not to go."

"I'm so terribly sorry, son. But, what about your broken bone? How bad is it?"

Peter adjusted the webcam so that Elliott could see him lying on his bed and wearing a brace over his shoulders.

"It wasn't a bad break," he said. "I wish it were much worse. I deserved for it to have been much worse."

"No, Peter, don't say that."

"They x-rayed me a couple of times and told me I had to keep icing it and make sure it stayed immobile. I have to sleep on my back with cushions."

He pointed to the brace. "This holds my shoulders back and keeps my clavicle stable. I didn't need surgery."

"How long will you need to wear it?"

"Three or four weeks. But that's not what's important. Tat's death has totally thrown me. I went to his funeral and seeing his parents and two sisters overwhelmed with grief was just horrible. I had to do some serious thinking about life."

"About life?"

"Yeah. I had convinced myself that the long-term didn't matter and things would work out. They always had. For now, I'd tour the world skiing and getting gigs to keep the money flowing. Lots of people in my generation have broken out of the mold. They've taken time off to explore and to get wild, thinking there'd be plenty of time before they'd have to live the cookie-cutter life.

"You worry that I'll get hurt and, forgive me for saying this, I've disregarded your warnings as coming from someone whose uptight life wasn't how I wanted to live."

He grimaced, and with a handful of tissues, he covered his eyes.

"I'm sorry. I've been so stupid."

"Peter, I love you."

They sat together silently for several minutes, so far apart in miles but, Elliott thought, thank God, so close in spirit.

Peter continued. "There's something else I need to tell you."

"Uh-huh?"

"I realized a long time ago that I'd never in my life accomplish anything close to what you and Mom have done in your professions."

"But your grades were great. How could you—"

"I know. But that's what I thought, and I would have been too embarrassed to admit it, because then you'd have made me talk about it."

"I wish you'd told us."

"Your pride when I got through dangerous situations in the wilderness safely just meant so much to me. I somehow came to think that the one thing I could succeed in, and not feel I'd failed in your eyes, was taking on bigger and more risky challenges and surviving."

Elliott looked off to the distance, processing what he'd heard. "I know you wanted to please me when you were young," Elliott said. "But is that what it's been about in your adulthood?"

"No, in my adulthood it's all on me. I think that I've somehow learned to only feel totally alive when I've flirted with death and survived. Every time I barely escape getting injured or killed, the rush is unforgettable."

"You have to nearly die to have this totally alive feeling?"

Peter slowly nodded. They peered into one another's eyes.

"That's got to change," Peter said. "I've never really believed I would actually die. Tat's death made it undeniable. And I know now how much I want to live."

With a downcast expression on his face, Peter signaled that he had finished. Through the wall, Elliott listened to Milena at her piano.

"I'm just remembering something Milena wrote in one of her letters," Elliott said.

Peter waited to hear.

"She knew her daughter was plagued by thoughts of inhumanities. They'd become demons and haunted her. Milena urged her daughter to resist those demons by having a life, demanding it. I'm thinking that you and I both need to listen to that advice."

As he spoke and out of the webcam's sight, Elliott used a Sharpie to print words in large capital letters on a used manila file folder. When it was finished, he held it up to be seen.

"COME HOME, SON. I NEED YOU."

Elliott watched as Peter yet again blotted his eyes. Seconds and then minutes passed until, finally, Peter held up his own sign.

"I NEED YOU, TOO."

23 ~ My Refuge

"Stop buggin' me, Elliott. Give it a rest. You'll know where we're headed when we get there. Just one thing you need to focus on right now. You listening?"

Theo pointed his finger at Elliott, his penetrating gaze demanding compliance. Elliott removed his handkerchief from his back pocket and waved it in surrender.

"Good decision, my boy. Today I'm your personal shaman, and I'm conjuring up a spell to cure all that ails ye."

Theo raised his left hand and held it palm down, hovering over Elliott's head. While swirling the last few drops of his cappuccino with a spoon and peering solemnly into the cup, he chanted, "'Double, double toil and trouble. Fire burn and cauldron bubble.'" He paused, continuing to swirl, and then added, "Relieve this boy's soul of all that damn rubble." Theo squeezed his eyes closed; his brow furrowed.

"Thanks to the universe, shaman," Elliott said, laughing as the two of them headed for the door.

Leaving the Starbucks on Fifteenth Avenue East, they walked west on East John Street and across the bridge over I-5, traffic barely creeping along in both the north- and southbound lanes. Not a cloud in the sky interfered with this full-out sunny day, seventy-five degrees at midafternoon, with low humidity and a slight breeze coming in from Lake Union.

Each of them was wearing shorts and sandals, daypacks slung on their shoulders. Theo showed off his muscular arms and sculpted abs with a tight-fitting bright-pink tank top that proclaimed, "I woke up like this." A Theo's Books baseball cap protected his bald head from the mid-July rays. He told Elliott he'd taken a day off for this excursion, and Rachel, his one employee, was minding the shop.

For Seattleites, this was payback time: a climatic return on investment for the interminable slog of all-too-many gray-sky months, days of drizzle or showers interrupted by the occasional gully washer. Sunscreens and barbecue sauces flew off the shelves as locals hustled to pack all things summer into a narrow window of opportunity.

"I will tell you this," Theo said, a singsong lilt in his voice. "The mission for this adventure is to bring some color into your life. For months now, both on the inside and the outside, all you've seen has been gray."

They walked on for several minutes, neither of them speaking, Elliott uncomplaining while he followed where Theo was leading. "We going to the MoPOP?" Elliott asked. The Museum of Pop Culture was a rock 'n' roll shrine that resembled a jumbled pile of overturned teacups, each emblazoned with swatches of color: gold, silver, red, blue, and purple.

"Nope, but not a bad guess, kiddo."

"The Seattle Art Museum or the Elliott Bay waterfront?"

"Not even warm."

Elliott shrugged and kept walking. As they approached the Seattle Center, once the site of a world's fair and now a seventy-four-acre urban park sprinkled with arts and sports venues, Elliott pointed at the Space Needle and said, "Ah, we're going up to the observation deck."

"No, but you're close. Hang on, almost there."

They walked past the International Fountain, where dozens of kids were running in and out of its gently sloping crater. Dancing water patterns shot from the nozzles on the fountain dome, and recorded music played from hidden speakers.

"Let's talk for a few minutes. I'm getting winded," Theo said. He pointed to a bench, and they both took off their daypacks and sat. The rhythm of the fountain's sprays was choreographed to Strauss's *Emperor Waltz*. "What's it been—eight, maybe ten weeks since you and Sandra dropped the bomb?" Each took a few swigs from his water bottle, gazing at the kids, hearing their shrieks whenever a nearby spout suddenly shot up and threatened a drenching.

"It's been just over three months," Elliott replied. "Still seems as if it were yesterday. And, you know, even though I've moved into the apartment, the whole thing feels unreal—like it'll go poof when I wake up."

"By the way, I ran into Sandra this past Thursday," Theo said.

"Where was that?"

"I went to an Edward S. Curtis exhibit at the Seattle Art Museum. She was there with a guy."

"It was probably Mateo, a colleague of hers at U Hospital. They've been dating for a while."

"You okay about it?"

Elliott nodded. "Yeah, I really am. Life goes on, my friend, and she should find someone to love."

Nearby, a father took a photo of his daughter who was riding the back of a life-size bronze killer-whale sculpture breaking the surface of the expansive lawn.

They sat quietly for several minutes and then Elliott abruptly chuckled. Theo turned and looked at him with a questioning expression.

"Strangely enough, there seems to be another shaman hovering over me," Elliott said. "You've got some competition."

Theo looked confused.

"It even gets better. My other shaman is an old lady and she has absolutely no idea that I'm under her spell."

"Unless you're suddenly hanging out with a lot of geriatric folks, you must be referring to Milena. But I don't get it. She's hovering over you, and she doesn't have a clue? What's goin' on?"

"Yeah, it's Milena." He looked off into the mid-distance, shaking his head. "When I first met her, I was charmed by her humor. She said she just might try getting stoned now that it's legal. Can you believe that? She's eighty-seven years old!"

A passing Black Lab nosed its muzzle into Elliott's daypack before the dog's owner noticed and yanked its leash, pulling it away.

"But it's what's happened the last few times she's invited me over that's really done it. I told you about when we stood looking at a painting in her living room?"

"I remember that."

"She said she imagined being in that Czech cathedral with her parents at her side. After first meeting her, I worried that talking with Milena would be depressing." Elliott turned sideways on the bench to face Theo. "But that's exactly *not* how she is. My God, she's enormously stronger, much more resilient, and optimistic than you'd ever expect.

Just listening to her has felt like an infusion of hope. Makes me think I might be able to crawl out of this hole I've been stuck in."

"Yeah?" Theo said. "And you're under her spell? Look, I don't know if Milena's a shaman, but something weird has quite obviously happened to you."

Elliott smiled.

"Okay," Theo said as he stood up, "follow me. We're almost there."

Walking past a billboard-size Paul Horiuchi mural, a mosaic collage with splotches of vivid color overlooking a grassy amphitheater, Theo led them to the ticket booth of the Chihuly Garden and Glass. Opened in 2012, the exhibition is a tribute to the internationally acclaimed glass sculptor, Dale Chihuly, who was born in Tacoma, a short distance south of Seattle.

"For today's spell to take effect, we'll need to immerse you in a sea of color. Believe me, this is just the place for that."

They walked slowly through the Glass Forest room with its display of delicate neon grass-like blades of white, rooted in mushroom-like pods, reaching for the black ceiling. Some blades were straight, others curved, and all were reflected in the black-mirrored surface of the platform.

The roof of the Persian Ceiling passageway was constructed of parallel steel girders that held up a flat glass-pane ceiling. Elliott and Theo peered up to see a multilayered array of brilliantly colored glass objects: platters, balls, and ferns. It was as if the two of them were under the sea, looking up to the ocean's sunlight-illuminated surface covered in a panoply of flotsam and jetsam.

They stopped for a while when they reached the Ikebana and Float Boats room. Here, three wooden rowboats rested on a black-mirrored surface. Each boat overflowed with various sizes of colored glass balls, blades of grasses, stems and leaves of plantings, sea urchins, and scallops.

"It's almost supernatural," Elliott said, gazing at the exhibit. "Glass is so fragile yet look what Chihuly portrays with it." He turned toward Theo. "Speaking of being fragile, since meeting Milena, I've begun to feel as if I'm able to wear someone else's skin. I can just shed my own and climb into someone else's and it's a lot thicker than mine."

"Hmm. Sounds like a chrysalis metamorphosis."

Elliott became more animated. "It's as if the gloom and doom can't touch me nearly so deeply when I'm seeing things through different eyes. Look, can we take a break? How about a cup of coffee? There's something else on my mind."

"Suits me," Theo said. "I'm tired."

A waitress took their orders after seating them in a booth in the exhibition's Collections Café. About a hundred pocket knives were visible in a display case beneath the glass top of the table where they sat, and dozens of accordions hung from the café ceiling. Shelf after shelf of transistor radios were displayed on a nearby wall.

"Chihuly is one passionate collector dude," Theo said. "Who'd have thought that stuff like this is art? Damn, I'd like to have that knife." He pointed to a silver one that was intricately engraved and double-bladed.

Their coffee was served, and Theo asked, "What's the something else? What're you thinking? The younger shaman's office is open for business." Theo sat back, winked at Elliott, and with his fingers, signaled, "Let's have it."

"Now, bear with me. This is going to sound crazy."

"No doubt in my mind that it will, indeed, sound crazy."

They both laughed.

"I really believe Milena's showing me how to take on a new persona," Elliott said. He shook his head. "You know, there are clinical terms for what I'm describing, and some of them are scary. Dissociative identity disorder is one of them."

"God, are you dissociating?"

"No, not at all. It's just a bit of well-controlled fantasy. No losing touch with what's real, just a very pleasant perspective, very different from my own, with which to see the world." Elliott paused, feeling a bit sheepish. "Among the slew of letters Milena writes every week, on Mondays she mails one to her daughter, Anneka, who's apparently a writer living in Mexico. She's about our age. Milena says she's bitter, somehow pathologically absorbed by atrocities in different parts of the world. Drowns her pain in booze."

Elliott stopped for several moments, lost in his thoughts.

"Milena says she occasionally includes poetry. Sometimes she tells about a book she's read or someone she's met. She wants her daughter to see life doesn't have to be hopeless, even if there's brutality in the world.

"Hell, I don't know if Anneka is letting anything her mother's writing to her sink in. But, my God, hearing about what's in those letters feels for me as if Milena is weaving me a new set of clothes, all out of spun gold. The more I'm getting to know her, the deeper I'm getting into being this new man. Am I making any sense?"

"Uh, just what do you mean by 'new man'?" Theo scratched his head and scrunched up his face, his eyes narrowing. "Is that just a figure of speech? I get the feeling that you wouldn't be acting so weirdly about this if that's all it was."

Elliott held up his right hand in a gesture that said "Wait." He took a brown eyeglass case from his daypack, opened it, and removed a pair of rimless glasses with thin gunmetal arms. Without saying a word, he put them on and looked at Theo, holding up his hands as if to say, "Ta-da!"

"You've never needed glasses. Since when—"

Elliott cut him off. "They're just plus-one off-the-rack, nonprescription glasses. Bought them at Walmart. Now take a breath before you say anything." As if he were concerned about being overheard, Elliott quickly glanced around where they were sitting before continuing. "I had an inspiration. I bought these as a symbol just to remind me what could be possible if I concentrated on thinking of myself as someone different: a guy who looks at the world as Milena does. And, so, when I'm wearing them, they're just a simple gimmick. They give me a choice to change viewpoint." He sat back.

"You need to wear them?" Theo asked. "Look, isn't this just a little strange? Couldn't you—"

"Okay, it sounds like I'm nuts, but I don't really plan to wear the glasses when I'm out in public. It's just a strategy to make me feel more hopeful about the future than I've been for a long time. So is it really that crazy?"

"Whoa, I don't know how to answer that." Theo paused, glancing into his coffee mug, slowly shaking his head. "I mean, maybe you can appreciate where your vivid imagination has taken you. But, man, you need to keep yourself from going overboard."

Elliott sensed his friend's alarm bells were blaring.

"Getting awfully close to the sun with your new set of wings, aren't you, buddy?"

Elliott grinned. "Repeating Icarus's mistake, you think? I'll be careful. It's just that I'm really intrigued about what those wings, as you put it, are making possible for me. Whether they're new wings or gold-spun clothes, it's so different than just trying to make myself think good thoughts about Rosalie or Peter. That'd still be me reacting to life. But as this amazing new person, I have so much more optimism. I'm loving being alive and feeling eager to discover what's possible for me."

Elliott paused, and then he spilled it all.

"Okay, before you jump all over me, there's one more thing. Those letters I told you about? The letters to Anneka?"

"Yeah?" Theo said, a hint of suspicion in his tone.

"I know. This is going to send you over the top. So here's the deal. About a month ago, I spotted one of those letters in our outgoing mail bowl and I took it. I—"

"What? But there's a law—"

"Wait. Breathe and just listen. I took the letter to my office and steamed it open."

Theo covered his mouth with his hand, his eyes wide in disbelief.

"I read it several times and then resealed it and put it in the corner mailbox outside my office building. Since then, I've read several more."

Theo was frowning.

"Yeah, it's a terrible thing to do. But, man, reading her words is just such a damned rush, an incredible jolt that reminds me what's possible in how to think." Elliott sat back, and with a voice of resignation said, "All right, go ahead and let it rip."

"Man, is it worth the jail time?" Theo blurted out. The veins in his neck had begun to throb. "Look, even if you're never caught, what you're doing worries me."

Theo drank the rest of his water and coughed several times. They sat there with neither of them speaking.

Elliott then was startled when Theo abruptly laughed and slapped his right hand on the table.

"Damn, I just realized you're a genius. A fucking genius!"

'What in hell, Theo?"

"So, I've walked in your shoes, and I just remembered it."

"In my shoes? What are you talking about? When did this happen?"

"Actually, it was a frightening time in my childhood, and right now it seems very relevant. I was fourteen years old. Just a few years before you and I met. I was beginning to realize that feeling aroused by boys made me different, and I was flooded with a sense of shame."

Elliott had a pained look of compassion on his face.

"It was a long time ago and I've moved on. There was another kid, my best friend, I thought, and one day I told him I loved him.

"So, hearing that another boy loved him must have triggered this guy. He yanked me into an alley and punched me in the gut and then kicked me in the balls. He said he never wanted to talk to me again. Then he called me a faggot."

"Oh no, Theo, I'm so sorry."

"I was shattered, but a few days later it all got much worse. I couldn't eat, slept almost round the clock, and kept telling my dad I was too sick for school. This was a year after my folks got divorced, and Tricia and I lived with him. After several days of this, Dad asked me if I'd let him in on what had happened. He said something like, 'Whatever it is you can tell me about it. I'm your dad.'" Theo's eyes were brimming with tears. "So I told him. I poured it all out, my being turned on by guys, the friend who'd beat me up, and the hurt I was feeling." He paused to take a breath. "And that's when the roof fell in. My dad did a one-eighty, insisted I was way too young to have any idea about my sexual orientation, and basically told me to man up. I can still see the disgusted look on his face. He got in his car and drove off."

"Damn him," Elliott said.

"I discovered that there was one place where I could hide out and escape the maelstrom of emotions that flooded through me. It was my refuge. Schmitz Preserve Park was close to our house in West Seattle. One of the old-growth trees had a hollowed-out spot in its trunk large enough for me to crawl into and sit up." He blotted his eyes with his napkin. "I hung out there, sometimes for hours, bringing a flashlight and a book to read. Being there comforted me, and when I went home, I was preoccupied with how soon I'd be able to get back to my tree. There was safety there, only there." Theo held his head in his hands. "Because of what had happened, I wanted to die. I even thought about how I'd make it happen. I'd take a rope from our garage and hang myself from that tree."

Elliott sat back and slowly shook his head, his eyes closed.

"Finally, my aunt took me to a therapist and insisted I talk about all of this. That therapist really saved my life."

"What happened in therapy?"

"Living in the tree was heading me down a road that dead-ended, and she helped me see that. It was checking out. I remember her words. 'You could decide to stay hidden in that tree and spend most of your time there. I know there's a part of you that wants to do just that.' She asked me to imagine something. 'But what if you could learn how to take the special feelings you have when you're in the tree out into the world?' I was skeptical.

"She had more to say. 'If you think your best choice is to seal yourself away, wouldn't you be denying all of the wonderful things about who you are? Your fascination with astronomy? How quickly you've been learning Spanish? Your being so generous with your classmate by tutoring him in math? Your love of reading? Doesn't it seem as if you'd be deciding that the real you doesn't deserve the right to live a full life? Even the real you who is attracted to boys? Wouldn't it really be setting the stage for killing yourself just as you've been thinking about?' I felt so terrible about myself that I almost told her that's exactly what I wanted to do, kill myself. But she had such a gentle and compassionate way of talking with me that I was able to think about the alternative she wanted me to picture.

"'Theo, you can take what you feel there in the tree and carry it in your mind,' she said. And with some visualization techniques, she showed me how to do that." Theo looked down at the table for a few moments and then turned to Elliott. "I stopped thinking about that rope. I stopped denying who I am."

"My fake eyeglasses," Elliott said. "You're thinking that when she taught you to carry those feelings from inside the tree to the outside world, she was giving you what the fake eyeglasses are giving me."

"Exactly."

Elliott held out his hand and they shook. "You're a good friend, Theo. I was afraid you'd disapprove."

"I might have. Except I realized I've been there. Been there and done that."

"Look," Elliott said, "let's pay up and take a walk. I've seen enough Chihuly glass for today."

They walked past the armory, now the site of several fast-food restaurants and a children's museum, crossing the South Fountain Lawn.

Theo said, "I'm beat. Let's stop for a bit."

They found an empty bench.

"Your folks got divorced, you discovered you were gay, your dad couldn't handle it, and you were fourteen—an incredibly fragile age," Elliott said. "Damn it. It's just not supposed to happen that way."

They sat there silently, each seemingly lost in his memories. Several minutes passed, and then Elliott turned to Theo.

"I cringed when you described your dad driving away after telling you to toughen up, leaving you so alone. That's how I felt after Todd died and my mom got so depressed, and my dad held on for dear life, mostly by writing in his journal hour after hour, day after day."

"How'd you survive?"

"I spent hours in the library, some of that time doing homework, but mostly reading books about reptiles, the great apes, birds, and—oh yes—I read about insects and butterflies, all of the different breeds of dogs, whales and porpoises, elephants, and, gosh, I'm probably leaving some things out. But, man, as I think about you and me at that time in our lives, I'm so glad that at least for a while until we learned how to survive, you had your tree and I had all of those books."

Theo nodded. "I wonder if that tree is still there. Someday, I'm going to go looking for it."

"Take me along," Elliott said. He patted Theo on the back, and they stood up. "Let's head back to Capitol Hill."

They began walking.

"Oh, by the way," Elliott said. "There's something I hope you can help me with. Milena asked me a question that reminded me I know next to nothing about my mother's line in the family. Do you have books on how to do genealogical research?"

Theo stopped and turned to face Elliott. "You bet. I'm on it. Now there's something you can help me with. Your fake glasses are fine with me, but nicking those letters? Promise me you're going to stop."

"No promises, buddy," Elliott said.

Crossing the bridge over I-5, the traffic in each direction was at a near standstill.

24 ~ How Can You Not Rage?

"Preso A. Hodrová, sexo femenino, no ciudadano, fecha de nacimiento 13 de Mayo del 1964." Prisoner A. Hodrová, female, non-citizen, date of birth 13 May 1964. That's what was printed with a black marking pen, all in capital letters, on the cardboard box that held possessions being returned to her—two keys, one watch (gold colored), one carry bag (blue cloth), one yellow-lined pad, one pen (silver colored), one pencil— all inventoried on the form she had to sign, a copy of which she received at the clerk's desk.

"Given the circumstances, the prosecutor is not going to charge you with a crime," the jail matron said, neither kindly nor with rancor; her eyes, however, averted Anneka's as they stood at the exit door. "There's an Alcoholics Anonymous meeting each night at seven in a basement room at the *parroquia*. I suggest you go." She was already turning away when she said those words, and Anneka sensed she had given the same advice to many before her. She wondered if any had complied.

It had happened at a *taberna* the previous night. One of two workmen sitting at the next table had shouted "Not now" at a girl, a kid she guessed was nine or ten years old. It was after eight, and the child had whined that she was hungry and wanted to go home. Dozens of bottles of cerveza littered the table. The ashtray overflowed and for well over two hours, the two men had been slugging them down, raucous with backslapping boasts. "No, Papa. I want to go home now."

During much of that time, Anneka had been studiously ignoring all that surrounded her, sinking into a cloud of inebriation. The girl's pleading voice broke through her stupor, and she looked up. Just as she did, the workman hit the child, a full-handed slap to the side of her face, knocking her to the floor. Immediately, the barroom became totally silent, every patron freezing in place as if in shock. The child then began to gasp, struggling to catch her breath before she scampered away from the table and hid under a chair.

Then, as conversations again continued, Anneka heard the other workman chuckle. Not one person responded to what had just unfolded. Like a thunderbolt, Anneka heard her father's wail, "We're killing the children," and pictured Enrique lying in the bed of his pickup and peering through his rifle sight.

Without further thought, Anneka grabbed a half-full tequila bottle from the bar, took three steps to the man's side, and swung it fiercely, smashing it over his head. Later, everything that happened next seemed a blur to her: the gushing blood, chairs tipping over, his daughter's sobbing, someone shouting for an ambulance, strong arms pushing her into a chair and restraining her, the handcuffs, and the jail cell.

What did not seem a blur, however, was the resolute righteousness that had surged through her when she witnessed the child being hit. In swinging that bottle, she felt an upwelling of Enrique's laser-focused dedication to exacting vengeance.

Sitting in her bathtub, soaking away the emotional grime of the past eighteen hours, the word *prisoner* and the unforgiving clank of the steel cell door slamming shut echoed in her mind. Yet she felt no remorse. She'd been drunk, without question, yet not so inebriated as to be oblivious to her surroundings.

There were red welts on each of her wrists caused by the too-tight cuffs. She looked closely at each hand, holding one and then the other up to the light, slowly rotating her wrists to inspect the swelling. Her skin would repair in a week or two, and the marks would disappear, but she realized she didn't want to lose them. Why? Trophies earned for a courageous act in defense of a little girl?

A hazy memory floated into her thoughts. She was young, maybe that girl's age, and she had rushed into her parents' bedroom to show her mother, drips from the newly inked numbers running down her left arm, proud that they were now alike. Her mother looked at her, horror registering in her expression—not the happiness that Anneka had expected—then suddenly yanked her into the bathroom, scrubbing it all away, all but the indelible sting from that vivid memory.

Now, quickly stepping out of the tub and pulling on her robe, she found antibacterial ointment in the medicine cabinet, smeared it on both wrists, and then wrapped them in gauze to speed the welts healing. What had represented an unquestionably bold act of fighting back suddenly led to perplexity. My God, there had been so much blood, and he didn't move. She'd heard one of the medics warning that they had to get him to the emergency room quickly. *I could have killed him.*

***

She put her mother's letter down and took a deep breath. More advice, this time to volunteer, to become a giver. *She has no idea whatsoever.* Shaking her head, almost in disbelief of what she was about to do, she walked to the phone hanging on the wall in her kitchen. She picked up the handset and stood there for a moment, undecided, and then returned it to the base.

Grabbing a bunch of carrots, she ran them quickly under cold water, and, taking a vegetable peeler and knife from the top drawer, moved to the cutting board. Refilling her glass, she took two gulps of wine and then, sloughing off the thought of procrastinating further, she reached for the phone and dialed her mother's number.

Milena answered on the third ring.

"Mom, it's me." She rushed to get out what she needed her to hear. "I'm really okay, and I'm sorry I've not been better at keeping in contact. I've needed time, though, and I still do. But there's more that I have to ask you to understand. I—"

Milena raised her voice. "Anneko. I'm so relieved that we're talking, finally. Sweetheart, how are you?"

"Mom, please. I'm really fine. Please let me say something. It's taken a lot for me to get ready to tell you this."

The handset cradled on her left shoulder, Anneka separated the carrots from the greens and began peeling the first one. "I don't think you've ever understood what your internment in Terazín and Auschwitz means to me, no matter how many years ago it happened." She heard a sharp intake of air on the other end of the phone line but ignored it. "That you were a victim, that my grandparents died, probably starving to death, and for that matter the whole Holocaust—I don't think you can appreciate how it all affects me."

"It's over, my daughter," her mother whispered.

"No, it's not, Mom," she answered. "It's now. Dad got it—at least, I think he did." She continued peeling, bits of carrot landing on the floor, one slice sticking to the window over the sink. "You said he'd been depressed for years before he killed himself, Mom. Even though I was young, I understood what tormented him. I remember his crying when he learned about that plane crash in Vietnam, the one trying to rescue all those orphaned kids before the North Vietnamese took over. Do you remember that? How hopeless he felt? I remember him saying, 'We kill children as if they don't matter, and we do it over and over again.' I also know he loved you, and he had to have imagined what you went through as a child in being ripped from your home. Those bastards!"

Now Anneka heard a sob come through the phone line.

"God, Mom, can I possibly not be haunted by all of that? How can I not feel hopeless if I live in such a world?" She began chopping the carrots, the knife blade slamming into the cutting board with each cut. "I remember you asking if I thought Holocaust victims should forever remain embittered. Right at this minute, as I think about it, I don't know. On the one hand, I can hardly wish to add even more pain to what you've already endured, but on the other hand, I want to scream out: How can you not rage against what they did to you, to six million of us? What they're still doing to children, Mom, now, at this very minute. How can any of us sleep?"

She nicked the index finger of her left hand, and it began to bleed, but she ignored it and kept chopping. "Mom, I can't answer how you should live your life, but I can make a choice for my own." She cut herself again, this one deeper. "Damn, can't I even slice a goddamn carrot?"

"Anneko, what's happened?"

"Business must not go on as usual." She left the cutting board and paced back and forth in front of the sink, the long phone cord flapping like a jump rope. "Reparations haven't even begun to be made in any way decently proportional to the horrors inflicted on people, and conditions continue to be ripe for it all to happen over and over again." She picked up another carrot and began cutting it. "Look at Rwanda, Mom. It was genocide, pure and simple, and it happened—hundreds of thousands of people murdered—decades after all of humanity had supposedly said 'Never again.' And Nigeria. My God, those babies!"

"Sweetheart, please. Have you hurt yourself?"

"Mom, the Holocaust must not revert to a simple historical footnote, because genocide hasn't stopped. If that means I live with a persistent darkness hanging over me, at least I'll be living authentically."

"Authentically? That's not how you—"

She interrupted, "And, please, there's something else that I want. Please stop trying to change me, to tell me being put in the camp happened to you and not to me, as if there's any glimmer of justice in saying that I get a 'get out of jail free card,' because I don't. I'm your daughter, and I'm also a human living in a grotesque, inhumane world."

"But, sweetheart, how can I watch you abandon any chance for living a decent life? I survived. We should be grateful for that. Must you be sacrificed because injustice still happens?"

"And what would you have me do? Forgive? Is that your remedy? The very idea of forgiveness for these horrors is an abomination."

For several moments, both were silent, Anneka's labored breathing the only sound.

"Mom, I'm going to say good-bye. I love you, and I promise we'll talk again soon."

Without waiting for her mother's reply, she softly placed the handset on the telephone base and stood there, just staring at it for several moments. She looked down at the cutting board, blood staining its surface and dripping down the face of the cupboard door.

She felt light-headed, and suddenly the floor was rushing up at her. The phone began ringing, its sound coming from far in the distance.

25 ~ Whether to Forgive

Milá Anneko—

I'm just back from working in my vegetable plot. Hector, the fellow who's next to me, had more beets than he needed, so we did an exchange. I gave him a half dozen cucumbers. He's such a nice man, always eager to help.

I am so grateful that you called yesterday, although I am troubled. I wish we could have talked longer. Please call again when you're able to. It's a gift to me, my daughter.

I went for a long walk after we spoke. Your words were heavy on my mind. When I closed my apartment door and walked down the steps, I was unsure where I was headed. Then, as if I were a Ouija Board, my feet being directed without my conscious intention, I found myself in the plant-filled aisles of the conservatory at Volunteer Park, that magnificent Victorian glasshouse that I took you to so many times.

I imagined you were there alongside me. When I saw that one of your fingers had a bandage on it, I held it to my lips for a kiss to make it heal.

Quite a few people had come to see the rare corpse flower. Its claim to fame is its putrid stench, a smell that's a lot like rotting meat. By the way, I learned its proper name is Amorphophallus titanum. Thank heavens it'll be another week before the plant blooms and the smell is strongest!

As I examined the many beautiful orchids and cacti, some of them quite rare, I replayed our conversation. You're wondering if I have forgiven the Nazis. It may surprise you when I say that at this point in my life, I don't really know. That's not how I felt at first, of course. What the Nazis did was pure evil, and my only wish was that their heinous acts be avenged.

Although it was more than seventy years ago, I have a clear memory of a guard they called Manfred. He was an ugly bully of a man who reveled in cruelty. I remember his gold teeth shining through his sneering grin as he mercilessly beat old and sick men, weak with starvation, who could not remain on their feet during the interminable prisoner counts. And Dieter, hardly more than a teenager, whose voice sometimes cracked when he screamed at us for taking too long in the toilet. He, too, took such pleasure in humiliating and brutalizing prisoners, particularly women and girls.

Milva was different. I've told you about her and the day she brought me a bottle of liquid soap. Do you remember? She encouraged me to dream while blowing bubbles that I was a princess and living free in the world. I taught it to you when you were a child. She was such a rarity.

I'm back. I began to feel ill, so I stepped outside for a few minutes. I didn't stay long because it's unseasonably warm today. While I was sitting on one of the wrought-iron benches in our front courtyard, my neighbor, Elliott, came by and kept me company. I've just now sat down again.

I can imagine you shouting, "You're not sure? How can you even consider forgiving them?" My answer to that requires some background. Let me begin, however, by saying that for Hitler or the others who designed and led the Third Reich, there's no question in my mind. For what they did, there can be no redemption.

But for those who followed them? I'm uncertain. Perhaps you'll understand if I first tell you about what happened in November of 1963, a year before you were born. President Kennedy had just been assassinated, and we were glued to the television. We watched the gruesome nonstop coverage of what unfolded in the days that followed: reporters interviewing horrified witnesses who were on that grassy knoll in Dallas, Oswald being caught and jailed, and then being murdered on live television.

Your father and I were in shock, just emotionally drained. Neither of us could sleep for days. At one point, though, he began to sob uncontrollably. The cameras had just shown John John, the president's toddler son, saluting the flag-draped casket as it passed by on a horse-drawn caisson. I misunderstood, thinking your father was grieving for the president.

That image of John John saluting had unleashed a firestorm within your father. In between his gasps for air as he wept, he told me more than he had said years earlier about a horrific atrocity his army unit committed in July of 1950 in Korea. Your dad was just twenty years old.

You know some of this story, Anneko, but not all of what I'm about to describe. I apologize. It will be painful to read.

After the North Koreans invaded, America sent its military to support the south. Weeks later, four hundred refugees, many of them women and children seeking safety, were caught between the lines that separated the Americans and the enemy. Your father's commander believed infiltrators were hiding among those innocent civilians. He gave an order to kill all of them. Your father's unit carried out that order.

My hand is shaking as I write the details your father told me. The killing spree went on for hours as survivors hid under a stone bridge to seek shelter. Some, using their bare hands, dug frantically in the dirt to create holes in which to hide. Others cowered behind piled up bodies. No one survived.

"Mileno," your dad pleaded, getting down on his knees in front of me, "we killed the children. Please forgive me." He choked and pulled at his hair, overpowered by the enormity of what they had done. "I tried to aim away from them while I was shooting," he cried. "But I didn't do anything to stop the killing. Please, Mileno," he wailed.

Day turned to night, and I sat with him in the dark for hours on the living room floor, gently rocking him in my arms until the cyclone that had torn into his soul abated. Thankfully, he then slept, and we never again talked about whether I could forgive him.

But what if he had asked for my forgiveness again? Would I have known what I really felt? I didn't have an answer.

Were those soldiers really monsters? I had to ask myself what I would have done if I had been a soldier in that American army unit in Korea and been ordered to shoot.

Dear God, I desperately want to think that I would have refused, no matter how much pressure and no matter how great the punishment I would face. But would I have?

I must tell you, my daughter, that when I look back at the years I spent in Terezín and then Auschwitz, I remember some things that I did, hoarding food is just one example, that made me feel ashamed. I did it to keep myself alive. But I also knew that others were dying of starvation. The food I hoarded could have eased their suffering, perhaps even made the difference between perishing and surviving until the camps were liberated.

There's something else I did, and this is a story I've told no one. Recalling it is immensely painful. Just weeks before the Soviet army reached Auschwitz, the conditions for prisoners were horrific. The gas chambers each day took many of us while others died of starvation or the illnesses that were so rampant.

A woman who slept next to me on the lower shelf was very close to dying. I had seen so many go through their last moments, and I knew what it looked like. I am horrified to tell you that I was eager for her to pass. Her shoes were much better than mine, and I wanted them. No, I needed them.

The moment came, and she took her last breath. I undid the laces of her shoes and began to remove them from her feet. While I was doing this, she suddenly opened her eyes and looked at me with an expression of abject horror. It lasted for only an instant before she did, in fact, die. But, that moment, seeing her recoil and feeling as if I were doing to her what we all experienced from the camp guards, has haunted me ever since. Dear God, to her I was the SS. Nothing has ever healed that shame, nor should it.

I believe many survivors of the Holocaust must carry memories such as this. We did things out of wretched desperation, and we did them sometimes at others' expense.

Could I have been a Manfred or a Dieter and brutalized prisoners? With every fiber of my being, I want to say no with absolute certainty. I must admit, though, that I believe the capacity to be sadistic is in all of us.

Might I have been one of the multitude of Nazis who played a part in the horror of the Holocaust, people like Milva who didn't torture prisoners, but nonetheless were cogs in the machine and helped to make it all happen?

Would I have stood with a rifle, aimed at those Korean refugees, and fired my bullets? When I think about what those soldiers did, undoubtedly good and kind and moral young people being ordered to comply with that ghastly order, I'm not so sure. I just am not sure.

Should they face charges? In my heart, I believe they should, every one of them. Playing a part in the commission of an atrocity, even if ordered to do so, must have consequences. They deserved to be tried and, if convicted, punished.

But can I forgive them? Could I forgive your father? The answers eventually came to me when I understood that I also needed to decide whether to forgive myself.

I realized that only I can fully know the state of mind I was in as a child in Terezín and Auschwitz. Those who were not there will never really comprehend the impact the conditions in the camps had on us, an impact that led me to do some truly despicable things.

When we try to conceive what might have been in the minds of those army soldiers to make it possible for them to do what they did, young people who I assume were raised to live a moral life, might we get it wrong? Might we fail to realize how trapped by authority they thought they were? Could we not understand the life-threatening danger they believed they were facing if they refused to obey? Might we not grasp the depth of grief and fear that motivated them to do what they were told regardless of how obscene it was?

Your father committed suicide when he could no longer bear to live with the searing shame and remorse he had carried for so many years. Because of your father, I have to believe that among those who commit atrocities, there are others like him. I found I could forgive your father, and I could also forgive myself.

Forgive the Nazis? Perhaps I do, but only for what they did to me. I believe Jewish tradition permits me that choice, although it does not permit me to forgive them for what they did to others.

This is a personal decision, and no one can make it for us. Whether you agree or disagree with how I think, I hope at least that you now understand it. For me, it lifts a heavy burden from my heart and allows me to live a full life.

And if looking at life through my eyes might offer you a way of reconciling yourself with living in a world in which genocide still happens, I pray you will try. Live, my daughter.

Love—

Tvoje máma

26 ~ Simply Drive Away

"I can't let it go. Every time I think about her and what she did, it makes me cringe." Bill was looking down at his lap as he spoke.

Abruptly he looked up to face Elliott. Throwing his hands in the air, he blurted out, "And I hate the thought that a middle-aged guy, a father and a professor for God's sake, is held hostage like this. Christ, it's been months of coming to see you, and I'm exactly where I started." He slouched deeper into his chair, his arms folded across his chest, biting his lower lip. "Damn her," he hissed. Bill's physical slump reflected the sag in momentum in their sessions.

Mired in a sludge of fury and grief, Bill was idling in neutral. At each session, Elliott would ask how he was feeling, Bill would pour it all out, and Elliott would empathize before offering suggestions that Bill quickly dismissed.

Nothing changed. From time to time there'd been a glimmer of possibility that he could forgive Jan for what had become an escalating pattern of abusive drinking that ultimately led to her death. However, each time Elliott thought that Bill might let go of his anger, a wave of acute sorrow sparked a renewed resentment. "How could she have done this to us?"

Helping him find an exit ramp from this closed loop had eluded Elliott. And then he had an inspiration.

"Bill, I think it's time for your relationship with your daughter to have a makeover. Tell me, do you and Kate talk much about Jan?"

In a tone of voice suddenly hostile, Bill said, "Of course we do. How can you even ask such a thing?" He walked over to the window and placed the palms of each hand on the glass as if he intended to push it out. He stood there for what seemed a long time and then Elliott saw his shoulders slump just before he returned to his chair. "No, that's not true, Elliott. Jan only comes up when Kate is screaming at me, something like, 'If mom were alive, she'd understand. You are just clueless.'"

"Is it possible, Bill, that because of your anger at Jan, the two of you are actually avoiding talking about her—the kind of talking that lets it all pour out?"

Elliott noticed the sadness in Bill's eyes. For several moments he didn't respond but sat there slowly shaking his head. "Yes. That's exactly what is happening. It just feels incredibly hard to bring her up. I've been so afraid that if I got started, I'd rant about Jan and Kate would be traumatized yet again, this time by me."

"Yeah. As much as you'd like for the two of you to talk about her, your anger is getting in the way." In the next several minutes Elliott channeled Milena. He talked about bringing the reality of Jan's death into father-daughter conversations, being brave enough to let it pour.

Remembering Milena's warning about the acidity of a single-minded focus on grievances, he said, "I need to tell you something, Bill. Until recently, I think that if I'd been in your shoes, I'd also have been held prisoner by my anger."

"I'm surprised," Bill replied. "But you've changed?"

"Yeah. My eyes have been opened to the price of refusing to let it go. I've learned that I needed to forgive."

"Okay, but how do you do that?"

"Let me tell you a story." Elliott walked over to his desk, picked up his journal, and turned to a page where he'd copied a poem from one of Milena's letters.

"A man in his mid-thirties died of cancer. As you'd expect, his mother's grieving went on for a long time. Eventually, as time passed, her loss became easier to bear. Yet she had setbacks. Years after he was gone, intrusive thoughts about his death washed over her. They pulled her back into grief with the power of a rip tide. She found a way to keep herself afloat, though, and even wrote about it in a poem. Want to hear it?"

Bill faintly nodded.

"In her poem she talked directly to those intrusive thoughts." Elliott began reading.

No one invited you into my home today
No one asked if you could call
You just showed up unannounced

intent on ruining my day
But I'm stronger now
I've learned to go on
So this year, I ushered you
into the closet
Locked the door
and left you kicking and screaming
I picked up
my keys
Got in my car
and simply drove away.

Elliott checked out Bill's expression before continuing. He was listening.

"Do you suppose, Bill, that your anger at Jan for being drunk is an intrusive thought? Your own rip tide?" This was a risk. Perhaps Bill would be ready to hear the choice the poem offered, but perhaps not.

"Could you usher that piece of your memory, just one piece among so many, into the closet, lock the door, pick up your keys, and simply drive away? Could you forgive Jan and perhaps forgive yourself as well for the wall you've let keep you from being there for Kate?"

Bill was quiet and Elliott suspected he was contemplating the possibility.

"You've been stuck in quicksand, Bill. Your anger is making it impossible for you to really grieve."

"Quicksand is something I know all too much about."

Elliott nodded. "I suspect you also know quite a lot about self-preservation."

***

A week later they met again. "I've been fighting the quicksand," Bill said as he took his seat. "And maybe even beginning to win."

"Tell me about it."

"That poem you read to me. It stayed in my mind, particularly the part about locking up the intrusive thought, getting in your car, and just driving off. With Kate, it had felt incredibly hard to bring Jan up. I pictured Kate resenting me for feeling angry at Jan, and then the two of us ending up screaming at each other."

"Has something changed, Bill?"

"After our last session, I went home, and Kate and I had dinner. She started heading for her bedroom, but I asked if she'd be willing to hang out with me for just a few minutes. She looked uneasy but agreed. We went into the living room and sat side by side on the couch. I looked her in the eye and said, 'I miss your mom, sweetheart. We don't really talk about her, and I think we should. At least I'd like to. Would you?'"

Elliott smiled.

"It was as if a dam had broken. Each of us admitted we'd been afraid to express our feelings about Jan, including our anger. Once we recognized what we'd been doing, our memories brimmed over. So did our tears. And, Elliott, I had my daughter back."

Bill talked about the sea change at home after he and Kate broke through the barriers and relived memories, watching some family videotapes, revisiting the arboretum which Jan had loved, and setting aside time to really talk.

Elliott almost laughed when Bill pointed to his beginning mustache. He'd actually enlisted his daughter's help in how to look cool, and that was her first inspiration. She'd also jumped at the chance to offer wardrobe ideas, and the two of them went shopping, this time for him.

More than anything else, Elliott thought, was Bill's changed affect. "I'm finally able to begin breathing again," he said. "And because I'm feeling alive, so is Kate."

Milena, Elliott thought, *you can't know any of this, but so am I. Feeling alive.*

27 ~ Taking Her Down With Him

At four thirty in the morning, two hours remained before the bus from Nuevo Laredo would reach its destination, an eleven-hour trip with one stop. Aside from the middle-aged couple sitting across the aisle from Anneka, almost all of the twenty-two passengers were asleep. For 350 miles, the couple had been bickering on and off, and just now the man slapped the woman who, after audibly gasping, was now cowering against the window, a coat covering her head.

Anneka jumped from her seat and, through gritted teeth, said in Spanish, "I saw what you did, you bastard. If you dare to harm her again, I will tell the driver to call for the police. Do you understand me?"

The man glared at her as she spoke, beginning to stand until his wife put her hand on his shoulder and pulled him back down. "*Por favor, señora, le ruego.*" Please, señora, I beg of you. She had a pleading look on her face. "Please forgive our disturbing you. I will be fine, I assure you. He will not repeat what he did. Tell her, Leonardo." Muttering something that Anneka was unable to hear, the man shrugged and then sat back in his seat and closed his eyes, turning his head away from her.

Anneka stood in the aisle for a few moments, deciding what to do. The woman nodded and, with a meek smile, also sat back and looked away. Anneka returned to her seat, her temples throbbing as she felt possessed by Enrique, by what he had become.

For the past three days, she had been scoping out reports of Los Zetas activities in Nuevo Laredo. Local and national officials were seemingly impotent in preventing yet another cycle of rapidly escalating violence, including murders by the crime syndicate. Among them was the discovery early in the morning just the day before of two beheaded bodies in the middle of a school playground.

This was the fourth trip she'd made in as many months to research story lines for the *New York Times* and scenarios for her novel. She'd done so despite being aware of the insistent travel advisories concerning that region for US citizens about violent crimes, including homicide, kidnapping, carjacking, and robbery. She had to risk it.

Each time, she'd stayed in an inexpensive hostel, not so much to be frugal but rather in the hope that casual conversations with fellow travelers, there and in the taverns and cafés where she hung out, might add to her insights about the drug economy. Among the tidbits of information that she'd gleaned on this trip were more rumors about a prominent Nuevo Laredo real estate investor. Word had it that he publicly called for safe streets and condemned drugs while privately profiting enormously as a Los Zetas lieutenant.

Anneka was about to write a scene in her novel in which he appeared. Quite intentionally, she'd use his real name. A different name would undoubtedly substitute when her book was published. For now, however, her writing was stimulated by her holding this man's evil image in her mind.

Anneka seethed. *So many predators,* she thought to herself. *Depraved predators.* As soon as the bus arrived and she was back in her apartment, she'd get back to her writing. At that thought, she felt both exhilaration and a sick feeling in her gut. Enrique was becoming more and more corrupted by his own actions. Her protagonist was taking her down with him.

***

Just after one in the morning, the elevator doors opened on the parking garage's third floor. It was nearly empty.

Cornelio Ochoa stepped out, quietly humming the folk song performed as an encore by a Chilean soprano. That evening he had attended an art show and concert. They were part of the Festival Internacional Tamaulipas in Nuevo Laredo.

He capped the evening off at a private banquet in a colleague's penthouse suite. He was a happy man.

He got his keys out from the pocket of his tux. In his midforties, Ochoa might have stepped off a GQ cover. He was tanned, trim, and had a streak of silver in his wavy black hair.

He paused, quickly scanning the surrounding space to assure himself he wasn't in danger. Then, walking over to his pearl-gray Lexus 570 SUV, he unlocked the driver's side door.

Suddenly, he became aware of a rustling sound. It was coming from the bed of a rusty pickup truck parked two spaces over.

He reached for the Glock 30S in his shoulder holster and began to swivel in a defensive crouch. Before he was able to raise his weapon and take aim, however, he heard a male voice. It was soft spoken but commanding.

"¡Alto! ¡Guardé silencio o lo mató!" Stop where you are and say nothing or you will die!

He stopped.

A rifle was pointed directly at his head.

"Good decision. Put your weapon on the floor. Stand up with your hands held out in front of you. Kick the gun over to me."

Ochoa complied.

When he got a good look at who had ambushed him, he saw an older, rather seedy man in faded jeans and denim jacket. He was kneeling in the back of a broken-down Datsun.

Ochoa came to a quick conclusion.

"Okay. Stay calm. I've got about sixteen thousand pesos in cash and a very expensive Bulgari watch. Take them. But I have to warn you, two men who travel with me are going to be here in the next minute or two." Feigning sympathy for his captor, he said, "They're very protective of me. If you're still here, they'll take you out without any conversation. Do we have a deal?"

As he talked, Ochoa removed the watch from his wrist and looked questioningly at his assailant as he very slowly moved his hand inside his tux jacket for his wallet.

Enrique responded with a sinister smile, holding the rifle steady. "A very fine performance, Mr. Ochoa. You have my admiration. Yes, I will gladly take your wallet and your expensive watch. But you and I both know that on Thursday evenings at eleven, you give your bodyguards the rest of the night off. No one is coming to rescue you."

Ochoa's confident demeanor rapidly began to dissolve. He realized this was by no means a simple robbery.

His eyes darted back and forth, surveilling the scene to begin formulating a plan for his escape, any plan. He began to perspire heavily.

The two of them were quite alone, and the man with the rifle knew his identity. Had he been set up?

Was this a territorial takeover? Were the five other senior leaders in this region also facing assassination tonight?

Abruptly, they both turned in the direction of the elevator. The car had begun to descend. Neither moved as they listened to the doors opening on the first floor and the elevator begin going up.

Enrique again pointed his rifle directly at Ochoa. "Absolute silence. Anything else, and you will not take another breath."

The car stopped one floor below. They heard two people laughing as they stepped off. In a few moments, a car engine started. The elevator remained where it had stopped.

Enrique stepped down from the truck, bent over to retrieve the pistol, and then sat on the hinged tailgate, holding his rifle aimed at Ochoa.

"You are not bleeding out onto the concrete right now only because you have followed my instructions. ¿Comprendes?" Do you understand?

Enrique's unblinking gaze and quietly stated question emphasized one unquestionable truth. He was entirely in control.

"Yes, yes, I do," Ochoa replied. "But I also want to make my remaining alive worthwhile to you. Are you in a position to negotiate? For my organization, I have that authority. Do you for yours? Can we slow things down here and take time to think through the options? How you come out of this could make you and the people you work for very wealthy."

His words implied he held a position of strength, but his voice trembled as he spoke.

"Now, before we get to that," Enrique said, "you will do the following. Lower your tux jacket from your shoulders so that it gathers around your elbows. Keep it buttoned."

Ochoa held his hands up in a questioning motion, but immediately did what he was ordered when Enrique gestured he was ready to shoot.

"Again, you are making good decisions, Mr. Ochoa," he said. "I am now going to hand you an open pair of handcuffs. You will cuff your left hand, pass it under the chain of this tailgate, and then cuff your right hand."

When Enrique stepped away from the back of the pickup, Ochoa made a sudden move to turn. But before he could begin to run, Enrique shot him, a carefully aimed round that grazed his right shoulder, the sound muffled by the rifle's silencer.

Ochoa staggered before regaining his balance. Acute pain registered on his face as he turned back to face Enrique.

"In the script for tonight's stage play, Mr. Ochoa, there is only one warning shot. Only one moment of grace. You have just enjoyed that privilege. For you now, any choice you make other than what I tell you to do will have only one consequence. You will die. Do you understand that?"

Ochoa nodded, his shoulders slumped in defeat. He took the cuffs from Enrique and followed the instructions.

"Before I ask you several questions, which, by the way, you will answer immediately and truthfully, let me help you to focus." Enrique took a photograph from his shirt pocket and placed it on the tailgate. "Lovely, aren't they?"

The color drained from Ochoa's face.

The photograph was of his wife and two school-aged children, Gracia and Orlando, climbing into the back seat of his wife's Mercedes. From the clothing the three of them wore, the photo might have been taken that morning.

"¡Dios mío!" Ochoa whimpered. My God!

***

Her stomach acidic, Anneka's body rebelled from a five-hour, caffeine-fueled writing stint. For days since she had arrived back from Nuevo Laredo, she had alternated between brief bouts of sleeping and long stretches sitting at the computer. At times, she felt as if Enrique held her consciousness captive, her fingers channeling his as the story unfolded.

It was seven thirty in the morning, and she became vaguely aware of the sounds of people showering, walking down the stairs, and leaving their apartments. Wrapping an orange-and-black afghan her mother had made around her shoulders, she stepped out onto the balcony.

There was life in the alley, children and adults going places, trucks delivering, smells from the bakery, and doors slamming. Feeling a desperate need to be a part of a living community, people with purpose in their days, out of the ominous darkness she had inhabited and into the light, she lay down on the balcony floor and closed her eyes. For the next four hours, she slept.

***

Ochoa had answered, immediately and truthfully, each of the questions that Enrique had asked. The names and home addresses of each of the five other cartel regional leaders. The places where large volumes of currencies were stored. The names and locations of each supplier. The points of distribution.

He'd withheld nothing. The code of silence he had on occasion brutally enforced when it was violated by others was now moot because of the plight he faced.

As he made these disclosures, three possibilities became increasingly evident. He would die at this man's hands; he would be killed by the organization he had just betrayed; or, highly unlikely, if freed tonight, he'd gather up his family and the cash in his home safe and flee. Even as he named each of these possibilities, he reconciled himself to the most likely of outcomes.

He would be dead within hours, maybe minutes.

"You are doing very well, Mr. Ochoa."

Enrique set aside the notebook he had been writing in and walked behind the truck and over to the Lexus.

"So well that I'm going to answer the questions you have been wanting to ask me."

Enrique leaned against Ochoa's car and crossed his arms on his chest.

His prisoner was kneeling on the concrete, his arms resting on the pickup's tailgate, and the right shoulder and arm of his shirt stained with blood.

"Who are you?" Ochoa asked. "Who do you work for?" he added.

"My name is Enrique Cordona, and I don't work for anyone. I'm a retired journalist. What else do you want to know?"

Ochoa looked surprised.

"You're not part of a syndicate? But how could you ... ? Why have you ... ?" He suddenly pulled violently on the tailgate chain, testing its strength. It held.

"Yes, of course, Mr. Ochoa. It's not making sense to you, is it?"

Enrique walked over to the pickup.

"While you are removing your bow tie, there's another photograph I would like you to examine," Enrique said.

He took the second photo from his shirt pocket and held it in front of Ochoa's eyes but said nothing.

"I don't recognize him. Why are you showing me this picture?"

For the first time in their interaction, Enrique's voice wavered. "His name was Adrian. He was sixteen years old. He died of a heroin overdose. Hand me your tie."

As Enrique was talking, he was simultaneously taking a plastic poncho from the truck's front seat. He left the bow tie in its place. He put the poncho on and buttoned it all the way up.

"My grandson, Mr. Ochoa."

He also took two disposable medical gloves and another object from the truck. He put the gloves on his hands.

As he did so, Ochoa watched, recognizing with a surge of horror that this could mean only one thing.

"You are avenging your grandson," Ochoa whimpered.

Coming up and standing directly in back of his kneeling prisoner, Enrique leaned forward and whispered in Ochoa's ears.

"Do you have a last wish?"

"Please," Ochoa sobbed. "Please spare my family," he cried as he heard the snap of the switchblade opening and felt Enrique grabbing his hair and pulling his head back.

"They are dead, Mr. Ochoa. Gracia and Orlando and Ana Maria are dead," he snarled.

With a rapid slash across Ochoa's neck, Enrique brought their conversation to the conclusion fated so many months earlier in an upscale condo on Seattle's Queen Anne hill.

***

Milá Maminko—

I sometimes feel as if you and I are on opposite sides of a very deep canyon, each of us standing on a rim shouting across to the other. I try to hear your words, but you are so far away. I step closer to the edge in the hope that I'll understand, but when I do that, I feel the earth beginning to fall away from underneath my feet and I must leap back to save myself.

Can you see me trying to hear you, Mother? Please ...

Tears stained the stationery. Anneka impulsively crumpled the letter and ran into the lavatory. She was sick.

28 ~ An Obsession to Exact Revenge

Milá Anneko—

I'm at the dining room table with one of my favorite photos of you in front of me. I laughed when Elliott saw it and said you reminded him of Katharine Hepburn. We figured out that he was remembering her playing a reporter in Woman of the Year. Did you ever see that film? She costarred with Spencer Tracy.

I had a light dinner tonight, just a bowl of kneydl soup. For me it's a comfort food, and after reading this morning's newspaper, I sorely needed it.

I'm a bit unsure whether I'll send this letter to you. It may end up in the trash. Some of the thoughts I've been having today are vengeful, and that's not an attitude I want to accept in myself. I particularly don't want my example to reinforce your remaining in the dark place you've been inhabiting for much too long. I guess I'll decide once I've finished writing.

Someone spray-painted "Holocaust is fake history" on the wall of Temple de Hirsch Sinai. I was disheartened. I'd been there just last month for the bar mitzvah of a friend's great grandson.

Today I'd committed to spending time with my Syrian refugee family. Cooking with Rima and then playing a game of chess with Quasim helped to distract me for a while from obsessing about what had occurred.

Why would a person do this? Can someone actually believe the Holocaust didn't happen, that it was just a conspiracy theory? In my mind, that conviction is incomprehensible, yet deniers keep popping up in our country and elsewhere.

There's a more likely explanation, I think. Rather than a statement of belief, claiming it is fake history is an assault. It's a spewing of raw hatred. The intention is to inflict emotional injury on a community of people who were nearly exterminated. It's no different than exclaiming Hitler was right.

There've been so many acts of anti-Semitic vandalism in the last year. Maybe the person who defaced the temple was somehow inspired to be a copycat.

The senior rabbi of the temple was quoted as saying he felt shock and sadness. As much as I admire him for his judiciousness in the face of such a provocative assault, I wonder if perhaps he, too, harbors—maybe unspoken—a separate and more vindictive attitude about the person who did this terrible thing.

Not too long ago I saw a story on the news. It focused on a ninety-five-year-old survivor of nine camps. I'm remembering something he said to the reporter. "If I could take you with me to Auschwitz for twenty-four hours, it would change you forever." He was making a point, of course, and wasn't implying that the reporter didn't understand.

But today I found myself thinking, what if such a trip back in time were possible? What if the person who spray-painted the graffiti could be brought to Auschwitz for a day?

So, my dear daughter, I simply let myself delve into imagining the experience this man would have. I assume it was a man.

To begin with, I would not want him to know that his life would return to normal in twenty-four hours. Deny him the benefit of being able to count down the hours and minutes until his ordeal would end. Instead, permit him to experience the utter despair of uncertainty as to how long it might last, perhaps even believing it could go on for months and years to come until the time of his death in the camp.

Let him be the victim of the cruel arbitrariness of the guards' brutality, the beatings and the forced hours standing in formation in freezing rain. Give him firsthand familiarity with the sadistic humiliation of having to race to and from the toilet without regard for his own bodily needs. Let him suffer from the bitter and unrelenting cold and hunger. Have him inhale the putrid urine-infested odors of the barracks and hear the death rattle from the emaciated man lying next to him on the shelf. Let him believe his turn for the gas chamber could come at any moment.

Let him be ignored when he tells them he is not an animal. Let him ask God why and get no answer.

In the vision I am creating, his ordeal would end in an instant. With all from the previous twenty-four hours fresh in his mind, he suddenly would find himself back in Seattle. He would be standing outside Temple de Hirsch Sinai with a can of spray paint in his hand just at the moment he was ready to begin writing that vile message.

What would he do? Do you have a guess, my child? I don't. But what I'd give to be there watching and to know what would be in his mind.

I stepped away to make myself a cup of tea. Then, suddenly, something else occurred to me. Perhaps my reaction to the vandalism is also giving me something much more valuable.

Might I be channeling you? Sitting here looking at your photograph, I'm wondering. Might my reflections today be offering me an insight, in a way that before had eluded me, into why you need to live in such dangerous circumstances in Mexico and write a book in which drug cartel criminals are vanquished? Why you are becoming an avenger.

I think it may be you who is wailing, Anneko. I fear that you are trapped there. How I wish I could send an invading force to rescue you.

Alas, I cannot. In lieu of that, let me at least tell you what I've learned about the risks in being taken over by an obsession to exact revenge. In a nutshell, the righteous one, unable to move on unless the aggressor first suffers, becomes doubly victimized. All else in life recedes. Sunsets and rainbows lose their radiance, the grandest gourmet feasts become tasteless, and the Rachmaninoff piano concerto no longer brings a soaring delight.

It's a toxic state of being. The acidity of this single-minded focus on grievances eats away at one's spirit. For me, that is intolerable. Even more so, the thought of you being imprisoned in the confines of this mind-set frightens me.

So, the man who did the hate crime will not take me down. Instead, I will resist by writing a message to him through the letters-to-the-editor page of the Seattle newspaper. "If you believe what you painted on the temple," my letter will say, "come speak with me. Let me help you learn the truth." Perhaps he'll see it.

I will resist by volunteering to go to schools and speak about the Holocaust with students. It's something I haven't been doing much of recently. It's necessary.

I will resist by cooking with Rima, by helping Elliott with his new vegetable plot, by practicing piano, and by writing letters to my precious daughter and to the many immigrants I've helped over the years.

I will resist by having a life. Demanding it. He will not take me down. This is a choice you, too, can make, Anneko. Having a life. Demanding it. Can you see that?

Love—

Tvoje máma

29 ~ Break Out of the Mindset

It was almost never like this in Seattle in August. That morning, though, standing at the window in his robe and looking out at the courtyard a little after seven, the fog was so thick that it obscured the top limbs of the western red cedar.

Sipping orange juice while waiting for the coffee to brew, Elliott was still musing about his previous night's dream. Theo was hiding in his tree. Out of shame for being gay and with the pain of his father's rejection, he wanted to die. But his therapist offered an alternative. Theo was learning how to take with him the tree's gift of self-acceptance. He was changing. He was healing.

Why that dream? He picked up his journal and, seated at his dining room table, jotted down the highlights. On the bottom of the page, he drew a large question mark.

The coffee had finished perking, and, as he poured his first cup, the answer became obvious. The dream had come to him as a bellwether. It was about Todd. Had he lived, his brother would be sixty-nine years old. It had been more than forty years. More than forty years of carrying shame.

Inevitably, whenever a client told Elliott how much they wished they could undo some reprehensible action from their childhood, now an indelible and haunting blot, he thought of what he did on that day in April of 1972. He remembered the rage that swept over him; his brother had broken his promise to come home. Elliott's unrelenting self-reproach tainted his happy memories of Todd teaching him how to pitch and his brother's patient encouragement at the ice-skating rink.

He needed to listen to Milena. She was showing him, through her letters to Anneka, that it didn't have to be this way.

It's a toxic state of being. The acidity of this single-minded focus on grievances eats away at one's spirit. For me, that is intolerable. Even more so, the thought of you being imprisoned in the confines of this mind-set frightens me.

Milena seemed to be speaking to him. In her words he heard encouragement to stop being trapped in the pain of guilt. *Have I been running away from Todd out of anger at him and shame for myself because of what I did so many years ago?*

He drove to the storage locker that he had rented after the divorce. The four cartons with his father's journals were toward the back, behind his bicycle and next to the locked filing cabinet with closed client files. He removed the notebooks that his father had filled from the beginning of 1971 through the end of 1972 and placed them in a Whole Foods cloth carry bag that he'd brought with him.

Back at his apartment, he began reading entries for January 1971. As he scanned his father's handwriting, he looked for any mention of the army unit Todd had been in while in Vietnam and, hopefully, the names of some of the men with whom he had served.

He was repeatedly distracted by his father's commentary about news events: the voting age being lowered to eighteen by a constitutional amendment, the opening of Disney World, and the Pentagon Papers being published by the *New York Times*. His father also ranted about Todd having to go to Vietnam at a time when so many Americans opposed the country's involvement there and a number of military units had already been pulled out.

Finally, in an entry dated December 8, 1971, he found part of the information he was seeking:

As of 10 Jan 1972, Todd's been given orders from Ft. Benning to Vietnam. He'll be assigned to H Company, 75th Infantry Ranger Regiment, 1st Cav Division. He's been promoted to Spec 4th Class E4.

Then, another hit about twenty pages later. The entry was dated January 28, 1972:

It's a relief that Todd's unit is led by a competent and well-respected CO, and that the morale among the troops is high. He knows of other units with leaders disrespected by the men they command, low morale, a lot of drug use, and even 'fragging.'

A few pages later he came to more of the information he'd hoped to find. He quickly realized he'd hit pay dirt:

Todd's company commander wrote a strong commendation for him after he led a group of men in resuscitating a soldier who was electrocuted while working on a generator. The CO, Captain Stephen Bryer, a West Point graduate, encouraged Todd to consider making the Army his career. The three other men who were commended for saving the soldier's life were Spec Randy Gierson from Tacoma, Washington, Spec Alphonso Romero from New York City, and PFC Timothy Jalen from Miami.

Elliott made note of each of these names and their hometowns. He decided to start with the commanding officer and soon discovered that there was an organization called the West Point Association of Graduates. The website had a link that could be used to find alumni. When he opened that site, however, he learned that outsiders can't access that data set. There was a phone number for the association, and he decided to take a chance. After the third ring, he was in luck. A real person answered.

In the next few minutes, his luck held. The man seemed genuinely interested in helping and walked Elliott through the pieces of information he'd need to track Todd's CO, who, it turned out, was a retired major general. The only roadblock at that point came when he told Elliott their policy prohibited him from giving out the man's current address and phone number without his permission. He would, however, contact Bryer and tell him about Elliott's request.

He turned his attention to googling the three enlisted men. He found that there was an architect in Olympia, Washington, by the name of Randy Gierson. He wrote down his website address and phone number before moving on to the other two men. No luck with finding an Alphonso Romero via Google, but perhaps he'd be in the New York City telephone directory. He noted down each of the steps he took as well as his plans for continuing the search.

The phone rang.

"You're Toddler's brother?" the voice on the other end boomed. "Man, it made me so happy to know you were looking me up. Oh, in case you think I'm a total lunatic, my name is Steve Bryer. I was your brother's CO."

A croak erupted from Elliott's mouth, and his throat clenched. He was unable to form words and suddenly feared Bryer would hang up.

"Oh crap. I've come on like a bull in a china shop. I'm sorry. Elliott, take your time to catch your breath. I'm not going anywhere. I'm right here."

Seconds passed, and all Elliott was able to say was "Thanks." Just as he worried he'd not be able to pull himself together, Bryer again took the lead.

"Okay, let me help. Over the years, I've had quite a few conversations like the one I believe you'd like to have with me. So let me fill you in with some of what I suspect you're looking for. By the way, 'Toddler' was our nickname for him. Your brother was a brave GI. Because of him, one lucky guy stayed alive. Todd got three other guys together and taught them how to do CPR. His courage in combat also made him stand out. Morale in our unit, including my morale, I want to tell you, got a boost because of your brother. When he was killed, Elliott, I wept. I wasn't the only one."

Elliott took a deep breath and let it out slowly. "You're bringing him back to life for me, General."

"I wrote to your parents, of course. I'm guessing you might have been too young for them to have shared that letter with you. Elliott, how old were you?"

"I had just turned nine."

Bryer sighed deeply. "There's no right age for losing a brother in war, Elliott. But you were altogether too fragile at nine to bear such a terrible loss."

In a strange way, Elliott thought, his saying that felt as if it were the first time anyone had acknowledged what happened to him. Perhaps this was exactly what he had set out looking for that day.

They spent a few more minutes talking, and before ending the call, Bryer invited him to check in again at any time. "You need to know that the family members of men I lost have a special place in my heart." He offered to send details about a unit reunion planned for the following year. Elliott would be warmly welcomed.

Elliott grabbed his journal and headed out the door, thinking he'd try to capture the experience he'd just had. He ended up at Espresso Vivace on Broadway.

He jotted down "Lessons from Theo's tree."

And then a thought. Would Anneka listen to her mother's advice and be inspired to search for a new way of living with memories of her father?

30 ~ Tree Spirit

"The wounds will heal, Elliott. I'll deal with this."

"We'll deal with this," Elliott said, correcting his friend.

Elliott had come by every day, first in the hospital and then to Theo's apartment where he was recuperating. In the last six days, they'd been to four medical appointments.

On the morning after the accident, Theo described what had happened. "It all seems so incredibly surreal." He reached for the plastic cup on his tray table and took a sip. "Some books had to be shelved. I was perched on the wooden stepladder and annoyed that I was feeling so goddamn wobbly. My legs had felt stiff for weeks. Normally, I'd have hefted a stack of books without giving it a thought. Rachel was in the next room restocking a shelf in the art history section, so I shouted for her."

While he was speaking, a nurse briefly entered the room and checked the monitor next to Theo's bed. As he left, he said, "Ring for me if the pain gets too uncomfortable."

"I waited a few seconds, and she didn't answer. *No big deal,* I thought. So I carefully came back down one step at a time and picked up three of the six Stephen King hardcovers. I held them with my left hand and took the first step up. I steadied myself and then took the second. Then, when I began to pull my right leg up to the third step, doing this on my own began to seem like a really stupid idea."

"What was going on with you?" Elliott asked.

"All I knew at the time was I couldn't raise that foot high enough. So there I was, teetering on the ladder."

"Good God."

"My center of gravity began to pull me over, and slowly the ladder tilted to the left. The train wreck I'd created for myself was unstoppable. I heard Rachel say, 'Theo, what are you doing? Theo, wait, I'm coming over.' And then I heard her scream, too far from me to do anything else."

"She's gotta be having nightmares about this," Elliott said.

"No kidding. Actually, she's all torn up. I'll get to that in a minute. It must have been over in a second, maybe two, but in my mind the fall was recorded in slow action, and it reminded me of the film of Mount Saint Helens exploding. The whole mountainside dissolved frame by frame."

"What happened next?"

"The books I was carrying tumbled from my grasp. I saw out of the corner of my eyes where I was headed, that I'd not land on the floor between the shelves and the counter. Instead, the counter display case was directly ahead. *There'll be broken glass for sure*, I thought. *Look away*, I quickly told myself, and began to turn my head to the right. I heard wood creaking, the rungs straining against their connections to the ladder. For some strange reason, I momentarily smelled bacon. *How bizarre*, I thought. Then, the tinkle of the bell at the store's entrance let me know someone had come in. That was instantly followed by the shattering of glass as the ladder and I crashed into the counter. I heard the scraping of wood as the force of my weight moved the case several feet into the main aisle. Two large, ugly shards of glass pointed up at me like punji stakes in a booby trap."

"Christ, Theo. Did you think you'd bought the farm?"

"Yeah, buddy, for a while I did."

Theo turned toward the window and was quiet for a few moments. "Then it was all a blur. I felt searing pain tearing through me like a lightning bolt, blood spurting into my face, and I heard Rachel shouting, 'Theo, don't try to move.' Someone must have called 911, because I remember the siren and then three firemen looking down at me on the floor. I was on a gurney and people were on either side rushing me forward. Someone put their hand on my arm to reassure me. I remember a woman in a white coat saying she was going to give me anesthesia so that she could remove the glass. She was looking at a clipboard, with a man in another white coat standing beside her. They kept talking, but I had no idea what they said."

***

Elliott walked over to the sink and, after returning the cold cuts to the fridge and the whole wheat bread to its spot on the shelf, he began washing dishes. With his bandaged left arm in a sling, the interminable time it took Theo to do the dishes was just one of a myriad of "gifts" that his recent adventure had sent his way.

"Okay, tell me what you learned from the neurologist."

Theo pulled himself up from the wicker rocking chair and walked over to the southeast-facing window where, when the mountain was out, there was a peekaboo glimpse of Mount Rainier between the two apartment buildings across the way. Couldn't see any of it that day, though, due to cloud cover.

"Dr. Greenberg confirmed this morning what she'd suspected. They had to rule out some other possibilities and finally came to a definitive diagnosis. It's Parkinson's."

Elliott whispered, "No."

Theo moved over to the armchair at the end of his dining room table, where he kept his business records for the store, and eased himself down.

"She's been pretty candid with me about what medicine can offer. Of course, she tried to emphasize the more positive stuff. For a while, they can jack up my dopamine levels, and that'll help. They can do a kind of surgery that involves deep brain stimulation to turn off part of the brain that's wreaking havoc with tremors."

Elliott watched as Theo reached over his laptop computer to the flyers and held them up for Elliott to see.

"There are support groups, and I can get lots of physical therapy, maybe three times a week. That'll supposedly help with balance problems." He laughed. "Could have used some balance training before I climbed up that fucking ladder."

They both laughed.

As they talked, Elliott offered no glib reassurances, no platitudes. Instead, he filled the electric kettle. Taking down two mugs from the cabinet above the sink, he moved some spices aside to find tea bags. He was simply hanging with Theo.

"Rachel started crying when she was here yesterday. She brought two books, one of them, believe it or not, had the title *Parkinson's Disease for Dummies*. Vile! Told her I appreciated having them. This news has hit her hard."

They both fell quiet as a jet headed to SeaTac flew overhead, and Lenin, Theo's thirty-year-old African gray parrot, squawked, his midmorning plea for a handout. Elliott placed a mug in front of Theo and stopped at the fridge on his way over to the cage where Lenin, perched on a branch wired to the cage top, got a mini carrot. They'd all been served, and Elliott sat across from Theo, peering into his mug, slowly swirling his spoon. The silence was heavy, interrupted only by Lenin's munching, the sound of a door slamming down the hall, and a car burglar alarm blaring somewhere in the neighborhood.

"Christ, Elliott, we're only in our fifties and already we're …." Unable to finish the sentence, he began to weep. Minutes passed. Elliott moved his chair closer, put a box of tissues within reach, and patted him on the back. Theo's crying slowed and eventually stopped.

"Up for going for a ride?"

Theo looked at him uncertainly. "Where to?" Theo asked, and Elliott laughed.

"Can't tell you because we're going on a mystery trip. C'mon. We'll be back in a couple hours."

Elliott helped Theo with his seat belt, and just after they pulled away from the curb, he popped a CD into the stereo. Theo likely wasn't surprised that it was classical music, almost always what Elliott liked to listen to when driving.

"This is Dvořák's Minuet number one in A-flat Major. Milena loaned it to me."

They spoke very little, listening to the music, and Theo kept guessing wrong about where they were going. When they drove onto the West Seattle Bridge, he asked if they might be headed to Alki Beach, maybe Lincoln Park, or possibly to the Fauntleroy ferry dock for a trip over to Vashon Island.

Then they turned onto Southwest Admiral Way. The entrance to a park with its low stone wall with pillars came into sight, and Theo said, "My God, I know where you're taking me."

Elliott pulled into a parking space on Southwest Stevens, the street adjacent to Schmitz Preserve Park. Elliott turned to look at him and quietly said, "Let's go find your tree, buddy."

"Will it still be there?" Theo wondered aloud. "It's been decades. What if someone else is in my tree? Damn, this is turning me back into a skittish fourteen-year-old. I can feel the acne sprouting all over my face."

"Time traveling, eh? Might be just what the doctor ordered," Elliott said. "Think you can find it?" They were standing just outside the entrance in front of a plexiglass-enclosed bulletin board on which there was a trail map posted. It was November 14, and the temperature was in the low fifties.

Theo looked around. The plexiglass was badly scratched. "This map isn't much help. I'm thinking the tree is somewhere in the middle of the park's fifty-three acres."

They started to walk, the woods thick with western hemlocks, Douglas firs, and Pacific yews. The earthy smell of evergreens, as well as the dense Indian plum shrubs, lady ferns, and huckleberries lining the sunlight-dappled path, was nearly intoxicating, a botanical prelude as the tempo of their excitement built.

Theo looked back and forth at the vegetation and trees on both sides. "I'm hoping something will jog my memory."

As they walked farther, the traffic sounds receded. About a hundred yards in, the pavement ended, and a dirt path continued until, at an intersection, several other paths headed off in different directions.

Theo led them on one of those paths, where, as they were walking up hill, Elliott spotted something just to the left of the trail and broke out in laughter. "Good grief, look what someone's done to your tree!"

Theo turned to look. An enormous fallen tree trunk emerged from the forest and ended at the path's edge. A gaping maw had resulted from a horizontal lengthwise split in the middle of the log. Sharp teeth had been carved on both the upper and lower parts of the trunk and painted white. The top half of the trunk had been painted green, and there was a menacing white eye etched into the bark toward the back.

"A damn crocodile. I can't believe it. Not my tree, thank God, but I wonder if the people who did this are the same pranksters who secretly put up a steel black slab monolith in Magnuson Park on New Year's Day of 2001. Remember that, from *A Space Odyssey*?"

"Oh yeah, in the best tradition of Seattle quirkiness, like the Fremont District's Troll and the Lenin statue. Hey, I've got an idea." Elliott insisted Theo stand in front of the croc while he snapped a photo with his iPhone. "Y'know, Captain Hook, this tells a much better story about why your arm's in a sling than that lame saga of a ladder tipping over."

"Hold on, hold on," Theo whispered, gazing uphill. "This area looks familiar. There's lots of old-growth, and particularly western red cedar trees, in this part of the park." He walked in that direction, somewhat unsteady when leaving the path and stepping over several nurse logs before he saw it. "This is the one."

Theo walked up to it slowly. He placed his right hand on the bark and held it there. Elliott stood back. He thought that if there was any truth to trees having spirits, at that moment Theo must be feeling the connection: safety, happiness, home.

Several minutes passed.

"C'mon, stand here beside me," Theo eventually said, and Elliott complied, placing both of his hands on the tree's bark.

Theo sat down and rested his back against the trunk. Elliott followed his lead and sat to his right, also leaning against the tree.

"Man, being here is exactly right," Theo said. "I'm remembering learning to imagine I was in here whenever I felt afraid."

"It's working, isn't it?"

"Yeah, it is," Theo said. "Leaning against this tree is giving me a mainline fix of tranquility and a keen reminder of what it was like."

Nearly an hour passed, and both of them dozed. When Elliott noticed Theo was awake, he said, "Y'know, much of what Milena is writing to her daughter in those letters is showing me a path. Like how she's doing it, for example, taking courses on a whole bunch of crazy topics is high on her list. She's also big on volunteering. And then, she encouraged Anneka to read some autobiographies of people who've survived tragedies such as the Holocaust and other genocides. The idea was to see how they managed to move on with their lives."

"Is Anneka buying any of this?" Theo asked.

"I have no idea," Elliott said. "I only get to steal mail heading south."

31 ~ 806 Walks

It was New Year's Day. In Seattle, the high would get only into the low thirties, but there was no snow, and the air was clear. Some sunshine was making it through the clouds. Elliott wasn't surprised that they were nearly alone on a morning when overcoming hangovers was the task at hand for many.

"How many times did we do this walk?" Sandra asked. "Got a guess?"

They took off from the boathouse as they always had, heading clockwise, and minding the rules about staying on the correct path. Hundreds, often thousands of people came to Seattle's Green Lake every day, and the regulars knew that bikers and runners did not take kindly to walkers encroaching on their lane.

He did some quick math on his iPhone calculator.

"Thirty-one years, probably every other week on average. So that's eight hundred and six walks. It's just under three miles all the way around. So, wow, we've done more than twenty-two hundred miles. Holy crap."

They both laughed. He wondered if she, too, was thinking about the miles they no longer walked together. In four months, it would be a year since the day they made the decision to divorce. He'd moved out shortly after that.

Sandra was all L.L. Bean that day: a tan Adirondack barn coat, faded jeans, a blue US Ski Team knit hat, and classic tan-and-black duck boots. He didn't remember any of these being in her wardrobe. On the other hand, she'd be surprised seeing him wearing his new Greek ship-captain's hat and brown leather bomber jacket.

She was fifty-three but looked to Elliott no older than maybe thirty-five or forty. He felt a pang, both of attraction to her and from the loss they'd endured when their marriage ended. It still stung. But, taking stock, he also realized neither of them was any longer who they were when they separated. Both had landed on their feet.

"How is it having Peter with you?" he asked.

Their son had arrived six weeks earlier and, because Sandra and her new husband had a guest bedroom in their West Seattle waterfront home, it made sense for him to move in with them. When Peter first returned, it was evident that his friend's death had put him into a tailspin. Elliott called a colleague who specialized in trauma. Peter began working with her the following week.

"For a while he seemed broken, Elliott. I didn't know whether to think it was just a temporary reaction to the accident or something much more serious."

They passed the kiddie pool, which would be jammed with toddlers at the height of Seattle's all-too-short summer, but on that day was just a slab of recessed concrete gathering yellowed leaves swirling in the breeze. Peter had played in that pool. Elliott remembered they had fretted the day their son broke into a crying spell because another kid wouldn't return his Mickey Mouse inflatable tube. And the day they watched him patiently teaching another child how to throw a beach ball.

Elliott realized that he was flipping back and forth between time periods. A toddler learning to cooperate with others, and a young man devastated by a friend's death for which he blamed himself. If only the pain he carried about Tat could have been kissed away with a hug, a colorful bandage, and a word of assurance.

"I'm optimistic he's getting past this," he said. "For one, therapy helped him look closely at the guilt part of his grieving. Each of those four guys, Tat included, could have chosen to skip doing that run. No one was coerced. When he heard himself talking it through in answering a therapist's guiding questions, he got it."

He paused for a moment.

"For another, having you and Mateo and the nest you're welcoming him to rest in was vital. He's also really into his new job with Theo. I had to laugh when Theo took me aside and said Peter was actually thinking about the career possibilities in running a bookstore."

"Is there a third reason, Elliott, why you think he's doing well?" Sandra asked.

She walked over to a bench and patted the seat next to her. He followed her lead and sat. Elliott had an impulse to take her hand in his but resisted.

A young couple walked by with two Australian shepherds on leashes. One was a black tri with a white bib and paws, a mostly black coat, and splotches of copper coloring. The other was a red merle, also with a white bib, and a coat that looked like a toasted marshmallow. He wondered if they were siblings. When the woman glanced over at him, he gave her a thumbs-up, and she smiled.

"Yes, there is," he replied. He turned toward her. "He's got his father back. Not the judgmental prig who harangued him at every turn, but the father he ought to have had all along."

Sandra reached into her jacket and removed a packet of tissues. She blotted her eyes and then spontaneously laughed.

"He told me about your conversation." She reached for his right hand and held it in both of hers. "Elliott, I am so full of love for you, and for Peter."

He stood and, with a knowing smile, pulled her up next to him.

"Let's walk. I wondered what he might say to you. I'm glad he did."

She was quiet for the next few moments. They watched a flock of ducks moving toward the shore.

"I'm sorry I didn't bring any bread," Sandra said.

Suddenly, she turned to him and bellowed.

"I just remembered what else he told me. Elliott Sterling, are you really stealing your neighbor's letters?" Her expression was a mixture of amusement and incredulity. "And steaming them open and reading them? Are you serious?"

He cringed at the realization that two women who had just passed them overheard what Sandra had said. But her reaction was contagious, and he began to chuckle, realizing she was dumbfounded that he would do something so entirely out of character.

He laughed and, in a flash, they were both doubled over. They staggered over to a nearby bench and sat. Minutes passed before they were able to catch their breaths. Just as they were quieting down, he got inspired and, taking his fake glasses from his pocket, put them on and turned to face Sandra. While they were both re-exploding, people passing by looked their way and smiled.

Sandra's cell phone rang, and she somehow calmed herself enough to answer it. She walked over to the shore and gesticulated with her hand as she spoke. The call lasted for several minutes, and when she returned to the bench, she had a serious expression.

"I've got to get over to the hospital. I've sent for a Lyft, and they'll pick me up in front of Starbucks." They walked in that direction. Checking her watch, she said, "Elliott, there's something else I want to tell you, but there's no time now. Will you come over to our house later this afternoon?"

"Sure. I can be there at six p.m."

***

Looking out to the Sound from the living room of the Beach Drive home, Peter, Elliott, and Mateo watched the lights aboard a ferry that connects Seattle to Vashon Island and to the Olympic Peninsula. Mateo had poured each of them a snifter of scotch while they waited for Sandra to return from the hospital.

Meeting him for the first time and engaging in small talk was so much less tense than Elliott had expected. Mateo reminded him of a Hispanic version of Mr. Kotter from the 1970s sitcom: bushy black hairstyle, mustache, and thick sideburns. In contrast with the stereotype of neurosurgeons, Elliott thought, he was low-key, even a bit self-effacing, with an easy smile. Elliott liked him.

And Mateo and Peter seemed to really hit it off. They'd been playing chess before he arrived. Just now, the three of them were debating the age at which most men are at their prime, intellectually and creatively. Peter was quoting Einstein, who believed it was before a man turned thirty. Mateo insisted that at the age of fifty-four, he had not quite got there yet. Perhaps another year or two. For Elliott's part, he questioned the premise.

"Isn't there a possibility," he asked, "of more than one peak? If I think about it, I was pretty hot at twenty and at thirty-five. Hell, I may yet hit my personal best at fifty-six."

Mateo and Peter groaned, and Elliott was just about to expound on his theory when Sandra walked in.

"Did someone say scotch?"

She walked over to the bar cart, popped some ice cubes into a glass, and gave herself a generous pour. After taking a sip, she kissed each of them on the cheek. Elliott suspected from her expression that surgery did not go well.

Mateo asked the question that was on all of their minds. "You okay, babe?"

She stood at the window and looked out.

"A twenty-three-year-old woman in a crosswalk got mangled by a drunk driver. She's alive, at least for now. But the four-month-old in the stroller ..."

Her sentence drifted off, and she dismissed taking it any further with a wave of her hand.

A pall descended in the room. Mateo walked over and held her in his arms. For several minutes, they were all quiet.

As if to signal that she was now ready to join the conversation, she went over to the cart, opened a bag of pretzels, and poured them into a bowl. Handing it to Elliott, she said, "I'm glad you're here." Looking around, she asked, "You fellows debating the future of humankind?"

They laughed. Peter replied, "You nailed it, Mom."

Seeing him in such good spirits touched Elliott. He was shaved, had gained weight, and the dark circles under his eyes had lightened.

"Mateo, shall we refresh the drinks and then tell these guys about our off-the-wall crazy plan?"

Peter and Elliott looked questioningly at one another, and it was evident neither of them had a clue.

Passing among them with the bottle, Mateo asked, "You've heard of Médecins Sans Frontières?"

Both of them had.

"A month ago, we were having dinner at Canlis," Sandra continued. "An elegant meal in an elegant setting. Following dessert, we were sipping brandy and listening to the pianist playing the theme from *Moulin Rouge*. Neither of us knew what the other one was thinking until it just spilled out. Something was deeply troubling each of us."

She looked at Mateo.

"It was Syria," Mateo said. "We both thought there is something obscene about the world doing nothing while so many civilians are being killed and so many others forced to flee from their homes. It turns out that each of us had been thinking about volunteering. We were greatly relieved that night when we realized we were on the same page about this."

Peter blurted out what Elliott also was thinking. "You're going into a war zone? There've been news stories about hospitals being bombed and medics killed in that country. How protected will you be?"

Something in the sound of Peter's voice led Elliott to hear the plea of a frightened son. Peter was indeed fragile, a carryover from the avalanche, Elliott believed.

But it wasn't only Peter who at that moment was feeling the weight of the news. The thought of Sandra dying had Elliott's pulse racing.

With raised eyebrows, Elliott let Mateo and Sandra know he had the same question. What they were contemplating would place their lives in danger without question. This was not a volunteering stint in rural America where there's a shortage of doctors. It was in a war-ravaged country where the shortage exists because the bombing by government forces has led MDs, many of the ones who hadn't been killed, to flee.

"We're going into this with our eyes open," Sandra said softly. "The protection comes from good communication so that all sides know just where the hospitals are located. But I wouldn't be honest if I didn't acknowledge that it doesn't always stop the bombing."

Elliott noticed Peter's eyes averting hers, instead seeking Mateo's. Elliott guessed he was hoping that his stepdad would somehow intervene.

Mateo got what was happening, the unspoken message.

"Your mom and I need your permission, Peter. Yours, too, Elliott. The action we're planning to take, from our perspective, is morally imperative." He looked back and forth between Peter and Elliott. "You are also owners of this family. Your voices are important."

Sandra agreed. "Your voices count."

They were all silent. In the distance, the ferry from Vashon to the Fauntleroy terminal sounded its horn to signal its arrival. Elliott stood and walked over to the window. Peter joined him. They were both looking out at the Sound.

"Unimaginable atrocities are being committed in parts of the world," Peter said quietly. "They happen because others don't stand in the way of the perpetrators. Mom and Mateo are feeling called to stand up. It's not on a whim. They swore an oath as physicians that recognized their special obligations to all of their fellow human beings."

Elliott turned to face Peter and put his arm around his shoulders, so moved by his son's capacity to rise above the fearful possibilities they were both picturing. Out of the corner of his eyes, Elliott saw Sandra silently mouthing "Thank you" to Peter.

"Dad?" he whispered.

Elliott looked him in the eyes for a long moment, taking in the sweetness of his son's empathy.

Elliott whispered back, "Okay."

"Become one with the mountain," Peter said. He looked at his mother and nodded.

"Is this your way of saying yes?" Elliott asked.

"Dad, it was Tat's way of saying 'Live life to the fullest, and don't hold anything back.'"

Elliott smiled at Sandra and Mateo.

"Become one with the mountain."

32 ~ Keeping Flames Alive

Theo had been there once before when he and Elliott installed a hanging bird feeder outside Milena's living room window. Elliott had climbed the ladder while Theo shouted instructions from the bench in the front courtyard. In a note taped to Elliott's door the next evening, she had told him how excited she was to already have caught sight of two Townsend's warblers, a bushtit, and two pine siskins.

She'd invited them to dinner. It would be a thank-you to the two of them and a welcome to Peter who was meeting Milena for the first time.

"A Czech beer is called for with the traditional meal we're having," Milena said as she handed each of them a bottle of Pilsner Urquell. She was wearing a white cooking apron trimmed with lace over her maroon skirt and tan blouse.

"We're starting with *zeleninová polévka*, a vegetable soup. And then the main course is *svíčková na smetaně*, which is marinated sirloin served with dumplings and cream."

Theo clapped his hands. He slurred the words several times while trying to say "*Mockrát děkuju*," and then almost succeeded before giving up and looking around apologetically.

Milena smiled in response. "I'm impressed! *Mluvíte česky?*"

"You've just heard my entire vocabulary," he answered, speaking slowly, pausing between each word. Theo was dressed for the occasion, wearing a navy blazer, black T-shirt, and gray slacks in the place of his usual jeans and sweatshirt. He used a cane to maintain his balance, and his right arm had a noticeable tremor.

The table was decorated with a red, blue, and white bohemian floral cloth. Candles were lit in two candlesticks on the table and a candelabra on the grand piano.

Before sitting, Milena walked over to her stereo and placed a CD in the player.

"I think you'll enjoy this. It's the third movement from Brahms's Piano Quartet in C Minor. It begins with a luscious melody played by cello and piano."

She took her seat and raised her bottle in a toast.

"*Na zdraví.*"

They clanked bottles and dug in, murmuring appreciation between bites. The music was indeed quite beautiful, Elliott thought, and ended just as they were finishing the soup.

When all had eaten, Milena and Elliott began clearing the plates.

"Music has always," Theo coughed to clear his throat. "It's always been important in your life, hasn't it?" Theo asked.

Elliott smiled, knowing the answer, and looking forward to the others learning about the children's opera Milena performed in while a prisoner in Terezín.

"Yes, it has, from as early as I can remember," she said, setting out dessert plates. "Elliott, show him the *Brundibár* book. My father was a pianist, Theo. I didn't have him for very long in my life, but his love of music is a thread that ties me to him forever."

Theo took the book. As he began to page through it, Peter came over to stand behind his chair, looking over his shoulder.

"It was not only the children who sang in Terezín, but also adults. My mother was one of a group who learned a very complex piece of music. It was *Requiem* by Verdi. I remember her telling me that when we sang, our imaginations would take us far away from the camp, back into a world with beauty and kindness."

As she spoke, Theo stood, grabbed his cane, and slowly walked over to a chair near the front door and removed a small book with a yellow cover from his backpack. Returning to the table, he said, "Milena, I found this on a shelf in my shop. The title is *The Terezín Requiem*." He handed the book to her. "I'd like you to have it."

Milena took the book and, going over to the piano, sat on the bench. She reached for the candelabra and pulled it closer to give her more light.

"This book I didn't know about," she said. They were all silent as she began to read the introduction.

Speaking very slowly, Theo said, "Josef Bor was a Terezín survivor. He tells the story of what Rafael Schaechter, a fellow prisoner, did as the choral group's conductor. From a single copy of the Verdi score, he taught one hundred fifty people the music. And when some asked why Jews should sing a Catholic funeral mass, he helped them see how relevant the *Requiem*'s lyrics were to what they were enduring. It was bold and courageous resistance."

Milena closed the book's cover, and placing it in both of her hands, brought it to her chest. In a moment, she looked up at Theo.

"I'm touched. Thank you."

"Elliott had told me about your parents," Theo said. "I read this last night, Milena. Learning what your mother did, what so many others did, knowing they were almost certainly going to perish, to demand their dignity, to defy the monstrosity of the Nazis, was a gift I took personally. Reading the book, I just felt so incredibly inspired."

Theo began to choke up.

"Some jerk spray-painted 'Holocaust is fake history' on the wall of a synagogue a while back," Theo said. "It's terrifying to watch the increase in anti-Semitic acts in our country. I will not stand by and just be silent." The others nodded in agreement.

"I wrote a long letter to my daughter about it," Milena said.

Several moments passed.

"Amen. Now, boys, maybe we can set aside our morbid thoughts. Is anyone in the mood for apple strudel, perhaps with a scoop of ice cream?"

They laughed as they saw one another enthusiastically shooting their hands in the air. Elliott guessed they all were relieved to have the heaviness lifted.

"The coffee will take a few minutes. But I'll serve the dessert now," Milena said. "Elliott, will you help?"

She carried the strudel from the kitchen, and he followed with a quart of vanilla ice cream.

Peter was over at the piano looking at the many photographs displayed there. A foot-tall glass sculpture in the shape of a flame caught his eye, and he brought it over to Milena.

"This is engraved with your name. It says, 'The hand you give keeps flames alive.' What was it for?"

Milena finished serving them and then said, "I'm proud of that, Peter. It was given to me for my volunteer work with refugee families. Typically, any agency support they're eligible for runs out long before people relocated to our country have really made the transition."

Peter looked fascinated. "So what do you do?"

"She cooks with ..." Elliott caught himself, almost blurting out details he could not possibly legitimately know.

Her eyebrows raised, Milena paused and then looked at him as if to say, "Go on." Elliott thought he spotted a hint of a smile before she turned to Peter.

"I'll give you an example. My current family fled Syria and, after years in transit, arrived in Seattle last October. The wife and I go to the malls, shop for food, cook and bake, sew, and practice English. The husband likes to play chess and write poetry, which I help edit. Their eleven-year-old daughter has speedily acclimated. She has such amazing courage and curiosity. We all go to a movie once a week and then have a conversation about it."

"But why do you do this?" Peter asked.

Milena paused for a moment and then set her fork aside. She took a framed photograph from the wall and held it up for them to see. Pointing to each figure, she said, "This is Antonin, and this is his wife, Magda. Iva, their daughter was seven years old when this picture was taken." All were wearing formal clothing and their faces were unsmiling. Milena again sat on the piano bench. "I had just turned fifteen when liberated from Auschwitz and had been in the camps for a little over three years." She looked at the photograph as she spoke. "I didn't know it for certain then, but both of my parents and their siblings had perished. I was an only child. There was no one else."

There was neither a sound nor any movement in the room. The dessert remained unfinished. Their attention was riveted on her and the unfolding story.

"I remember thinking it would never end, that I'd never again go on a trip to a new and exciting place, that I'd never again eat ice cream or slowly savor chocolate melting in my mouth. That was the hardest aspect of the Holocaust. It would never stop. If I somehow escaped the transports and managed to stay alive, that's where I would spend the rest of my life. So, when we were liberated, even though we'd heard rumors that it was coming, the emotional adjustment to freedom was difficult. And like everyone else, I suffered physically. A lack of vitamins affected my vision.

Roger Roffman

"I returned to our Prague apartment and discovered that another family now lived there. When I explained who I was, they closed the door in my face."

Milena looked around at each of them. Elliott guessed she was gauging their capacity to understand.

"Magda and Antonin, our Christian neighbors across the hall from before we were taken to the camps, still lived there. They found me sitting on the hallway steps and took me in. I became part of their family. A Jewish child. Had Hitler not been defeated, they'd have been persecuted for doing that. When I woke the next morning in the bedroom they gave to me, a suitcase lay on a chair under the window. In it I found all of my family photographs, my parents' wedding *ketubah*, many letters my parents had saved, and all of my mother's recipes."

She took a tissue from her pocket and blew her nose.

"I had lost everything, but because of Magda and Antonin, I had so much more than only my memories. Then, in 1948, they took me with them to France when they fled the communist takeover in Czechoslovakia, and I lived with them until I completed what you call high school. At that point, I immigrated to this country." She looked at Peter and smiled. "Are you beginning to understand why I volunteer with refugees?"

"Payback," he said softly.

"Yes," she said. "And for what they did for me, I'll not be able to pay it back. There will never be enough time."

Then, holding it up in the air, Peter emphatically pointed first to the sculpture and then to Theo and then back to the sculpture. Elliott saw a blush beginning to take over Theo's face.

"No way." Theo waved his arm back and forth. "What she does is way out of my league." His voice was increasingly hoarse and his volume very low. "Besides, I get all the benefit by having a totally obedient and worshipful gofer hanging around my shop and driving me wherever I need to go."

Milena seemed confused, and Elliott explained.

"Peter began working in Theo's bookstore this week. So far, there hasn't been bloodshed, but I'm not taking any bets."

She laughed.

"Help me with the coffee, Elliott?"

They walked into the kitchen.

"Is Peter coming to terms with what happened to his friend?"

Milena poured the brewed coffee into a white carafe and took a pint of milk from the refrigerator.

"Yes, I think he is," Elliott said. "He's seeing a good therapist. I'm also so grateful that he and I have turned a corner in our relationship."

"You've changed, Elliott," she replied, and patted him on the back as she walked over to a cabinet for the sugar and creamer.

"And Theo? How is his outlook?"

"Theo's caught his second breath. For a very brief time, he was thrown by the diagnosis. But he's picked himself up. He began volunteering at Gay City by helping with their library, and he told me how relieved he is to have Peter at the store. They've been pals since Peter was a kid. I don't know if it would interest Peter, but Theo seems to be thinking about eventually turning the business over to him."

"Fingers crossed," Milena said.

"And Anneka?" Elliott asked.

"In my darkest moments, I fear I will never see her again. It's as if this book she is writing is devouring her spirit." Milena rested her hands on the counter and slowly shook her head.

"She wrote to me this week about an article she's writing. It will unmask a leader of one of the drug cartels who professes to be a real estate developer. If she does that, surely there'll be a bounty on her head. But I had a premonition this morning that she wanted to abandon the writing. I pictured her desperately searching for some way, but the book had taken on the power of a whirlpool and was pulling her under. I shudder to think she may be running out of time."

"I wish I could speak with her," Elliott said. "If you're right, and she's seeking some excuse to escape the trap she finds herself in, perhaps I'd be able to help."

Milena turned to Elliott, an imploring expression in her eyes. They stood there silently for several moments. Then, Milena shrugged and picked up the coffee carafe and carton of milk.

"She's a strong woman, Elliott. She often tells me I'm overprotective, and I probably am."

Elliott followed Milena back to the table, where coffee was poured, and they chatted about a storm forecast for the next day. Peter, with pride in his voice, told Milena about his mother's plan to go with Mateo to Syria as volunteer surgeons.

"Such brave people," she said. "Brave and inspiring."

Elliott thought about how Peter's magnanimous reaction to Sandra's news touched him, helping him to overcome the stab of fear he had first felt.

The evening came to a close, and, after Theo and Peter left, Elliott helped with the cleanup. Just before heading to his apartment, he took another look at the glass sculpture. The inscription moved him: "The hand you give keeps flames alive."

Standing there holding the sculpture, he remembered that poet's line, the one he jotted down at the poetry slam: *Looking always for what might be mine.*

He wondered whether Milena was once again unknowingly pointing the way for him—the possibility of finding life's meaning that had been so elusive. Finding it through work and by giving. Possibly even giving to her.

33 ~ What Have I done

At a few minutes before nine in the morning, the bookstore aisles were empty. Since closing time the previous day, Queen Esther, the resident Persian cat, had had her empire all to herself.

Later that morning, a group of retirees would arrive in a van from Horizon House and pore over guidebooks about Provence in the travel section. A smattering of mothers with toddlers would sit on bean-bag chairs during story time, listening to a reader tell of the adventures of an elephant who can flap his ears and fly. The crime novel aisle would be busy as this was the first day Patricia Cornwell's newest forensic thriller would go on sale. And, in the community room where author readings take place, an Al-Anon meeting would convene early that evening.

This morning, however, it was just the three of them. Peter and Theo had asked Elliott for the meeting. His son had broached the subject two days earlier while they were eating a spaghetti dinner he'd cooked in Elliott's apartment. Peter would not reveal the meeting's purpose.

"What's going on? You and Theo want to talk with me, and it has to be scheduled?" His initial smile quickly became a frown, and the tone of his voice took on a hint of worry. "And we've got to go to the bookstore for this?" He cocked his head. Putting his fork down, he pushed his chair back from the table. "C'mon Peter. Is someone in trouble?" He folded his arms across his chest. "Things going downhill with Theo?"

"No, nothing like that, Dad." Peter avoided looking his father directly in his eyes. "Theo's doing okay, and I'm fine. It's just that there's something important we want to tell you. You need to know about it, and we want to support you while you take it all in."

Take it all in? Elliott felt a bolt of apprehension, fearing that whatever it was, it could not bode well. Unconsciously he glanced over at his desk, where he'd last left his journal.

They finished eating, and Peter washed while Elliott dried. Their conversation had moved on to other topics, but the mood was heavy.

The unspoken issue seemed to suck the air out of the room. They'd meet at the bookstore two days later at nine in the morning.

***

In the hallway outside Theo's office, a room now shared by both Rachel and Peter, a grandfather clock that had been in Theo's family for generations quietly chimed the hour. Peter unlocked the front door when Elliott arrived. He hugged his father, but there were no lighthearted greetings between them this morning.

Elliott had been ruminating about the possible topics and was eager to get on with it. He followed Peter to the sitting area with two leather chairs next to the biographies section. Elliott nodded at Theo, sitting in his wheelchair.

Elliott noticed a stack of books on a table next to Peter. His son led off.

"Dad, how much do you really know about your grandfather? I mean your mom's dad."

Elliott looked questioningly first at Peter and then at Theo. Of all the possible things he'd thought this conversation might be about, his family background wasn't even on his radar. But Peter had used the words *really know*. He was all the more confused.

He sat for a moment, trying his best to manage his surge of emotions. He'd asked Theo for help in learning how genealogical research is done, but that was as far as it had gone. He'd not gotten started.

What do I know about my grandfather?

"Well, actually, almost nothing. His name was Bernhard Bauer, and he was a cattle farmer in Austria. I never met this grandfather and can't remember my mother ever saying much about him. When war was looking imminent in Europe, he sent my mom from their family home in Vienna to live with relatives in the US. She heard from him only very sporadically over the next few years."

He paused, noticing that neither Peter nor Theo were looking at him. Their eyes were instead downcast. He realized he had begun to sweat.

"Word came that he and his wife had been killed. Apparently, a violent storm devastated the region and blew down their farmhouse."

The silence in the room hung heavy for several moments.

Then, looking up with a compassionate expression on his face, Theo said, "My friend, there's a different story you need to know about Bernhard Bauer, but first let Peter tell you what he and I have been doing."

"For God's sake, please do."

"All right, I know you're feeling stressed by all of this, so I'll be quick," Peter said. "After Theo told me you wanted to know about your mom's side of the family, he and I began looking into our ancestry. We have a number of books on how to do the research."

Peter took two of the books off the table next to him and handed them to Elliott, who cursorily flipped through one book's pages before setting them both aside.

"We dove in and uncovered a trove of information."

Elliott looked back and forth between the two of them.

"And ...?"

Peter continued the story. "For the past week, reading about our family's history has just about been all I've done."

Looking at Peter, Elliott said, "You've found out something about our background, about my mother's dad, that you're afraid will upset me."

Both Peter and Theo nodded.

"It's knowledge you need to have, Dad."

"And, Elliott, it's not just history. You need to know it because of Milena," Theo said haltingly.

"What are you talking about?" Elliott sputtered. "How can my grandfather possibly have anything to do with—"

Peter cut him off and, from a file folder, took a newspaper photo and handed it to Elliott.

Elliott peered at the photo. He noticed immediately that the man was wearing a Nazi uniform.

"Bernhard Bauer wasn't Austrian, Dad. He was German. And he didn't die on his farm because of any severe storm."

Looking more closely, Elliott felt a growing sense of horror as he saw an unmistakable resemblance between himself and this man. It was their eyes and the lines of their chins.

Setting aside the photo, Elliott subconsciously tented his hands in front of his face, bracing himself. He closed his eyes and shivered. It had something to do with Milena? With a flash of insight, he realized what had to be coming.

"Dad, he was in Himmler's Schutzstaffel, the SS. Bernhard Bauer was a Nazi SS officer."

Elliott bolted from the chair and stood at the window looking out. Peter and Theo said nothing, giving him time.

"Oh my dear God."

His arms wrapped around his chest; he rocked on his heels and slowly shook his head. Minutes passed.

"How is it possible I didn't know?" Elliott muttered, turning to face his son. "Could my mother not have known?" He held his hands up, his facial features darkened in a grimace. "Would they have hidden it from me?"

"That'd be my guess," Peter replied. "Maybe your folks planned to tell you when you were older, and then Todd's death, when you were nine, changed everything. Your mom, in particular, was obsessed after that with trying to protect you from harm."

"Protect me from harm by denying me the truth?" Elliott again faced the window and looked out.

"Dad, take a look at this." Peter stood and held up a xeroxed copy of a page from a newspaper. "This tells us how he actually did die."

Elliott took it from Peter. It was from the April 24, 1947 edition of the *Milwaukee Journal*. One article, highlighted with a yellow marker, was titled, "Lidice Deaths Are Avenged—Nazis to Be Hanged."

Quickly scanning the story, he spotted his grandfather's name. Bernhard Bauer was among six defendants in a trial who had been convicted and sentenced to death. Nine others were given life prison terms.

"Lidice?" Elliott asked. "What's this about? What did he do?" He looked again at the article. "Good God. He was hanged?"

"Sit down, Elliott," Theo said. "This won't …," he coughed, "this won't be easy to hear."

Theo opened a file folder and removed a stack of copies made from newspapers and sections of books. He handed them to Peter.

"We've pulled together these materials for you to read later," Peter said, "but for right now we'll give you the highlights."

Elliott sat. Peter glanced at his dad with an unspoken question. Was Elliott ready to hear the details? Elliott responded with a rapid nod.

Peter read from his notes on a lined yellow pad. "Lidice was an agricultural village in Czechoslovakia. When that country was occupied, a resistance movement grew and began to sabotage the Nazis. One of Hitler's favorite lieutenants was sent to suppress it. His nickname was 'the Hangman,' and he executed thousands of resistance fighters."

Elliott realized he'd been holding his breath and exhaled.

"In May of 1942, the Hangman was assassinated. Hitler ordered massive reprisals. Lidice was targeted. Later it turned out to be false, but it initially looked as if one of the killers had connections with Lidice. The entire village was leveled. Every one of the men …"

Peter stopped. He cleared his throat.

"Every one of …." He choked on the words and dropped his notes on the table. "Dad, Bernhard Bauer was one of the senior officers."

Elliott winced.

Peter continued. "It was June 9, 1942. Ten trucks of the security police rolled into the village. They rounded up all of the men and took them to a farmstead, where they locked them in a barn. The next day the men were taken out, ten at a time, stood against the barn wall, and shot. One hundred seventy-three men were killed."

Elliott held his head in his hands, his eyes closed, and tried to stop himself from hyperventilating.

"Every one of the women and almost all of the children, nearly three hundred in all, were taken to concentration camps, where most were gassed."

His head throbbed as the story of the horror of that day unfolded.

"All of the farm animals were slaughtered, all of the buildings were burned and then leveled by bulldozers, all of the fruit trees were uprooted, and the lake was filled in. After the village had been entirely destroyed, a barbed wire fence was put up. A sign warned that trespassers would be shot."

"My mother's father did that?" Elliott croaked.

Peter stopped. Elliott looked up as his son silently read the notes that followed and saw the pained expression on his face. Elliott realized there was more.

"Dad, we learned that thirty Jews from Terezín were brought in trucks to the village. They were forced to dig the common grave and bury the Lidice men."

"Oh Jesus," Elliott shouted.

He stood and waved his arms back and forth, gesturing for Peter to stop.

"That could have been Milena's father," he said. "Please stop. I need …. I've got to …."

He moaned, walking between the shelves of books toward the front door and then turning back. His heart was racing.

"What have I done? How in God's name could I have let myself …."

He paced back and forth, wringing his hands.

Peter and Theo stayed in their chairs. Queen Esther jumped up into Theo's lap and settled. The grandfather clock quietly chimed the half hour.

Elliott stopped pacing and grabbed the pile of xeroxed copies. Flipping through them, the words on those pages were just a blur, and he returned the copies to the table. Again, he moaned.

"What have we done to her? My grandfather and now me. How in God's name—"

"Dad, please. You can't think you're responsible for what Bauer did. You hadn't even been born yet. What happened to the people of Lidice was grotesque, but you have nothing to do with it. Do you hear me?"

Standing at the window, Elliott mumbled, "Grandfather and grandson. We were both thieves. It's as simple and as shameful as that. We stole from Milena and her family and her people."

He unexpectedly pictured the wooden dough bowl in the lobby of their building. And he remembered Milena's reason for placing it there.

It was to cradle letters on their way to Anneka, to symbolize their family heritage.

What have we done?

At that moment, he thought of Anneka and her obsession with seeking vengeance. If Anneka knew that Elliott had been stealing and reading her mother's letters, and if she knew of the horrors his grandfather had inflicted on her family, on her people, would Elliott be a target?

34 ~ I'm Frightened

Anneka propped up her head with both hands, her unfocused eyes staring through the monitor. A vivid and troubling image, one she had created in the paragraph she'd just written, was seared in her brain.

A nineteen-year-old boy lay twitching on the ground. His head was nearly severed from his body. Blood was still pumping from his neck. Enrique stood next to him, slowly taking aim before administering the final blow. This mission was completed. He calmly wiped the blood from his machete by rubbing it across the boy's T-shirt.

"For my grandson," he said.

Feeling the bile rising in her throat, Anneka rushed to the balcony. She stood there looking out at children wearing backpacks and returning to their homes after school. Some of them were only a few years younger than the cartel member whom Enrique just had killed in her story. She heard the sound of someone playing a piano.

Leaning on the railing, she watched a boy who had stopped to retie his shoelaces. Her gut roiled from the toxicity of her protagonist's transformation. He had become a sinister, bloodthirsty killer and would never be the same.

"The children, Anneko. We're killing the children," her father had said. *God, what am I doing?* Anneka thought. *He was just nineteen years old.*

She, too, was changing. Darker.

Hearing a knock on her door, Anneka assumed it was her neighbor. Felipe often asked that she water his plants while he was on a training deployment with his army unit. Checking first to be sure the security chain was fastened, she pulled the door open a crack, starting to ask, "Hi, when are you …" and then abruptly stopped. In front of her stood a tall and silver-haired gringo wiping perspiration from his forehead, a backpack on the floor beside him. He wore a Harris Tweed sport coat, badly wrinkled khakis, and cordovan loafers. His disarmingly friendly smile was thwarted by a look of worry in his eyes.

"Anneka, my name is Elliott Sterling. I'm your mother's next-door neighbor. May I talk with you?"

"*You're* Elliott?" Her look of surprise rapidly morphed to one of fear. "What about my mother?" She suddenly felt her legs becoming wobbly. "Is she dead?" Anneka raised her right hand to cup her mouth.

Elliott quickly added, "No, she's fine. Really, Anneka, she's alive and she's fine."

For a moment she stood there speechless, her shoulders briefly relaxing before again tightening. "So my mother sent you?" Her voice rose. "Without telling me? No, without asking me?" She began to close the door.

"Anneka, please. Milena doesn't know I'm here." His voice was desperate. "I didn't tell her."

Momentarily undecided, she hesitated, then undid the chain, stepped back, waved him inside, and pointed to the chair next to the bridge table, where her computer was set up. He sat and she took the seat where she normally worked.

"I apologize for not letting you know I'd be coming, but I—"

"Okay, Mr. Sterling." She spoke with a crisp assertiveness. "You're here and obviously traveled a long way, so I'll listen." She glanced at her watch, a signal to him that this was going to be quick. "I'll tell you right at the outset, though, that if you're on a rescue mission, you're going to be disappointed." Anneka crossed her arms on her chest, her raised eyebrows and a cock of her head an order to proceed.

He focused on his hands, picking at the cuticle of his thumb, and then looked up at her through the corner of his eyes.

"I've been rehearsing what I'd say much of the way down here, but now I ...." His sentence drifted off.

He stood, removed his jacket, and sat again, placing it neatly folded on his lap. He rolled up his sleeves and his gaze returned to his hands.

"All right, I'll just spit it out. Your mother doesn't know it, but she has pretty much turned my life around during the months I've known her. I'm a different man because of her."

She remained silent. She knew he was hoping for some indication, any glimmer of warmth, to suggest she gave a damn about how his life had changed or the fact that her mother had been his savior. She'd give him nothing.

"Uh, so I'm here because it feels like a way I can pay her back. At least, that's one of the reasons." He cleared his throat, and then rapidly spurted out, "She's frightened because of the danger you're in by being a reporter here, and she's—"

"Yeah, yeah," Anneka abruptly sat forward and scowled. "And she's hoping I'll see the errors of my ways and come home." She bit her bottom lip. "Look, you're inserting yourself right smack in the middle of a dispute my mother and I have been having for, oh, I don't know, many months at this point." Her voice rose to a near shout. "She's smothering me." Anneka slapped her right hand on the table, and he flinched.

Seeing his reaction, she grimaced, a hint of apology in her expression.

"Yes, there's some risk." She picked up a pencil and began tapping it rapidly on the table. "Actually, there's a great deal of risk. It's something I've got to do, and my overprotective mother is insisting that I'm broken and need to be fixed. And"—she wagged her finger at him—"here you are, the fixer."

Elliott shook his head in disagreement and, with a tone of urgency, said, "No, no, not fixed, Anneka, protected. There was a newspaper story just last week about a journalist being murdered down here. He wrote about the cartels. It was gruesome."

Anneka sighed and rolled her eyes. Shaking her head, she walked to the kitchenette, where she poured the last few drops of wine into a glass and tossed it down. She opened another bottle and refilled the glass almost to the brim.

He was probably thirsty, she thought, and for a moment considered offering him something. No, he wouldn't be there that long, and she didn't want him to feel welcomed.

She watched him look around at the apartment's austere furnishings and then step out onto the balcony. He picked up her sketch pad, and she saw him looking back and forth between the image on the open page and the rear security door of the bakery across the alley.

"Put that down," she shouted. "Grab one of the folding chairs and take it out there."

In a minute, they were settled. A delivery truck passed by, narrowly avoiding a pedestrian who ducked into a doorway.

"My mother's written to me about you. She, uh, she told me you're having a tough time."

Anneka drank half of her glass, paused for a moment, and then gulped the rest. She put it down on the balcony deck, where it tipped over and rolled to the wall and stopped.

She sat up and turned to face him. "Let me try to explain something that my mother has never understood." Her diction was clipped. "Or maybe understood, but never accepted. Do you want to hear this?"

She shot a questioning glance in his direction.

"Absolutely."

She took a deep breath. "I'm the daughter of a Holocaust survivor." She watched Elliott's gaze shift to her left forearm, which she had been unconsciously rubbing. "That obscenity could only have succeeded if much of the world let it happen while sitting on their goddamn hands." She furrowed her brows and emphatically waved her hands to make the point.

"For much of my life, I've stood by silently while atrocities were being committed—Rwanda, Burundi, Srebrenica, Sudan—so many of them." She tightly balled both of her fists. "Then, just a year ago, nearly sixty children in a village in northeast Nigeria were burned alive. Children, Elliott. It was the Boko Haram. They set fire to the children's dormitory and shot or stabbed any who tried to escape. And the fact of the matter is that it most likely happened because I'd visited there to do some interviews just a few hours earlier."

"Grotesque," he muttered. "And you think your visit may have prompted it." He shook his head.

She leaned over, reaching for the glass.

"Children, Elliott," she rasped. "One of them, a precious twelve-year-old boy named Gbadebo who told me all about himself and his school. That did it."

Returning inside and refilling her glass, she called through the open door, "Now, no more. *No. Fucking. More.*" She slammed the cabinet door shut. "If we want to claim we're civilized, we've got to fight back. No other choice."

She walked directly to face Elliott where he was sitting, her wineglass spilling as she gestured.

"Enrique, my avenger, is doing just that, and through him my voice will be heard."

His eyes widened.

"I'm filing articles for the *New York Times*, but I'm also writing a book. It's about the Zetas cartel. It shows one man battling their horrific violence, even if he's just pissing in the wind. It's fiction, but it's telling the goddamn unvarnished truth. And it's doing something about it."

Elliott leaned forward in his chair. "Your avenger?"

She nodded. "Enrique. He's deeply wounded, living with a dagger embedded in his heart. At this point in my story, he's assassinated three men and one boy. There'll be more, many more."

Her voice grew husky, and her words began to slur. She pictured the death toll she was creating, remembering that nineteen-year-old boy's twitching corpse. She felt Enrique's merciless thirst for vengeance thrashing in her chest.

Elliott closed his eyes and folded his hands, pressing them against his face. Moments passed, and then he looked at her.

"Aren't you taunting fate? What about the personal danger you're putting yourself in?"

She paused, undecided how to answer. Would it be worth it, she asked herself? Worth trying to get this man to understand what actually had brought her to this country? She teetered on the verge of shrugging his question off. He'd not get it.

"Doesn't someone need to do it? Can we all stand by and just be bystanders? Tell one another it's such a shame?"

She waited, expecting him to counter her. But Elliott didn't seem poised to pounce with an argument. Indeed, something about this man gave her the sense that he was genuinely concerned.

Her gaze fell on his backpack. He'd come such a distance.

"Give me a minute."

Anneka walked into the bathroom, splashed water on her face, patted it dry with a hand towel, gargled with mouthwash, and gave her hair a quick brushing before returning to the balcony.

Pointing her finger at him, she said, "I don't want to be misunderstood. Got it?"

"I'll do my best."

"It's personal, deeply personal. My father ...," her voice cracked, "my father killed himself."

From his nod she saw that he already knew this.

"Milena told me about his suicide." He was quiet for the next few moments. "But weren't you just a child when that happened?"

As she spoke, her eyes looked up at the ceiling, as if she were picturing the scene.

"I was thirteen. When I came home from school that day, he'd been brooding in his study. I knew he was desperately unhappy." A sob rose from her chest. "I wanted his help in memorizing my Spanish vocabulary, but he brushed me off. He kept repeating to me, 'We're killing the children. Oh my God, Anneko. Oh my God.'" She blotted a tear with her sleeve. "He was in such agony. This was in 1975. The North Vietnamese were days from entering Saigon. Operation Babylift was under way to fly orphans out of the country."

"I remember that," Elliott quietly said.

"A plane full of those children crashed and burned. Seventy-eight children died. When I went in to see him after coming home from school, his normally neatly combed hair looked wild, tears were running down his cheeks, and he was pacing back and forth, wringing his hands."

"That was so long ago. Don't you—"

"No, no, you have to understand," she almost shouted. "I left him alone cleaning his pistol. I guessed what he was planning, but I didn't really believe he'd do it. I couldn't. I went to my room, changed my clothes, and started making flash cards so I could test myself."

She stood up and began pacing.

"What happened next will forever haunt me." She ran her hands through her hair, walking back and forth, and avoiding his gaze. "Fifteen minutes later, I heard the shot. Our house had been so quiet, but in an instant, it was as if a cyclone had hit. Mother shouted, 'Anneko, what was that?' A train going by blew its whistle again and again. I ran to his study, and when I saw his body on the floor and all that blood, I began screaming hysterically. Mother came in right behind me and, dear God, I can still hear her wailing, 'No.' And that fucking train whistle kept blowing and blowing and blowing as if something terrible was happening on the tracks."

She coughed several times and blew her nose. Looking directly at him, she saw compassion on his face.

"If I had told her, she could have stopped him." Her eyes implored him to get it. "For me, it's as if it happened yesterday."

His hands formed a tent, the fingers of one hand tapping against the fingers of the other, as he seemed to take in what Anneka was saying.

"I knew some of the story," he said. "Your mother told me how guilty he'd felt."

Tears ran down her cheek.

"There was more. He kept reliving the day his army unit in Korea massacred innocent people, many of them women and children. It was an obscenity committed by those men. They ...." She wrapped her arms tightly around her chest. "Those soldiers made certain they stopped any infiltrators. The babies were just collateral damage.

"Mother recently told me details I hadn't known. My dad had convinced himself that he might have stopped the carnage if he'd spoken up. But he didn't. Along with the others in his unit, he aimed his rifle and fired. He didn't say anything and," her face was contorted in anguish, "and I didn't say anything.

"People died. My writing this book, living here, and doing the research interviews, is saying something. It's speaking up. It's paying back, for my father's cowardice and for my own. And for that beautiful free spirit, that little Nigerian boy, whom I promised I'd write to."

She slumped back into her chair, emotionally spent.

He looked away for several moments.

This is the time, she thought. He'll start arguing with me, telling me I'm carrying too much guilt and should think about myself differently. Or maybe he'll feel overwhelmed and won't have any advice. We'll see.

"You really have to be here," he said, looking her straight in her eyes. "For you, this is not a choice. It's a moral obligation. Because of what your father didn't do, what you wish you'd done, and for that little boy, you must write this book. It's taking a stand that for you couldn't be more important."

"Yes," she whispered.

He'd not told her what to do or how to think, she realized. There was no *but* in how he'd replied. He'd simply accepted what she'd told him.

"Yes, Elliott. Thank you for that. Thank you for seeing me."

Anneka sat up and looked over at him. Her face had a flicker of a smile. She stood, walked back to the kitchenette, and filled her electric teakettle and switched it on. She took two mugs from a shelf, scooped tea into her tea ball, and reached for the ceramic pot. They were both silent as she stood there, waiting for the water to boil, and then, almost as an afterthought, she called to him, "What do you take with tea?"

"Just a little milk. Thank you."

Several minutes passed with neither of them speaking. Standing at the counter, she shouted over her shoulder, "Well, I've bared my soul. It's your turn. Does your soul need some unburdening?"

"I don't understand," he said hesitantly.

Anneka handed him his mug.

"Why don't you lay down that heavy pack you've been carrying," she said softly, a hint of curiosity on her face as she turned toward him. "The guilt pack," she said, "not that one." She pointed to his backpack.

Then she saw the color as it began rising in his neck.

"How … how long have you known?" he stammered.

Seconds passed with no reply. Then she rose slowly, walked behind his chair, and gently placed her right hand on his shoulder, leaving it there for a moment before going to the closet next to the front door, where she removed a storage box. She found a red expanding file and opened the flap. After a few moments of flipping through the contents, she took out a single sheet of paper and glanced through it quickly before handing it to Elliott. She then sat down with her mug of tea.

"Almost two months," she said. His hand shook as he began to read.

Milá Anneko—

You'll likely be surprised to receive two letters this week. You see, I've made a strange discovery that at first troubled me, but then—after I'd given it some thought—appeared to be rather wonderful. If you're entirely confused at this point, I'd not be surprised, but bear with me.

I've written to you about my neighbor, Elliott. He moved into the next-door apartment five months ago and I've become quite fond of him. He's a psychologist, and when one of his clients took her life, it threw him into a tailspin. Eventually, when the darkness that had imprisoned his spirit continued for months, he and his wife decided to divorce. They'd been married for thirty-one years. And then there was his son. Elliott was unhinged at the decisions his son was making about his life.

Elliott's about your age, actually, and he was clearly adrift at this new turn on his journey. I took him under my wing, treated him to some home cooking, and began to realize how much comfort he took in unburdening himself when we talked. He also asked so many questions about me!

A week ago, I took four letters downstairs and put them in the bowl for outgoing mail. A few minutes later, I worried that I'd forgotten to put stamps on the envelopes. Just as I came down the stairs to check, I saw Elliott pick up one of the letters, tuck it into his briefcase, and leave the building. It was the letter to you. He had no idea I had watched this drama unfold.

Elliott looked up, his face gray with shame. "I'm so … it's unforgivable. I don't know how I can ever—"

Anneka had been watching him as he made his way through Milena's message. With her right hand, she signaled him to stop talking. "Finish reading it. You may be surprised."

He returned to reading.

When you phoned me a week later, it was evident that you'd received that letter. My initial reaction was to be dismayed, but that turned into confusion. I decided to hold back on confronting him.

This morning, I listened for the sound of his apartment door opening and, after he'd left for his office, I checked and, once again, my letter to you had disappeared. So, here's what your mother, the intrepid detective, has deduced. My fragile next-door neighbor is opening and reading my letters to you, then posting them, believing that no one is the wiser.

You'll be wondering at this point why I might see this as wonderful, so let me tell you. Something in his childhood deeply wounded this man. I don't know what it was, but it's clear to me that it plagues him. Now, I'm watching him change in ways that are astonishing him and delighting me.

I think that reading my letters to you has had something to do with it. Yes, he's being deceptive, but in a way that I applaud him for, having the bravery to break out of his rigid shell and take a huge risk.

So, my child, it appears that you and he have been sharing my letters and, for my part, I am pleased, really pleased. I wanted you to know this and ask that you extend a generosity of spirit to this man whom you've never met. Will you do that?

I'll write again next Monday. If there is anything I don't want him to read, I'll write that in a separate letter and drop it in a mailbox. Until then, I love you, Anneko.

Tvoje máma

Elliott wiped his perspiring forehead with his handkerchief. A sheepish grin on his face, he said, "I feel like a thief who's been given a pardon and then won the lottery." He held his hands as if they were encircling an unseen globe. "What a gift. Your mother is absolutely right. Those letters have forever changed me. But Anneka, I violated your privacy and I—"

"There's a reason you've needed those letters. Tell me about it. What did my mother mean when she said you'd been wounded as a child?"

Elliott squirmed in his chair. He closed his eyes.

She waited. Moments passed. He sighed deeply and then opened his eyes, looking at Anneka. "Your mother knows part of it," he said. "She knows about my brother getting killed in Vietnam, and my parents suffering so badly that they were no longer able to do what moms and dads are supposed to do with a kid like me. I was nine years old."

He stood, looked out at the alley, and gripped the railing with his hands. "Your mother was incredibly prescient," he said. "I told her that I slump into a depression each year on the anniversary of Todd's death, and she asked if I'm carrying guilt, somehow punishing myself." He turned and faced Anneka. "She was right. That's exactly what's been happening. And I've avoided thinking about the reason. It's just too painful." He bit his lip.

Anneka patted his chair, signaling with a tilt of her head that he should sit. "Today's the day. Open the drapes and let the light in. I'd like to know."

He paused for a moment and then sat.

"I did something terrible the night we learned my brother had been killed." Elliott slowly shook his head. "Hours had passed after the army officer and chaplain left, and my father was preoccupied with trying to console my mom. I closed the door to my room and, and ..."

He moved from his chair to sit on the floor of the balcony, his arms wrapped around his knees and his back resting against the wall.

"I tore up his football jersey, the one he wore in his last game before he graduated. He asked me to keep it for him until he returned from Vietnam. I tore it to shreds, and then I set a match to the pieces and burned them. I ripped up the letters and postcards he wrote to me and the photos of him in his uniform and the Vietnamese paper currency and the insignia patch from his unit. All of it!'

As she listened, she heard Elliott's voice become that of a nine-year-old. His eyes were closed, his fists clenched. "You lied to me," he whimpered. "You promised me you were going to come back, that nothing would happen to you."

She watched as his chest heaved. Minutes passed. Elliott blew his nose and wiped his eyes.

"I've never told this to anyone. It was as if I'd killed him a second time. I hated myself."

Tears streamed down Anneka's cheeks. "You were nine, Elliott. I was thirteen. Today's the day, long overdue, for both of us to forgive ourselves. Yes?"

He nodded.

"Yes," she said. They sat quietly.

In the distance, the *parroquia* bells were ringing. A mother called for her children to come in. Smells of freshly baked tortillas wafted in the air.

"I'm just remembering what you said when you came in the door. What was the other reason why you came here, Elliott? Something other than to pay my mother back."

He stood, reached for his mug, and leaned against the railing. He took a deep breath and slowly exhaled. "Four days ago, I learned something that horrified me. My son looked into our family's background and discovered that a grandfather who I thought was an Austrian farmer actually was a Nazi SS officer."

Anneka gasped.

"He was one of the commanders who led a unit that destroyed a Czech village called Lidice. After a high-ranking Nazi was assassinated, supposedly with the help of people who lived there, Hitler ordered that the village be leveled in reprisal. The citizens were either shot on the spot or sent to camps, where they were gassed. The details are gruesome, simply gruesome."

"You only just learned about him?"

"Yes, and I also learned another part of the story. Jewish prisoners from Terezín were trucked to the village to bury the murdered men. My second reason for coming here is to ease my conscience. Two generations in my family have stolen from yours."

In a moment, the expression on her face registered recognition. "Oh," she said, "I see. One of them might have been my grandfather."

She gazed at her hands and for several minutes picked at a cuticle. The silence was heavy. She tilted her face up, her eyes closed, and kneaded the muscles in her neck.

When she looked at him, she saw he was glancing at his backpack. She guessed he was thinking he should leave, maybe get out of there quickly before she exploded with anger. Or at least prepare himself to bolt.

But, then Anneka chortled and began to giggle. And her giggles turned to cackling. Seeing his look of confusion only propelled her further into raucous doubling up laughter,

"What a god-awful thought," she said when she finally was able to catch her breath. "How fucking absurd fate can be."

Anneka set her mug down and took a step toward him. "Oh, Elliott." She held out her hand, and when he took it in his, she gently pulled him to his feet. For several moments, they stood there facing one another.

There were no words, just the sound of the bakery owner locking his security gate across the alley. Elliott's arms encircled her and pressed her to him. She rested her head on his shoulder.

"You and I have had a fair exchange," she whispered in his ear. "My mother gave you a new window through which to see the world and yourself. And you. You've looked through that window and understood me. I say that's a good deal all around."

Sunset hues of pink and blue were reflected in the upper-story windows of the building across the way. In the apartment below Anneka's, an eighteen-year-old student was practicing Beethoven's Moonlight Sonata on the piano.

The trucks had all completed that day's deliveries, and the only shop still open was the Old Town Café halfway down the block. Six people sat at two outdoor tables illuminated by hanging paper lanterns. The pungent aroma of beef being grilled drifted up from a balcony on a lower floor.

They remained in an embrace, swaying slowly to the Sonata rhythm, and continuing to hold one another in the stillness that followed the music's ending. Elliott looked into her eyes before caressing Anneka's cheek, then bringing his lips to hers, at first with only a hint of touching, and again, and then with a fierce passion.

Hours later, they lay together, their bodies entwined.

"Are you awake," she asked.

"Mm-hmm."

She turned to face him. "I'm frightened about what's happening to me."

"I'm here."

35 ~ To Abandon Enrique

He and Theo were sitting with their backs against the hollowed-out tree trunk. Patches of sunlight filtered through the leafy canopy, and the forest's carpet had a smell of musky dampness. One hour passed, then another, neither of them keen to detach from the old-growth cedar's infusion of restorative tranquility. He felt at peace.

Someone tapped him on the shoulder. Elliott heard a woman's voice. It was vaguely familiar.

"Breakfast's on."

As his eyes focused, he saw Anneka standing next to the bed in her robe and chewing a piece of toast spread with cottage cheese. She smiled as she watched him blinking the sleep from his eyes.

"Hi."

"Good morning," he said, stretching his arms and shoulders.

She tousled his hair.

"You'll find the toaster and a loaf of whole wheat bread on the counter. I've cut up some fruit and cooked a few hardboiled eggs. Coffee's hot."

He dashed into the bathroom, making a grab for his pants and toiletry bag on the way. In a few minutes, he stepped back into the bedroom and put on a clean shirt taken from his pack.

Anneka was out on the balcony working on a sketch detailing the spider's web of power lines that crisscrossed the alley. He poured coffee and sat next to her. Watching her draw, he reached behind her and scratched her back. Without looking up, she murmured, "Hmm, that feels good."

A van pulled up to the bakery's rear entrance, and two men began unloading what looked to be sacks of flour. The owner checked off items on a clipboard as they were carried inside.

He waited while she continued sketching. Then, when she looked over at him and smiled, he said, "I want to know what's frightening you." For a moment she appeared to be studying his face before returning to her drawing pad.

"We'll go for a walk."

After finishing breakfast, they left her apartment building, heading north. Elliott took photos as they walked down the cobblestone streets, getting Anneka to pose in front of several intricately carved wooden doors of centuries-old mansions. Their walls were painted in vibrant pastel colors, and many of the windows opened onto wrought-iron balconies festooned with resplendent bougainvillea vines.

She wore tan slacks, sandals, and a blue jean shirt. Her long brunette hair was piled on top of her head along with her oversize round eyeglasses. He remembered telling Milena that her daughter's lanky look reminded him of Katharine Hepburn.

Pointing to the *parroquia* spires and domes she said, "Let's start at the church." They crossed El Jardín, dotted with Indian laurel trees that had been pruned into round or oval shapes with flat tops. The food vendors were beginning to be busy.

When they entered the church, Elliott looked up at the crystal chandelier suspended from the brick-arched ceiling. Walking down the patterned tile aisle, Anneka led them to a pew on the left about halfway to the altar.

"When I first moved to the city, I came here just about every day," Anneka said. "It's been a long time since my last visit."

"Why is that?"

For several moments, she gazed at the altar.

"Being here gave me a kind of spiritual grounding. The work I've been doing has taken a toll. It's corrosive."

She was wringing her hands.

"No matter how egregious the corruption or how gory the violence in the pieces I wrote for the *Times* or for parts of my novel, I felt cleansed after I'd been here, even if I'd just dashed in for a few minutes."

"And now?"

"Now," she said, her voice barely a whisper. "Now, it feels as if I defile this place just by my presence."

He swiveled in his seat to face her. "Defile a church? How can you believe that? Aren't all of us imperfect?"

She rapidly shook her head and placed her hand on his arm.

"There's a difference, Elliott. Most people come to church to acknowledge their sins and pray for forgiveness."

"And you?"

"I'm committing sins." Her volume was low, but she spoke with a clipped diction. "For that matter, I have no intention of stopping. And I certainly don't deserve absolution. I don't want it."

"What can you possibly be talking about? I just don't get ...," Then, the consternation that had clouded his face morphed into a smile. "Oh, it's what's happening in your novel."

She seemed surprised that he'd not tracked her meaning.

"Yes. It's Enrique. With each killing, he becomes more ruthless. Making him so bloodthirsty is infectious. It's infecting me. I despise the person I'm becoming, but it's a price I have to pay."

He took her hand, pausing for a moment to consider what he'd say.

"But you're just inventing his assassinations, not carrying them out." He squeezed her hand to emphasize his point. "It's only a story, Anneka. Even if you're feeling sinful because of what you're writing, it's still fiction. No one is getting killed."

She pulled her hand away.

"You see, it's not just what's on the page. Writing this book is fueling my own rage. Now, I actually think I could kill someone."

Resting her arms on the pew in front of them, Anneka slowly shook her head.

"One day not too long ago I came close, much too close."

The *parroquia*'s bells began tolling, a resonant sound calling the faithful to prayer. She waited.

When the ringing stopped, she told him about the inebriated man who had cruelly slapped his child when the girl pleaded to go home from the tavern.

"In a flash, I felt as if I were Enrique, and I smashed a bottle over that guy's head. He nearly died. And, as horrified as I was later at what I'd done, at that moment I wanted him to die."

In her eyes, he saw a blaze of fury.

"Has something like that happened again?" he asked.

"No."

"So, why—"

"But I'm frightened that it will." She paused to think. "It's almost as if I know that when it happens, I'll feel relieved. No, that's not quite the word. When it happens, I'll feel realized."

Near the main altar, a priest was speaking with a young couple, pointing toward the entrance and then to several other places in the church as he spoke. Elliott wondered if this was a wedding rehearsal.

"Your destiny? You feel destined to kill?"

"At times I think it's inevitable."

"So that's what frightens you."

"That's one thing."

"There's another?"

"Yeah, there's another," she said with a hint of sarcasm. "I'll tell you the other thing, but you will judge me, and I will not listen."

He looked for a smile, but she was dead serious.

"Can't promise what I'll think."

She used the fingers of her right hand to list her conditions. "Don't try to argue with me." Then, finger number two. "Don't tell my mother."

He felt a chill. "What's the other thing that frightens you, Anneka?"

"My father suffered for years. Somehow, he eventually summoned up the courage to end it. If I've felt any destiny at all, it's that I'll follow him. When the time comes, I want to have the same courage."

"Oh," he blurted out. Feeling as if he'd been punched in the gut, Elliott bolted out of the pew and quickly walked over to a chapel to the left of the main altar where an image of Christ had been sculpted from cornstalks and orchid bulbs. He stood there silently, hunched over, his eyes closed, and his hands jammed into his pockets. Minutes passed. Anneka remained in the pew.

He thought about Peter. With Rosalie's suicide in his mind, he had ripped into his son when he imagined Peter, so addicted to death-defying stunts, accidentally killing himself.

He considered leaving, but then turned and walked rapidly back and stood next to Anneka.

"All of those letters from your mother?" His voice had an edge of anger. "Haven't they made any difference in how you think about your life? Not any of them?"

She focused on her folded hands in her lap.

"I think her letters make it worse. I drink to blot them out." With a pleading expression, she said, "I disappoint her. Mother wants so much for me to live life her way."

She took a handkerchief from her purse and dabbed at her eyes.

"I can't do what she wants. I simply can't, Elliott. Those letters are exactly right, but only for you. After figuring out that you were reading them, I think she became optimistic they'd have the effect she hoped, at least in your life if not in mine. Now, she's writing them to you."

He felt exasperated.

"Do you actually think Milena's stopped caring about you when she writes her letters?" He held his hands up in a questioning gesture.

"No, not at all. Maybe it's just that she's got a far more willing reader in you than in me and she knows that."

An organist began rehearsing. Elliott recognized Gabaráin's "Lord, You Have Come to the Seashore." Minutes passed with both of them silent.

Elliott again reached for her hand.

"Look, there are some things I want to say to you. Are you willing to listen?"

"Please don't—"

"No, it's not what you're thinking. I won't judge you. My thoughts could even be useful. Will you hear me?"

It was almost imperceptible, but she nodded.

"When I listen to you, I mean really listen, what stands out for me is how badly you want to abandon Enrique."

"What do you mean? I don't—"

They were looking directly at one another.

"I think you've realized that his character in your novel has become insidiously evil. He has poisoned you and it's undeniable where this is leading for you personally. It's destroying you."

She avoided eye contact.

"And you want to live. Let me tell you what I've heard. I've got four examples. The first involves our coming to this church."

"What about it?"

"You said you feel that you defile this place, yet you brought me here this morning. We could have gone somewhere else, anywhere. There must have been something you wanted to experience by coming here."

She turned away.

"Maybe the cleansing you once felt?"

A young mother walked down the aisle with a baby in a carrier strapped to her chest and two toddlers holding her hands. They walked to the bank of tiered votive candles to the right of the main altar.

"The second is about the killing. On the one hand, you want Enrique to avenge, and you see yourself avenging, too. On the other hand, you're terrified because what he and you are becoming violates your morality."

Anneka knit her brow and quickly turned to face him.

"Yes, but it's necessary that I—"

He pushed on. "The third is how you describe your mother's letters."

"No, Elliott, don't—"

"You're unhappy that she tries to change you, but you keep those letters in a file. And you get drunk to keep yourself from letting her messages sink in. You can't see life the way she wants you to, but I think you want to. You hearing me?"

Twisting her handkerchief, she said nothing.

The young mother's baby began to whimper. She slowly rocked on her heels in an attempt to give it comfort.

"Here's the fourth. When I asked you to tell me what was frightening you, you were willing to talk about it. I think you actually wanted me to hear what's really going on in your thinking. That you're looking for a way out, Anneka."

"Elliott, I—"

"So, if you want me to understand why you're frightened, be honest. Talk to me about both sides of the arguments that are going on in your head. Some part of you wants to live very differently. Isn't that true?"

"I don't know how I can …." She spoke with a pleading tone, squirming in her seat.

"Tell me about it."

She looked down.

They were both startled when the baby's piercing shriek echoed in the church sanctuary. The two toddlers began to cry.

"Anneka, talk to me, please," he said, his voice more insistent.

She turned to face him. It looked as if she was about to reply when her cell phone buzzed. It was an incoming text. Glancing at the phone's screen, she then looked at her watch.

"There's someplace I need to be," she said as she slid from the pew and quickly walked toward the exit.

36 ~ Giving the Cartels a Green Light

"Where are you going?"

They stopped to talk in the church foyer.

"To a panel presentation at the municipal building. It's going to begin in ten minutes, and I just learned about it. The mayor's office organized it. They've had a heap of angry messages from citizens about drug violence. One of the speakers is a guy I've had on my radar. He masks as a fine upstanding civic leader, but, if the rumors are true, he's a regional kingpin in Los Zetas."

"How'd you learn about him?"

"I talked with some people in Nuevo Laredo, where he's based. He's a real estate investor, a heavy hitter. But that's his cover. My neighbor, Felipe, is in one of the military's drug interdiction units, and he told me they think this guy is a multibillionaire and pretty high up in the cartel hierarchy."

"Do you really need to be there?"

He remembered what Milena said Anneka planned to do. Picturing her confronting the guy at this meeting made him shudder.

"Just to listen and observe."

There was a darkness in her facial expression.

"Being in the presence of evil fuels my writing," she said.

His apprehension doubled.

"I'm coming with you."

"No, Elliott. This is my thing, and you've got no reason to be there. We can talk when I—"

He was adamant. "You're not going alone. Let me take you in my rental car. We'll get there quicker."

Indecisive, she stood at the church entrance for several moments and then shrugged. "Okay."

The meeting was in a small auditorium on an upper floor of the baroque municipal building.

About forty people were in the audience, nearly filling the room. Elliott guessed that many were in their fifties or older, their attire casual for the most part. There was a smattering of younger folks, more formally dressed and probably taking time off work to attend. What looked to be a group of American expats filled two rows on the far right. A uniformed police officer stood at the entrance.

Five people were on the dais. Anneka told him they were a lieutenant from the police narcotics unit, a municipality council member who chaired a committee on public safety, a deputy mayor, the real estate investor, and a woman who became an activist after losing a son to drug violence.

The meeting was under way when they arrived. The council member was speaking about the meeting's purpose and how it would be structured. He then introduced the first panelist.

Elliott and Anneka were seated in the second row from the back. Even with his very limited Spanish, Elliott quickly recognized that the tension in the room was palpable. Audience members were restless, some were whispering to one another, and the deputy mayor looked and sounded defensive.

Anneka translated parts that Elliott missed. The speaker reeled off lots of numbers. More money in the budget was being allocated to violent-crime reduction. It was a large increase over what the previous mayor had spent. More uniformed police had been hired. There was more interagency cooperation. More training was under way.

While he was talking, the woman on the panel looked increasingly frustrated. From her deeply wrinkled complexion and flowing salt-and-pepper hair—hippie-like, Elliott thought—he guessed she was in her sixties. Unexpectedly, she interrupted the speaker and made a comment. From the look on her face, whatever she'd said seemed clearly hostile. Elliott heard murmurs of agreement from the audience.

Elliott leaned over and whispered, "What's going on?"

"This woman just nailed him. He was doing the typical politician's shuffle of boasting how much is being done. She demanded that he talk about results. As you can tell, what she said mirrored what the people who've come to hear the panel want to know. By the way, the son she lost was a cop, straight, not corrupt. He was one of seven police officers murdered last year by the cartel."

"God, that's terrible." Elliott cringed with a sudden thought of what it'd be like for him if Peter were killed. "But isn't she putting her life on the line by rocking the boat?"

"That's exactly what she's doing." Anneka balled her hands into fists. "So what's really happening here," she continued, "is that the meeting is just another effort to quell activists by giving lip service to meaningless anti-cartel efforts. Keeping the lid on citizen outrage is the actual purpose, preventing the public from organizing and throwing people out of power. She's pushing back, and my guess is she thinks she doesn't have anything more to lose."

The deputy mayor wound up his remarks, and the audience's scattered applause was indifferent. He looked impatiently at his watch before taking his seat.

The council member introduced the next speaker, señor Cornelio Ochoa. The real estate investor came to the podium. His tailored navy suit, crisp white shirt, and gold-colored tie contrasted sharply with the attire of most in the audience.

Anneka translated for Elliott. Seemingly oblivious to the mood in the room, the speaker smiled broadly and profusely thanked the panel organizers and the audience for attending to such an important issue in the life of the community. With a patronizing tone, he then launched into a pronouncement about the one valid way of thinking about drug crime.

Anneka whispered, "He's speaking to us as if we were grade-school pupils."

"For decades we've heard what we must do to make our streets safe." He paused, looking into the distance as if to let his words sink in. "We've been told over and over again how to make our homes and our communities more secure." He shook his head, a scowl on his face. "The answer we've been given is that we must pour massive amounts of taxpayer wealth into virtual armies of law enforcement personnel." Again, he shook his head.

"They've told us we must legislate longer and harsher prison terms for drug crimes." He counted each item off on the fingers of his right hand. "We must extend the death penalty to a litany of activities. We must triple and quadruple our prison capacity."

With a cocky shake of his head and a flick of his wrist, he said, his volume rising, "This lady on the panel asked the right question." He turned to briefly acknowledge her. "What about the consequences? Is it working?"

The activist didn't return his gaze.

"My answer to her has two parts. The first is that of course we must invest in adequate law enforcement, and of course we must hold law breakers accountable. But decade after decade we've watched this utterly failing approach drain our public coffers."

He looked out, and Elliott watched as several in the audience were nodding in agreement.

"There's got to be a different way of thinking about it. My friends, it's not working! More than that, it never will!"

He stopped and looked keenly at the audience, as if daring anyone to disagree.

"Want to know how to pull the rug out from under organized crime?" He waited several moments before continuing. "Invest in jobs. My dear neighbors, we must invest heavily and smartly in community economic development. And let me tell you what will happen then."

His hands were raised as if he were about to declare victory.

"What will happen then is that those who prey on others will have opportunities they don't now have, never even dreamed of. When they have the kind of employment that truly offers an alternative, crime will no longer be their one and only choice. Believe me."

Anneka was furiously jotting some notes on a pad of paper. Others sitting nearby were animated, shaking their heads in disagreement, scowling and muttering. From the corner of his eye, Elliott spotted the policeman who had been at the back of the room move halfway to the front and lean against the wall.

"Imagine how we would benefit," the speaker said. "All of us. First, the criminals would finally have a chance to pull themselves up legitimately. But the rest of us would also benefit. Imagine new training programs, hospitals, schools, roadways, power plants, airports, public transit, hotels, shopping malls, and modern sports and recreation centers." He was expansively waving his hands as he spoke, his white teeth gleaming through his salesman's smile.

"I tell you, we have a choice. Believe me. We can continue to throw good money after bad, building massive armies of police and enormous prisons. Or we can invest in economic development and foster a prosperous and secure future for every man, woman, and child."

He had a triumphant look on his face. Gathering his notes, he prepared to sit.

"Fuck it," Anneka muttered. Then, before Elliott could stop her, she jumped to her feet and waved her arm to catch the speaker's attention.

"Just a moment. I …"

The council member chairing the session tried to cut her off, saying there'd be time for questions after all of the speakers had presented. She ignored him.

"Very interesting indeed, señor Ochoa. And how generous of you to come all the way from Nuevo Laredo to speak with us." Her voice was dripping with sarcasm. "You invite us to think about how we will all benefit from this grand scheme. But isn't it the case, señor Ochoa, that the true beneficiaries will be real estate investors and developers like you?"

The speaker's confident expression didn't change, not even a glimmer of reaction to being challenged. All eyes were on Anneka, and the woman sitting next to her leaned over and said something under her breath. Elliott guessed it was a word of encouragement.

"Oh, wait. I'm not done. I have two more questions for you to ponder." She quickly looked down to review her notes. "While you piously tell us that we must spend money on crime, just a lot less than most officials know is the absolute minimum needed, aren't you really creating a fairy tale to justify taking the heat off the cartels and their thugs?"

More in the audience turned in their seats to watch Anneka. She became even more animated and emphatic.

"Aren't you in fact lining your own pockets, pockets by the way that we're not supposed to know about, if the cartels get a green light to do whatever they wish?" She sat down and repeated it all in English to Elliott.

He heard gasps and felt stunned. The undercurrent in the auditorium became electrically charged. The police officer was now standing just a few feet away from them. Two more entered from the back of the auditorium. They were carrying assault weapons.

The activist on the panel was applauding enthusiastically, and the council member conferred with the police lieutenant and deputy mayor. It looked to Elliott as if all in the audience were anxiously leaning forward in their seats.

The speaker smiled. His voice was quiet.

"*¿Es la señora americana?*" Is the señora per chance an American?

"Entirely irrelevant," Anneka responded, waving her hand dismissively. Elliott could tell she was shaking with fury.

"Yes, we have heard from many Americans about how we ought to live and to raise our children. We've heard that we must build a wall between our countries. Oh yes, and we must pay for that wall." His smile was replaced with a look of scorn. "So much advice coming from a country that has entirely lost its credibility to lead."

Someone close to the front applauded.

"Those gringos have insulted our culture. They've claimed those who go north, men and women simply seeking a better life for their families, are rapists and thieves and addicts. They sneer at us, saying we infect the wholesome United States with our cast-offs."

He looked directly at Anneka, and for several moments their eyes were locked, his finger wagging.

"My answer to you today, señora, is no thank you. My answer is we are tired of gringo insults."

Moving from the podium back to his seat on the dais, Elliott watched as the speaker glanced over at two men wearing dark suits and seated on the far left of the front row. He saw both of them nodding. Elliott's pulse quickened, and as Anneka began to again stand to retort to the speaker's dismissal, he grabbed her arm and held her.

"Anneka, don't. Please!" She yanked her arm away but let the moment pass without any further confrontation.

The police lieutenant was introduced and began to read in a droning voice from a sheaf of papers in his hand. It appeared that there were no others in the audience ready to grab the baton and go after the developer.

"We've got to leave," Elliott whispered to her. "Now! We've got to get out of here. Let's go while we're still safe because there are so many witnesses if anything were to happen."

Anneka refused. "I'm an American. They wouldn't dare harm me." Despite the certainty of her words, Elliott could tell she was unnerved.

"Do it for me, then. They know I'm with you, so I'm in as deep as you are."

He started to stand and was surprised when she acquiesced. They made their way to the exit at the rear of the room. Many in the audience smiled, and a few gave her a thumbs-up as they passed.

Once they were in the outer hallway and standing at the elevator, his heart was racing. They'd be back in her apartment within a quarter of an hour. What they'd do after that, he didn't know. But getting out of that building safely was top priority.

The elevator seemed to take forever to get to their floor. From behind the conference room doors, he heard some angry shouting. Had Anneka's example emboldened others? She turned and started heading back to the room, but Elliott pleaded with her.

"Don't."

The elevator finally arrived, and the doors began to open. Before they could step in, however, Elliott heard rapidly approaching footsteps behind them.

He began to turn. Rushing up were two men. He recognized them; they'd been sitting in the front row.

One of them said, "*Al señor Ochoa le gustaría hablar contigo.*" Señor Ochoa would like to speak with you. Elliott saw the man take a pistol from his waistband.

When he and Anneka didn't move, one shoved them into the elevator while the other pushed the button for the basement parking garage. Instantly Elliott knew this was the one moment when something, anything, could be done to prevent the inevitable. If he didn't act, they'd surely be beyond help. The doors began to close and then, just before they slammed shut, Elliott stuck his foot onto the track.

When the doors popped back open, two of the speakers from the panel were walking in their direction. The pistol quickly disappeared. Wagging his finger, the deputy mayor was loudly dressing down the police narcotics unit lieutenant. The two of them boarded the elevator, ignoring the others, and the berating continued all the way to the garage where they stood aside to permit Anneka to step out first.

One of the men had Elliott's arm in a firm grip. Yanking it free, Elliott grabbed Anneka's hand and, pressing the remote on his key fob to unlock the doors, pulled her out of the elevator and twenty feet over to his car. After shoving her into the passenger seat, he ran for the driver's side door. Gunning the engine, he drove toward the ramp. In the rearview mirror Elliott spotted their abductors racing after them on foot, then turning and heading in the opposite direction when they apparently realized that catching his car was impossible.

Just after they shot out of the garage exit, he shouted, "Where the hell am I going? Give me directions." A moment later he jammed on the brakes after almost hitting two jaywalking teenagers. "We've got to get our passports from your apartment."

"Take this next left," she said. He turned onto the narrow street she pointed to only to find that they immediately became penned in between a school bus from behind and a white sanitation truck that had stopped and blocked the street in both directions.

He thought about abandoning the car but quickly pushed that idea away. They'd be all-the-more vulnerable on foot. For the next five minutes, they could only inch along as the garbage truck repeatedly stopped to permit the driver to heft trash barrels from the curb and empty their contents into the hopper. Ten minutes later they turned into the street where Anneka's apartment building was located. A large black SUV, its windows heavily tinted, was idling in the middle of the street just outside her building's entrance. As Elliott drove past, two men in the front seat were visible through the SUV's open window. They were looking directly at him and Anneka.

He swerved around the SUV before its driver could react and sped to the next corner. "We can't stop! Tell me how to find the embassy."

"I'm not sure," she stuttered. "It may be this way," pointing to a freeway on ramp. "But, Elliott, maybe I'm wrong. I can't …." He heard the fear in her voice. Just then, their car rocked violently as the SUV rammed them. Anneka turned in her seat and looked just as they were about to be rammed a second time. "Oh, my God." The second hit was even more violent, forcing their car to sideswipe a parked pick-up truck, pushing it sideways onto the curb.

"We've got to get away from them," Elliott shouted as he made a right turn and raced through a residential neighborhood, grateful there weren't people in the crosswalks. Steering the car became a struggle and he wondered if one of the tires might have blown.

The SUV stayed right behind them as the two vehicles sped block after block. Outrunning their pursuers was impossible. Making a snap decision, Elliott said, "There's only one thing I can do. Anneka, you're going to need to trust me."

"What are you going to do?" she screamed.

He accelerated to ninety miles per hour putting a city block between their car and the SUV. Then, swerving onto a side street, he unclasped first his and then Anneka's seat belts. After spotting a postal delivery man walking toward an apartment building's entrance fifty feet ahead, he abruptly braked to slow down and then reached across and opened Anneka's door. "Jump, Anneka. Fold yourself into a tight ball. Try to roll when you hit the ground. I'm sorry," he shouted as he pushed her from the car and sped ahead, repeatedly honking the horn to get the postman's attention.

In his rearview mirror Elliott saw her crawl behind the postal delivery van where she couldn't be seen by the black SUV as it careened around the corner and came speeding toward him. He was relieved that, at least for the moment, Anneka was safe from them. But how badly had she been injured?

Thick smoke was coming from the right front wheel well and the car's steering was increasingly difficult. The SUV slammed again into his rear bumper and very nearly pushed him off the road into the gulley alongside it. He wrestled the steering wheel to regain control, his car swerving wildly from left to right.

A railroad bridge above the road was just ahead. Glancing through his mirror, he held his breath and braced as the next hit rocketed his car into the concrete bridge abutment on the right side of the road. Without his seatbelt on, the impact propelled his body forward, smashing his head into the windshield.

37 ~ Don't Let Them See You

Peter felt himself falling, spiraling deep into a maelstrom. It was as if a trapdoor on which he stood had suddenly tripped. When he abruptly woke to the sound of his ringing cell phone, he was still submerged in the nightmare. Tat was also tumbling somewhere in the darkness below. They were both most certainly going to die.

Peter was in his room at Mateo and Sandra's West Seattle home. Milena was on the phone. It was 6:00 am.

"I need your help, Peter." She was in tears. "Please, will you come to my apartment as soon as possible?"

He swung his feet to the floor, momentarily grimacing from the pain in his shoulder. He rubbed his eyes. "Yes, of course," he replied. "But, what's wrong?"

He heard her trying to answer but straining to form the words.

"What about dad? Couldn't he—"

He turned on the nightstand light and put on his slippers.

She cut him off. "Peter, I must talk with you." He pressed her for the reason, but she would not say more. "Get here quickly."

He knew it had to somehow involve his father. Reaching for his robe, he ran down the hall to wake Sandra and Mateo and tell them about her call.

Both peppered him with questions, none of which he could answer. The three of them quickly dressed and, with Mateo driving, headed to Milena's apartment. On the way there, Sandra tried to phone Elliott. The call went directly to voicemail.

Rushing into the building, Peter used his key to enter Elliott's apartment. The lights were off, and the rooms were empty. His father was not there.

Wearing a robe, Milena opened her door before they could knock. The anxious look on her face further telegraphed alarm. Something horrific had to have happened. All eyes were on Milena who was looking pale, perspiring, and breathing rapidly.

"Are you okay?" Peter asked.

"It's ... it's both of them," she said, clearly looking as if she were about to faint.

Before she could fall, Mateo grabbed her by her waist. "Let's get you over here," he said. He nodded in the direction of the couch. Sandra piled several throw pillows at one end and then the two of them assisted her in lying down.

After taking her pulse, Mateo said, "We'll need to elevate your legs. Peter, a cold washcloth, please."

Several minutes passed. She lay there with her eyes closed. They could see her lips moving although they couldn't make out what she was trying to say. Mateo stayed at her side while Peter and Sandra looked for any evidence in her apartment of what might have happened, finding nothing.

Color began to return to Milena's face. She opened her eyes.

Mateo again measured her pulse. "That's better," he said. "Do you want to try sitting up?"

She nodded. With Mateo's help, she slowly moved to a sitting position. Sandra handed her a glass of water and Milena took two sips. She motioned for Peter to sit next to her. Mateo and Sandra pulled two dining table chairs over.

She spoke slowly. "I have to tell you what happened. A few hours ago I had a phone call from a hospital in Mexico. My daughter, Anneka, had fallen from a moving car."

"Oh, no!" Sandra said. "Is she alive?"

"Yes. Thank God there was someone there who witnessed it and called an ambulance. They took her to an emergency room. They're currently running tests and told me they'd phone again by noon."

"How was Elliott involved?" Mateo asked.

Milena looked at Sandra and then Peter. "Your father had gone to Mexico to see her without telling me. Did you know?"

All three shook their heads.

"When she arrived at the emergency room, they tried to ask her questions, but she couldn't speak. They said there weren't any obvious physical reasons for that, but their assessment was still underway. She could write, however. She gave the nurses my name and phone number."

Milena paused, looking down at her hands clasped together in her lap. Quietly, she said, "Anneka also wrote that she and Elliott were being chased. He saved her life by pushing her out of the car and then leading away the people chasing them by speeding off."

Milena began to sob and reached for a tissue. "She thinks they may have killed him."

Sandra gasped, reaching for Mateo's hand. Peter jumped to his feet and walked to the window, his hands wrapped around his torso. His mother stood and took him in her arms. No words were spoken.

Mateo reached for his cell phone and attempted to call Elliott. There was no answer.

"Is that all you know?" Mateo asked.

Milena nodded. "Hopefully they'll tell me more when they call back."

Sandra said, "What should we do in the meantime?"

Peter, looking at his smartphone, said, "I'm going to call the U.S. Embassy. There's a contact number on their website." He keyed in the number and waited for an answer.

Mateo looked at Sandra. "Do you think Elliott might have told Theo what he was going to do?"

"I'll call him and ask," she replied.

Once he reached the embassy, he had extended conversations with five different staff members, each of whom required that he state the same information before determining that they'd need to connect him with someone else. Finally, he spoke with a case officer who seemed to know what had to be done. He asked for a photo and a detailed description of Elliott.

Peter rushed back to Elliott's apartment, searching for a current photograph. The only one visible was the one of him along with his mom and dad on the table next to the couch. But that had been taken at least twenty years earlier. He began randomly opening cabinet doors and felt increasingly desperate until he realized he'd entirely overlooked his own smartphone where he quickly found a recent snapshot of Elliott.

He emailed the photo to the case officer and accompanied it with his father's age, height, weight, color of his eyes and hair, and a statement that he was physically fit. Four hours passed and they waited for a return phone call. None came.

Just a few minutes before noon, Peter's phone rang. He noted the call's origin. "It's the embassy." He walked over to where his mother was sitting. Milena, Sandra, and Mateo all stood. He placed his phone on speaker and answered the call.

It seemed to take forever while the case officer reviewed the procedures he had used to look into Elliott's status. A bulletin had been issued to all police departments, records of people arrested in the previous week had been searched, and hospitals with emergency rooms had been given Elliott's photo and details.

Finally, the case officer told them that one plausible answer emerged. A man meeting Elliott's description had been in a car that crashed into a bridge. He was brought to a hospital the previous evening with no identification.

"Is he alive?" Peter nearly shouted into the phone.

He was.

Milena, Sandra, and Mateo erupted with tears and shouts. Peter took the phone into the kitchen so that he could hear. The case officer said the patient was still unconscious and the full extent of his injuries was uncertain. But the doctors believed his life was not in danger. He would live.

When Peter ended the call, Sandra turned to Mateo and said, "I want you to help me find the earliest flight to Mexico. I'll phone my chief and ask that he reassign or postpone my cases."

"Peter, once I know more about what Elliott will need for rehabilitation, you'll need to begin checking out each of the possible facilities. And Milena, we'll want to do the same for Anneka." Sandra looked at her watch and then searched in her handbag for a note pad and a pen.

"No, Mom. I'm going to go to Mexico."

The three of them stopped what they were doing and looked at him. For a moment, no words were spoken.

"But, your clavicle, Peter. You're not fully healed, and you're not finished with physical therapy. Really, I don't think it's a good idea and—"

Mateo interrupted. "Let him go, Sandra. It's the right thing for him to do and it's the right thing for his father."

For a moment, Sandra looked confused.

"You, Milena, and I will need to be here, ready to make any arrangements that are necessary to get Elliott and Anneka back to Seattle and into whatever kind of rehab facility they'll require."

"Mom?"

Sandra nodded and smiled. "Yes. Go to your father and Anneka, Peter." They hugged. "We'll do this as a team, with you as our point man."

Peter took the first flight out of Seattle. Upon landing, he grabbed a cab and then, at the hospital reception desk hit a brick wall. The administrator insisted on reviewing in detail evidence of Elliott's identity as well as his medical coverage.

Peter begged for them to schedule this interview for a later time and to let him speak with Elliott's doctor. The administrator was adamant about following the necessary procedures. More than an hour later, he told Peter to go to the fourth floor waiting area where the physician would meet him.

When he stepped off the elevator on the fourth floor, the physician was waiting. "He's still unconscious," the doctor said as the two of them quickly walked down the hall and into Elliott's room. "Both an orthopedic surgeon and an ophthalmologist examined him. I need to get to the ER right away, so here are their preliminary reports. I'll be back to speak with you as soon as I can."

A single bed occupied the room. Two nurses were finishing changing the bandages over Elliott's eyes. Before leaving one of them smiled at Peter and placed a chair for him next to the bed. Respiration and heart function data were displayed on the nearby monitor. Elliott's head had been shaved. Several large bruises were evident.

Peter took his father's hand and gently squeezed it. "Dad? I'm here." There was no response.

He sat and read the two medical consultation reports. When finishing with the second of the two, he cringed. He needed to phone home. Stepping into the corridor, he took out his phone.

Sandra answered. "It is dad," Peter said. "He's alive and the doctor doesn't believe his life is in danger."

"Is he conscious?" she asked. "Are there any serious injuries?"

"He's still unconscious. There are bruises all over his head and his left leg has a compound fracture. But, it's his eyes that ...." Peter choked up.

"Peter?" He heard the urgency in her voice.

"I'm on the other line," Mateo said. "Peter, has something happened to your father's vision?"

"Yes, he ...," Peter coughed to clear his throat, "when his head hit the windshield, his eyes were injured badly. The ophthalmologist says dad won't see again."

"My dear God," Sandra said. Peter heard her crying and Mateo quietly speaking to her.

"Mom, I'll go and sit with him until he wakes. I'll phone you again as soon as he's able to speak."

An hour later Elliott began to stir. Peter took one of his father's hands. "Dad?"

"Peter?" Elliott whispered. He tried to sit up. "Don't let them see you. You mustn't be here. Hide quickly, son."

"Dad, dad, it's okay. You're safe." Peter eased his father back down. "You're in a hospital. No one will hurt either one of us here."

"Hospital? How did ...? Why can't I see? What's happened to my ...?"

Then, after a moment in which he was silent, Elliott's body stiffened. "Oh, my God, the crash. Why can't I see? I'm going to be able to see again, aren't I?"

Elliott took a breath and then cried out, his body bucking on the bed. "Anneka. Did they find her? You've got to get the police to look for her. Peter, please. They're killers and they're going to murder her." Hearing his shouts, the two nurses returned to the room.

"Dad, Anneka's here in the same hospital. They're treating her and ..."

Elliott moaned, tried to sit up, and then screamed in pain. In his extreme state of agitation, he was unable to hear what Peter was trying to tell him.

With Peter holding one of his arms and a nurse holding the other, they gently restrained him. The second nurse injected him with a sedative. "You need to be calm, Mr. Sterling," the nurse said. "This will help." In less than a minute, Elliott was asleep.

Over the next several days, Elliott was in and out of consciousness and underwent imaging procedures for his leg. Bone fracture repair surgery took place on his third day of hospitalization.

When he came out of anesthesia on his fourth day, Peter and Anneka were sitting on either side of him on his bed.

"We're here, Dad." Peter watched as Anneka caressed Elliott's cheeks and then leaned over and kissed him. There were bruises on both of her legs and each wrist was bandaged.

"You're alive. Thank God, Anneka. Were you hurt?"

She lifted his hands so he could feel her head shaking back and forth.

"I'm so relieved. I knew you could have died when I pushed you, but there wasn't another option. You're really okay?"

Again, Anneka held Elliott's hands to either side of her head. She nodded.

"Why aren't you speaking?"

"Dad, Anneka's going to be fine. Her doctors believe it's an emotional condition that will eventually heal."

"You can't speak?" He took her hands in his.

She squeezed his fingers and, for the first time since his accident, Elliott chuckled and then began to laugh.

Peter gasped. "Dad, what the fuck?"

"Anneka, you laughed after I told you about my grandfather. It was so horribly absurd that laughing was the only possible way to react. And now, here we are. Look at us. Could it be any more ironic?"

Elliott felt Anneka's laughter, even without her giving it a voice. With one arm around her neck and another around Peter's, Elliott pulled each of them toward him in a hug.

"Peter, I'm remembering something your friend Tat said."

"What did he say?"

"He said, 'Be one with the mountain.'"

"Be one with the mountain, Dad."

38 ~ To Shed My Own Curse

Dear Todd,

Just saying your name is choking me up.

Forty-eight years ago today you died. Grief descended on me like a volcanic spew and for decades darkened everything in my world.

Peter came by this morning with some groceries, but also to check on me. He knows the significance of this date.

I told him I wished I could talk with you. I'd tell you that although I have a hole in my heart that can never be filled, my life is no longer defined by its shadows.

Miraculously, my life has changed.

For the first time since it started when I was nineteen years old, I'm not sinking into the depression that hit every year on this date.

And I wrote the final chapter in my journal and closed its covers. I'm no longer hiding in its pages.

I'm alive again.

Even after losing your sight, Dad? he asked.

In some ways it's only because of that, I said.

Peter was quiet for a minute. Then he walked over to sit beside me on the couch. He gave me an idea. Actually, it was a gift.

Write to your brother, he softly said. Put a letter to Todd in that wooden dough bowl in your apartment building's lobby.

So here I am, in faith that you'll get this letter, speaking into the voice recorder Theo bought for me. That's all I need this morning: faith.

In the first few months of being blind, I tumbled through a whirlpool frenzy of questions, never ending it seemed. Who was I if I could not see? Would I forever be perceived as an invalid? Would I be smothered by my self-pity? Could I relearn how to be independent? Would needing to reassure those I love be an endless burden?

With the passage of time, however, there've been rays of hope. For example, a blind therapist I've known for years told me I might find sightlessness to be a therapeutic advantage. Last week when I held sessions with clients for the first time since the crash, I knew she was right. I was able to hear so much more than ever before.

Then, two weeks ago, I was introduced to Jade. She's a one-year-old black lab in training to be a guide dog and we've been matched. Soon she'll come to live with me. There is lightness even in the dark, I'm learning.

Still today, for a very brief time on many mornings when I wake, I expect to see the world as I once did. I expect to be able to move through space without assistance. And I expect to be able to take in who and how each individual is by looking into their eyes. Even so, as time passes, the momentary emotional plummet when I remember I've lost my sight is gradually disappearing. On some days, I wake immersed in my new normality.

And then there's Anneka. In that first month she didn't talk. With Milena she cooked some of their family's favorite dishes. They worked together in the p-patch plot and went for long walks. She read for hours on the couch in my living room and listened to music.

Strangely enough, in one dramatic moment she spoke for the first time. And in another, you appeared. I felt certain of it. You were there beside me.

We were attending a performance of Verdi's Requiem. In the Jewish in Seattle magazine, Milena had read that this event would educate the audience about what had happened in 1943 and 1944 when Jewish prisoners in Terezín were secretly taught the lyrics.

Meany Hall, just off Red Square on the University of Washington campus, was nearly full when we arrived. Milena described for me a photograph that was projected on a screen above the stage. It was of the concentration camp gate with the Arbeit Macht Frei sign. It means work sets you free. What an obscene lie.

When the conductor came out, instead of raising his baton, he spoke to all of us in the audience. He said that in the midst of the suffering and grotesque brutality, the Jewish prisoners fought to preserve their dignity and build a community. Through education and the arts, they resisted.

Just before the chorus and orchestra began the Requiem, we heard a long, lonely wail of a train whistle echoing throughout the auditorium. The whistle was an ominous reminder of the transports. Milena and her parents had been brought to Terezín in a cattle car.

I was sitting on Anneka's left holding her hand. I felt her begin to tremble. I remembered her describing the foreboding sound of a relentless train whistle moments after her father killed himself.

But then the chorus of 150 women and men began to sing. My heart was filled with the grandeur in Verdi's score and the splendor of the chorus members' voices. Milena leaned over and whispered that she pictured her mother having been part of this more than seventy years earlier, as young and as beautiful as many of the singers we were hearing.

Anneka began to calm. Her body was relaxing, and the trembling stopped. I even felt her swaying slightly in her seat.

The music paused and a film clip was shown of an elderly survivor who had sung in the chorus back then. She said it had given her the will to survive. "I can't describe what the music sounded like, only what it meant to me."

Then Anneka quietly said, "Babička."

"Ano," Milena said. "Yes. It was babička."

Anneka was saying "grandmother" in Czech. In the days since, as her speech has returned, she's talked about the courage those prisoners must have had to take such a risk. The concert we attended was titled, Defiant Requiem. I think she's on her way to finally figuring out how she can live in a world in which genocides occur. It's about defiance, learning to defy guilt by not letting it prevent her from having a fulfilling life. Her mother's example illuminates the way.

Just as I heard Anneka saying her first word, a powerful shiver surged through my body, and I felt a change in the texture of the air. You were there. Anneka and Milena must be seeing you, I thought. Surely, if I moved my hands around me, I'd be able to touch you. I didn't do that, though. It was unnecessary. For me, there was no question because I heard what you told me. You said that I, too, needed to be defiant in order to shed my own curse.

The truth is that I am a survivor, but not of a war or of imprisonment in a camp. Like several of my clients, I think I've been emotionally hobbled. For them, violating their moral code by some action they took or failed to take while in a war led to a moral injury. I think that after you died, Todd, my destroying all reminders of you was just such a violation.

I couldn't see the chorus members as they sang, but I could hear their profound message as well as yours. I heard that I can choose to defy my deadening shame. I can understand and forgive that nine-year-old for what he did. And following Milena's example, I can live my life making choices to enrich its meaning.

Anneka and I are recovering. We talk for hours, imagining our future and reveling in the gifts of renewal we're both receiving.

I'll stop now. But there's just one more thing for me to say. Often in her letters, Milena includes a poem. I'll end with one for you.

Thundering echoes persisted,

silenced neither by my reverence
for the written word nor the
depth of my emotional abyss.

Look to the warriors, she said
and learn how they choose to listen
to a chorus, not solitary tones,
hearing each track of life's symphony.

Later today, Theo, Anneka, Peter, Milena, and I will plant a western
red cedar seedling next to Theo's tree in Schmitz Preserve Park. That's
where I will visit you and will remember.

I love you, Todd.
Elliott

39 ~ Eager to Meet You

Dear new neighbor,

A very warm welcome to our building! I live upstairs in Apartment 4 and I am eager to meet you.

I don't want to simply leave a post-it note on your door. What kind of welcome would that be? So, if you're free, please join me tomorrow evening at 7:00.

I'll offer you a taste of my homemade koláčky and a cup of strong Czech coffee. Perhaps I can help you begin to settle into your new neighborhood. I'd also like you to meet my daughter and son-in-law.

Very sincerely,

Milena Hodrová

Epilogue

Liberate Me

June 24, 1944

It's just before dawn. Did they hear us?

Replaying in my mind the previous day's events, I'm unable to sleep and will instead write. Someday, I pray to God that if I do not survive, my diary will help tell the world what happened.

Tens of thousands of us have been subjected to unspeakable barbarism in this place of savage horror, not daring to protest for fear of being tortured, even executed. Yesterday, in response to the unending degradations inflicted on us and on all of our people, we answered them.

Yesterday we looked them in the eye and shouted, "Shame."

Just sixty of us remained, fewer than half of our full chorus. Sixty plus the maestro and Gideon, our pianist. So many of our members had already been transported to the east. And yesterday, commanded to do so, our performance was for representatives of the International Red Cross and a group of high-ranking Nazi SS officers. Adolf Eichmann was among them.

Earlier in the day, the commandant walked the visitors past a park where the children played soccer or rode on hobbyhorses and were required to make it look as if this were normal. I watched Milena with a group of other children, such expressions of joy on their faces, being fed bread and butter and then chocolate. The visitors looked on and smiled, oblivious to the fact that once they left, all of this carefully orchestrated pretense would be instantly dismantled.

And so we sang. We previously had performed Requiem fifteen times. This time was different. This time we sang to all of mankind.

But were we heard?

I was startled by Rafi's physical appearance as he stepped up on the podium. He's thirty-nine years old, but weight loss and the burden of the unforgiving demands he makes on himself have taken their toll. He looks so much older, even in the several weeks since I last saw him.

He brings steely discipline to his role as conductor. Every one of us in the chorus knew full well how quickly he'd rebuke any singer whose focus lapsed.

We stood there, all eyes on him, and waited for his signal, but he paused, his head lowered as if in prayer. We held our breaths. Moments passed. Finally, he raised his head and took time to look each one of us in the eyes, a gift to us of deep compassion on his face. He raised his arms.

We began with three descending notes, sung in a near whisper, followed by drawn-out phrases of melody, so sweet and innocent, as if in a lullaby.

"Requiem aeternam dona eis, Domine, et lux perpetua luceat eis." Eternal rest grant unto them, Lord. Let perpetual light shine upon them.

Did the visitors understand the fierce resolve in our voices when we sang the dies irae? Four resounding chords played fortissimo on the piano proclaimed the coming day of judgement. We sang out at full volume:

That day of wrath shall consume the world to ashes.

What trembling there shall be when the judge appears.

How stern will be the judgment.

In lieu of the trumpets in Verdi's score, the pianist rang out a summons to all to come before the throne. Honza, our bass soloist, and Dominika, our mezzo-soprano, predicted the reckoning:

Death and nature shall be stunned when mankind arises to answer before its judge.

The book where all is written shall be revealed.

Within is contained everything by which the world shall be judged.

When the judge sits upon His throne all hidden things shall come to light.

Nothing shall remain unpunished.

That day of wrath shall consume the world in ashes.

That book would contain all of the truths of what the Nazis had done and the names of all transgressors. The day of wrath would see a decisive defeat of the Wehrmacht and the utter destruction of the Nazis. The very ground upon which our extermination was being carried out would erupt in a massive upheaval, the earth quaking in protest. That was our meaning of the dies irae.

When, finally, we came to the last section, Libera me, I remembered how adamant Rafi was when he taught it to us. "The Latin" he said, "is 'Libera me, Domine, de morte aeterna in die illa tremenda; quando coeli movendi sunt et terra: dum veneris judicare saeculum per ignem.'"

Pacing back and forth in that cold dank cellar, he said, "It translates to 'Deliver me, O Lord, from everlasting death on that awful day when the heavens and earth shall be shaken: when Thou shall come to judge the world with fire.'"

"But when we sing these lyrics," he said, "in our minds the Latin will translate to 'Liberate me!' We will sing in defiance. Our meaning will be 'Set me free!'" He repeated himself, this time shouting. "Not 'Deliver me,'" he yelled. "'Liberate me!'"

And so, yesterday, as we performed for the Red Cross visitors, we came to the final pleas, each of us very nearly drained by having sung of the maelstrom of terror from imagining God's judgment on that day of wrath. In my mind at that moment, I was in the nave of St. Vitus Cathedral, standing with Tomas and Milena on either side of me.

We sang in hushed and desperate prayer. "Libera me. Libera me." Deep in our souls, however, our voices were thundering.

Liberate me!

Can you hear us?

About the Author

Roger Roffman was born and raised in Massachusetts, but has been a Washington state transplant since 1972. He retired from the University of Washington School of Social Work faculty in 2009 and subsequently wrote a memoir, *Marijuana Nation: One Man's Chronicle of America Getting High from Vietnam to Legalization* that was published by Pegasus Books in 2014. *Looking Always* is his first work of fiction. Roger and his wife, Cheryl Richey, live in Seattle.

FOR MORE INFORMATION ON TITLES AVAILABLE FROM
ALL THINGS THAT MATTER PRESS, GO TO
http://allthingsthatmatterpress.com
or contact us at
allthingsthatmatterpress@gmail.com

If you enjoyed this book, please post a review on Amazon.com and
your favorite social media sites.
Thank you!

Made in the USA
Monee, IL
10 October 2021